What if all life's ups and downs aren't about you? What if the people you've known forever live a different life than you've imagined? What if God asked you to see your worst enemy through His eyes? Darcie Gudger asks readers these introspective questions via her debut novel, *Spin.* Readers will identify with many of the usual suspects of high school hallways as they reconsider if the grass really is greener on the other side.

–Laura L. Smith
author of *It's Addicting*

Spin

Guarded Book 1

Darcie J. Gudger

Mountainview Books, LLC

Spin

Edited by Carol Kurtz Darlington

ISBN: 978-1-941291-04-7 (paperback)
ISBN: 978-1-941291-05-4 (ebook)

This book is dedicated to

Robert and Jeanne Yetter

Parents extraordinaire who modeled the love of all things books and reading. Who endured countless crazy crafted stories over the years. Who never doubted my words would be published one day. Well, that day is here.
Thanks for believing in me when I didn't.

Acknowledgments

This book has been thirteen years in the making so I fear I may forget some names. And they are not in any particular order.

Without my faith in Jesus Christ, none of this would have ever happened. Not this book, not my life. Life is cruel. Jesus never left me hanging. My relationship with Him is the only reason I breathe today.

If it weren't for the Lake Lehman High School band program, color guard would be nothing but random flag waving. Under the direction of John Miliauskas Sr., the band and color guard were undefeated for decades. Mr. M. taught me work ethic. The kind of persistence needed to write a book. Todd Marcocci, my guard instructor, is the reason I am *still* involved in color guard twenty-four years later!

John and Kyle—Thanks for not throwing me out of the house. I love you both. Kyle, you are so patient with me when I drag you from one guard rehearsal to another. You poor thing, you've been going since you were born!

Jenn Carrasco—You define the words "loyal friend." Without you, I'd be stuck in the dark ages of color guard. It is a blessing to have a friend with whom to share life and spinning.

Michelle Field—The world of pageants was and still is rather foreign to me. You helped me develop the role of pageants in Wendy's life, making it a powerful force to help secure her future. You gave me a new perspective and appreciation for something I did not understand.

Samuel Schiller—We met online through a writers' group and you were willing to take a look at my scenes involving the police and detectives. You helped me make those interactions real and not cliché. Thanks.

Dave Spinks—You helped me with school administration questions years and years ago when I first plotted the book.

Sheridan, Columbine, and Evergreen guardlings—You guys have *no idea* how much you inspired me over the years. And Evergreen, how much you fuel my fire in the present with your passion and love of all things guard and books! Now all you guard kids can say there is a book featuring your world!

Grandma Sally, Becca Whitham, Heather Caminiti (now Harner), Kayla and Kim Woodhouse—my crazy crit team—oh, my word. What to say? You guys tore my manuscript apart again and again and again until it made sense. We sharpen each other's skills, and I love you guys for being brutal. Making my manuscript bleed red.

Jim Walters—Aside from my parents, you believed in me when I didn't. When I wanted to quit and throw my computer under a steam roller, you would say something to me at random to keep me going. You even called me a writer out of the blue in church this past Easter Sunday. In front of all those people. It struck me to the core. I am blessed to have you as my pastor.

Mike Medina—Thanks for that impromptu photo shoot. You know how to shoot a girl.

Esau, Chloe, Blob, Carson, and Caleb (even though he is dead)—I know how hard it is to have Mommy on the computer when you want your bellies scratched, or food bowls filled. Chloe, you tried to help me type a few scenes by dancing on the keyboard . . . but I had to cut it. I'm sorry. I love you, my furries!

And last but so not least, C. J. and Tracy Darlington—Yeah, you're my publisher now, but you were my friends first. For a looooooong time. We go way back. You guys saw this project in its infancy. When it was an idea I was kicking around. Who knew, ten years or so ago when I spilled a pumpkin latte on Tracy, that we would be in this place now. Back then we dreamed of our words in print. And here we all are. God works in the coolest ways. His hand *is* in all of this. Thank you for being a part of my life. (And I promise to tie my hands down next time we see each other).

Kisrie Kelley counted pencils impaled in the ceiling—six. Yesterday it was three.

Despairing groans echoed off concrete walls pulling Kisrie's attention from the abstract artwork above her head. Paper packets plopped rhythmically on desktops. Mr. Plank approached her desk. She squeezed her eyes shut, lips moving, pleading for mercy. Oh please be a B, at least a B. A dull thud announced the arrival of her English essay.

Dare she look? No. She couldn't do it.

Glancing back up at the ceiling, she cocked her head and examined the yellow pencil-missiles in the cork-boardy tile. If only she had her zoom lens, she could escape into her favorite world. Capturing pictures of the mundane life around her.

But unfortunately, life would never be kind to *her* in that way. She'd never be able to do what she wanted to do. And facing the music of graded English essays would always be her demise. Why couldn't she excel at something *normal*? Something that would make her accepted and popular. Even if it had to be the dreaded schoolwork, at least she'd be included by the smart-nerdy types. As it was, her awkward ways, chubby figure, and love of all things Nikon made her a bit of an outcast. Who was she fooling—*the* outcast. Color guard, Jacque, and Tammie were the only things motivating her to show up to school every day.

The dreaded essay lay on her desk. She knew it was there but chose to ignore it and closed her eyes. The volume of groans and complaints around her grew. She imagined the sounds as ocean waves on a sandy shore. She could run away and escape there. It wouldn't be hard. No one would notice Kisrie Kelley was missing.

An expletive from the back of the room made her jump in her seat, and her eyes popped open. Head dropped down. Air rushed from her lungs, rattling the cover page emblazoned with a giant *D*. Her hands worked their way from her lap to her throat and massaged the growing knot. Mom was gonna be furious.

Anything less than a B in the Kelley household equaled failure.

Dread worked its way through her insides. She wound her fingers into her curly hair. What would Mom do? Probably make her do laundry for six months—by hand. Outside. She'd have to boil the water herself and stir the laundry in a hot cauldron under the brutal September sun. And then bang it between rocks until her hands were raw and bruised. No. Even that wasn't bad enough. Imagining brutal punishments equal to medieval torture methods sent chills rippling through Kisrie's body.

Her hand shook as she pinched the corner of the first page and flipped it over.

Red ink. Next page? Red ink. Next?

Red ink. Everywhere.

Only a tourniquet could stop this kind of bleeding.

Kisrie retracted her hands deep into the sleeves of her dad's old CU football sweatshirt. Jeepers creepers, you'd think a relative would have some compassion when doling out grades. Demanding she call him Mr. Plank at school forged a crack between uncle and niece like an earthquake under the Earth's crust. Tanking her GPA rumbled that crack into a canyon.

"Mr. Plank, I think you gave me the wrong grade." Wendy Wetz's nasty voice reverberated through the room. She slid out of her chair, crushing the returned paper in a fist. Kisrie tried not to stare at Wendy's skirt. The hem hovered an ant's hair below her rear. Kisrie's big toe wouldn't fit into that skirt. So not fair.

"Please check your tone when you address me." Mr. Plank stretched his index finger skyward then pivoted on one foot toward his desk.

Oooh, this was gonna be good. For once, Kisrie agreed with Wendy. If only Kisrie had the guts to argue with her uncle. One challenging word from her mouth and Mom would know about it by the time Kisrie swallowed. That weird twin telepathy.

Wendy pressed her lips together, sliding her jaw from side to side, no doubt for a dramatic pause to show Mr. Plank who she thought was in charge. Too bad she opened her mouth. This couldn't end well. "I had a four-point-oh." She glanced at the ceiling. "I *was* ranked first in the sophomore class." She tossed the wad of paper from hand to hand.

Mr. Plank stopped. Light danced on his shiny head, green in tint from the fluorescent bulbs. He lowered his chin. "Your point?"

Wendy smashed her essay onto her desk like a bug. She ran her left hand through her glossy hair. "A scholarship. That's the point. I—"

"Ms. Wetz, if you have any issues with my grading practices, you can leave me a voicemail with at least three dates that are convenient for you and your mother to meet for a conference." Mr. Plank clasped his hands together. "Meanwhile, I will begin class."

Kisrie twisted in her seat searching for BFF number one, Jacque Gonzales. Hopefully, Jacque wasn't so wrapped up in flirting with some dumb boy she missed the drama.

A square of folded purple notepaper skidded across Kisrie's desk. She brushed it onto her lap and noted her uncle's location.

She unfolded the note and read:

Ol' Wetbottom thinks she's queen. R u ever gonna get a phone? U need 2 b able 2 txt.

"Yeah, right. Keep dreamin'," Kisrie mumbled and slid a glance at Jacque.

"You say something, Cow Pie?" Wendy's angry eyes turned toward her.

Talking to herself. Great. Why couldn't the Kelley family curse skip a generation and spare her the humiliation? And where was Harry Potter's invisibility cloak when she needed it?

Scratching her arm, Kisrie blurted, "Uh, way to go Wendy. Way to stick up for your grade."

Yeah, sure. That was *so* much better.

Wendy's shiny lips shaped foul words.

"Points of Persuasion." Mr. Plank's increased volume signaled the teacher's tolerance level had reached maximum. That and he turned his back on them and faced the white board. Not a good sign. The green marker squeaked like a wounded mouse. Kisrie feared her uncle was gonna pound the marker through the wall into the next classroom.

Wendy yanked a notebook from her Gucci bag and slammed it on her desk, flashing her middle finger at Kisrie.

Kisrie flinched. Tuning out her uncle, she stared at the comments on her paper. "Fragment. Off topic. Source citation. I'm disappointed, Kisrie." Uncle Evan's voice leapt off the paper into her head.

Clenching and unclenching her hands, Kisrie fought the urge to pull a Wendy and crumple the offending document. Excuses for the saturation of red ink shouted in her brain.

Points of persuasion. Pay attention. Her whole future was in jeopardy. Mom would go after the camera. Then she'd never be able to prove to Mom how good she was. Mom expected her to be a chiropractor. Being a chiropractor meant studying the kinds of things Kisrie couldn't wrap her brain around.

Her camera was her life. The one thing she loved *more* than color guard. If Mom took away photography, Kisrie would keel over and die.

No eating in the library. What a stupid rule. The librarian hovered like a vulture. Circling. Waiting. But this vulture would bust her for smuggling in food.

Kisrie shoved her unopened brown bag into her backpack and returned a copy of *Seventeen* to the periodical rack. Less than ten minutes remained in the lunch period. But where could she go? The band room? Nah. Watching couples make out in the corners would turn her queasy stomach into a barf machine. Only one option left.

Kisrie clomped down the stairs and scanned the cafeteria for an empty spot.

Dropping her backpack onto an abandoned table in the back corner, Kisrie sighed then sank onto the bench. She yanked out the brown bag and dumped it—a ham-and-turkey sandwich on bricks of sprouted-grain bread and a baggie of red pepper slices. No matter how hard her health-conscious mother argued, veggies did not substitute for Doritos. No comparison. And what was up with the no dessert thing?

A tray stacked high with Chick-fil-A sandwiches floated by on the extended arms of a boy wearing a Nuggets jersey. Kisrie stared at the fried poultry sucking in the drool forming at the corner of her mouth. Maybe she should get a job so she could buy her own lunch.

Reaching deep into her backpack, she found her stash of peanut butter cups melted into a mound of sugary goodness and foil. Maybe the shed wasn't the best place to hide the contraband, but Mom had an uncanny ability to sniff out what she considered edible profanity. An in-house hidey hole would have to be Mom-proof.

Holding the bag up to her nose, Kisrie inhaled the salty-sweet scent before diving in. Maybe full of chocolate she could focus on excuses for her English grade.

Popping a peanut butter cup into her mouth, she rehearsed potential lines to deliver. "Uncle Evan mistook my paper for someone else's . . . Maggots crawled into my brain, taking control of my thought-processing center . . . Uncle Evan was out at a bar, and someone poured a vial of a mysterious substance into his drink . . ."

"Can you believe these stupid lines?" Jacque slapped a plastic tray onto the table.

Kisrie gasped. She was talking out loud to herself again. Who heard?

"Like, by the time I get my food, there's no time to eat."

Kisrie opened her mouth to reply, letting in more air than she intended. The peanut butter cup lodged in her throat. Eyes watering, she opened her mouth, hoping air would rush in.

"Mr. Plank axed your paper too? I got another. Big. Fat. F." Jacque punctuated each word by slapping Kisrie over the head with her English paper, oblivious to the life-and-death crisis unfolding.

"Jaaa . . . !" Violent coughs fought their way around the candy.

Jacque's eyes widened. "You're choking! Oh! Kisrie's choking!" Jacque squealed, hopping from one foot to the next and flapping her well-manicured hands. Kisrie let go of her throat long enough to grab Jacque's lacy camisole top and yank her onto the bench.

"Ghhaa . . ." was all she could get out before she started gagging.

"Water, yeah. I'll get some," Jacque said and rushed away.

A crowd of spectators gathered. Fingers pointed and faces contorted with laughter. At her expense. No one moved to help. "Someone pound on her back," a voice cut through the noise. A male student bumped into her.

"A choking cow! Cow Pie is choking!"

"Back off!" Ms. Glisp, the gym teacher, marched in, right-angled arms swinging.

Blackness edged Kisrie's field of vision. Her lungs burned. She was gonna die. Here. In front of the whole world. Panic flapped through her chest like a startled goose. She pounded on the table with her fist.

"Get back to your seats, all of you! What's wrong?" Ms. Glisp's face hovered inches from Kisrie's.

Kisrie barked. The candy shifted, filling her lungs with precious air. Ms. Glisp grabbed her arm and led her out of the cafeteria.

Stopping in front of a water fountain, Ms. Glisp spoke. "Try to take a sip, and keep coughing. Sounds like whatever's in there is loosening."

An invisible, giant fist squeezed Kisrie's throat. She was a goner! Why wasn't anyone dialing 911? She beat her chest as the teacher nudged her.

Kisrie leaned over the fountain. Slimy brown chewing tobacco glinted up at her under the fluorescent lighting. Her stomach bucked. There was no way. Barfing seemed like a good idea, but the candy was lodged. Kisrie turned on the gym teacher, ducked, and ran toward another fountain. But she didn't get far. Glisp's fingers clamped around Kisrie's arm, and next thing she knew, she was being dragged back to the tobacco spit pit.

Her lungs burned. Green spots danced in front of her eyes, and her esophagus felt like the Sahara Desert had taken up residence along with a few camels. She had to get to water. *Clean* water.

Kisrie planted her feet and spun on her heels with all her might. Glisp's fingers dug channels in Kisrie's skin as she pulled free. She staggered toward another fountain about thirty yards away. It better be clean!

Footsteps drummed on the tiles behind her as she pawed at the button.

"Drink." Ms. Glisp hovered over Kisrie's right shoulder and clapped her hands together rapid-fire.

Closing her eyes, Kisrie obeyed. The peanut butter cup broke free and landed on the drain. Now two water fountains in the school held slimy, gross prizes. Kisrie tangled her fingers in her hair, flopped on the floor and exhaled, "I can breathe! I can breathe—oh, sweet air!"

Ms. Glisp's voice broke through. "Get off the floor, Miss Kelley."

Kisrie opened her eyes. A crowd of students hedged them in with the water fountain and hacked-up peanut butter cup.

Oh, great.

"Kisrie?" Ms. Glisp put her hands on her hips and raised an eyebrow.

"I'm . . . I'm okay." Kisrie's eyes darted around looking for an exit.

"Lunch is almost over. Go clean the chocolate off your face." The teacher waved at the crowd to disperse. No one moved. "Ten sets of suicides for anyone who doesn't move in the next three—" It was like a light flicked on in the midst of a cockroach convention. Ms. Glisp rubbed her hands. "They scatter every time. Now go clean up."

Kisrie bolted then collided head-on into a panicked Jacque. Water sloshed down the front of Kisrie's shirt.

"Oh, here's your water. Oops!" Jacque patted at Kisrie's dripping chest. "I thought you were gonna die on me. Here." Jacque swung a backpack toward Kisrie. "I got your bag too." The corner of her mouth crooked up.

"Thanks, Jack, but I really gotta get cleaned up." Grabbing her pack, she took off running. As she skidded to a halt in front of the bathroom door, the bell rang. Terrific. Let's just add a tardy to the long list of Kisrie's misdeeds of the day.

Two cheerleaders burst out of the door, eyeing her like she was a rotting corpse. One paused in the doorway. "Oh, girl. Might as well put a bag over your head and spare us all."

She hunched over and sidestepped inside. Hairspray haze hung in a low cloud.

Kisrie's backpack landed with a splash in a puddle of water on the vanity. She leaned over the sink and lifted her face to the mirror. Bloodshot eyes. Great. Couldn't wait to hear the comments. Splotchy face. Perfect. Annoying and random curls clung to her nastified, sweaty scalp. Cupping her hands under the stream of cool water, she splashed her face, hoping to reduce the redness. So much for her makeup. At least her mascara and eye liner were waterproof. Now if only she had some Visine. Or better yet, a new head.

Kisrie shuffled to the handicap stall, backpack dangling from her elbow. She hung her pack on the door hook, lined the seat with paper, and settled down to do her business. As she reached for the toilet paper roll, she heard the door to the hall open. Not wanting to be noticed, Kisrie hoisted her knees to her chest so her feet didn't dangle under the stall door. There was no way she was gonna go to class until the redness in her face and eyes subsided. She held her breath and rocked back against the icy, cold plumbing. Hopefully, these people would be in and out. And hopefully, none of them was in a wheelchair.

Loud laughter punctuated by foul words assaulted her ears.

"So, Wen, what're you gonna do? I mean, like, Mr. Plank can't get away with this, ya know?"

Kisrie pulled her knees up tighter. Ugh. Wendy and her goony friend, Sabrina. No mistaking that nasal voice. Now she *really* didn't want to be discovered.

"I'll think of something. My grade can't drop if I plan on competing in the pageant. Not to mention, Iona will be mad enough to make me pay in ways I don't want to think about. I mean, she had one of her reporter friends help me write that paper."

"Do you think Plank caught on to ya?"

"How could he?"

"Mr. Plank needs to go down, Wen."

What did Sabrina mean by that? Kisrie rolled in her lips and bit down to keep from making any noise.

"Sabs, quit sucking on your lip gloss. It's so infantile."

"It tastes like Skittles."

Kisrie's heartbeat whooshed in her ears. They *had* to hear it.

"Forget the Skittles! Sabrina, can't you see I'm freakin' here?" Wendy swore. "Help me think. I need to come up with a way to get back at Plank. People like him shouldn't be . . . around . . . kids." Something slammed on the counter top. "Sabs, I got an idea!"

"Okay."

"Remember that coach over at Falcon who was caught with the captain of his volleyball team?"

"Um, no."

"Let's spread the same rumor about Plank."

"But he doesn't coach volleyball."

"That coach is in jail. On the sex offender list."

Icy prickles raced up and down Kisrie's bottom and legs until they went numb. Her heart hammered against her ribs. This was getting very bad, very fast. Should she do something?

"I mean, think about it. What if we say Plank's willing to fix grades for a price?"

"I don't know, Wen. What girl in her right mind . . . He looks like that guy who plays Scrooge and smells like a musty, old book."

"Think about how many kids are ineligible for sports because of Plank. He's obsessed with low numbers. Like, I don't think he can count above seventy. The girls' softball team hopes to go to playoffs? Not without their pitcher. She has Plank for AP. Trust me, this rumor will fly."

"Okay. So?"

"You're gonna tell Carolee that you heard Plank gives A's for certain favors. Make it steamy."

"Ewww. That's just gross."

The hall door opened, cutting off their conversation. Kisrie avoided falling off the toilet by sinking her right cheek in. Cool water lapped at her bottom. Spider legs crawled up her spine. Had she flushed? Just what she needed to brighten her day.

One of the girls squeaked.

"Why aren't you in class?" The unmistakable hall Nazi whose voice could overpower a crowd at a Broncos game. Kisrie heard a hard-soled boot tapping a quick staccato.

"Heil!" Wendy shouted. Door hinges squeaked. Noise from the hall . . . silence.

Stale air seeped from Kisrie's tight lips. Her wet rear was the least of her worries. The magnitude of Wendy's plot sat on her like a diaper-clad sumo wrestler. What should she do? Muzzle Sabrina?

Take a shower, that's what. But there was no time. Kisrie slid off her perch. Cold water ran down the back of her leg. So gross. Not only was she wet, but she was a health hazard. She had to get the potty water off.

Kisrie stared at the toilet paper dispenser for a moment and shrugged. It would have to do.

She grabbed the torn end and pulled. A tiny piece broke off. She pulled again. A smaller piece.

"What's up with this cheap paper?" Yikes. Gotta keep the comments internal.

Furious determination flared in her chest. She squatted under the roll and pulled. A toilet paper blizzard swirled around her.

So. Not. Going to work.

Pushing up to her knees, Kisrie huffed and grabbed the paper roller dispenser. She pulled. Pulled harder. The plastic gave way and the cover popped off.

The freed roll fit onto her fingers. She spun it round and round until all the paper lay in a pile on the floor. She was gonna need *all* of it to dry off.

Without tearing it, she wadded some in her hand and patted her bum. But the paper stuck.

She pulled. It broke. What good is toilet paper if you can't wipe a wet rear with it? Seriously!

Time was running out. Hall Nazi was sure to knock down the bathroom door any minute, discovering her in her compromised state.

She twisted to examine the damage. Her backside and thighs looked like she had leprosy. White paper dotted her skin. Hopefully, the paper would fall off after it dried.

Kisrie pulled up her pants. What to do about the paper on the floor?

She stooped and scooped it up then pushed it into the toilet. School toilets had a violent flush. It would all go down, right?

She flushed.

The paper swirled.

Then stopped.

"Oh no! Oh no! Oh no!" Kisrie pushed at the pile of paper. The water kept coming. It splashed over the sides. She grabbed her stuff and ran from the exploding toilet. She had to get out of there before she was connected to yet *another* disaster.

Peering from the cover of the bathroom door, Kisrie saw

the hall was clear. She sprinted toward the band wing, leaving the sounds of the gurgling toilet behind.

Once ensconced in the safety of the guard room, she leaned against the wall and took a few deep breaths. The issue with her uncle had to be figured out while she finished drying.

Should she go to the office and tell Dr. Martinez? Tell him what? Wendy could easily say Kisrie made it all up. Kisrie rubbed her eyes. Her memory pulled her back to Lakewood Elementary where the gym always smelled like sweaty little boys and dirty socks.

Wendy had used four-letter words on the playground. Kisrie tattled. For three days, Wendy had to stay after school for an hour. Behind the buses after school on the fourth day, a Hello-Kitty backpack made contact with Kisrie's face. "Gonna rat me out again, Cow Poop?"

It took Aunt Zena, school psychologist and Mr. Plank's wife, two days to coax Kisrie back to school. Meanwhile, Wendy's mother, Iona, brought in some lawyer dude, wanting to sue for violation of First Amendment rights.

Ever since then, Kisrie dreaded going to school. It didn't matter how many tears she cried or how hard she banged her head on the wall in hopes of giving herself a concussion, her mom dragged her to school.

As the years passed, Wendy turned tormenting Kisrie into a weird, demented sport. Aunt Zena had been the only reason Kisrie hadn't run away from home in hopes of being adopted and sent to a Wendy-free school.

Yeah, right. Like she was gonna go rat on Wendy again. Who'd believe Wendy's stupid story anyway?

The unmistakable scents of stale urine and beer greeted Wendy as she approached the entrance of her apartment building on Colfax Avenue. A loud snort erupted from a putrid man as he rolled to his side on the second step. She cut a wide circle around him. Last time, she got too close and he made a grab for her.

Nasty. This place and all of its people were just nasty. She was way better than this.

The urge to escape propelled her up three flights of stairs, two steps at a time. Pausing in front of apartment 31B, Wendy bent at the waist to catch her breath. Hopefully, Iona was either alone or not home.

Home. How can you call a place home when you're required to knock before entering?

"Come in!"

Wendy turned the key in the lock, pushing her body against the door. Iona lay on the couch in a teal-and-brown silk robe. Dark bottles littered the floor. The place was trashed. As usual.

"Drinking again?" Wendy dropped her bag onto the floor and walked toward the kitchen area.

"Nah, just working. One of the celebs had a friend needing good company. Made almost two grand."

Wendy rolled her eyes and pulled open the refrigerator. She hated the way Iona made money. Professional escort services? Ha! Wendy wasn't some snot-nosed, two-year-old. She knew how the world worked.

Nothing in the fridge caught her attention. She slammed the door.

"So, how'd school go today? You get that English paper back yet?"

Wendy took her time walking to the bar separating the kitchen from the living area. She leaned on the counter, flipping through the mail. "Yeah."

"And?"

Wendy scooped up the mail and flung it against the refrigerator. "That idiot Plank gave me an F."

"What?" An expletive flew across the room and echoed in a string of unsavory words. "That paper was written by a professional." Iona picked a pack of cigarettes out of the couch cushions and shook it while smacking the bottom side. "Ahh, come on!"

"So you told me." No more letting Iona's friends come anywhere near her schoolwork.

"Said he wrote for the *Boston Globe.* Cost me good money too." Iona slid the cigarette between her lips and lit up. "That Plank's proving to be a pain in the—"

"Gave me a C on that other lit test two weeks ago."

Streams of smoke raced from Iona's nose. With a sudden display of yellowing teeth, Iona swung her legs off the couch and patted the empty space next to her. "Have a seat. Talk to your ma."

A thin smile tugged at Wendy's mouth while she crossed the room and dropped onto the couch. Moments when Iona appeared interested in Wendy's life were rare. Better take advantage of this and pretend it was a normal mother-daughter chat. In a normal home. Under normal circumstances. Then again, since when was cooking up some nefarious plot normal?

"Come on, girl, are you gonna speak or what?" Iona's eyes

glittered in anticipation. She scooted closer. Wendy launched into a detailed description of the career-destroying rumor and how it was gonna spread. Iona *had* to be impressed.

"You think it'll work?"

"Of course it'll work."

"Principal's gonna buy it?"

Wendy jerked away from Iona and leapt to her feet. "What, you think I'm going to screw this up?"

"I'm just remembering a time in middle school when you accused that little Asian boy of stealing petty cash from Mr. Godfrey's drawer."

"He was suspended."

"Until they found the money in your lunch box." Iona rocked her body to the side then settled back down again. "I need a drink. Go to the fridge and grab a Coors Lite for me."

So much for normal. "Get your own booze. I've got homework."

"How badly do you want to win that pageant?"

Wendy inhaled long and slow. "That's a stupid question. You know the answer," she said on the exhale. Win this circuit, and then when she was old enough go for Miss Colorado, Miss America.

"Well, you gotta make it personal then."

"Personal?"

"Who's gonna believe hearsay? Without details and specifics, your story's gonna be laughed at. But, if you speak from experience—"

"What? You want me to say *I*—?" Wendy couldn't even complete the thought in her mind.

Pushing at a cuticle, Iona chuckled. "Well, I guess you're stuck with me, kid. You can kiss that scholarship money goodbye."

"There's always next year. I could enter the pageant next year and win the scholarship."

"Next year? The longer you wait, the harder it'll be to get your grade point average in the range they want. And you could be hit by a bus and have your pretty face ripped off. Then what'll you have?"

Wendy's stomach felt like a pile of vipers, writhing and snapping at her insides. The sharp pains intensified, piercing her abdomen. Iona was right. If this F wasn't raised, the law of averages would work against her. She had to get a good college degree to prove she was more than a hot body, and time was running out.

"Okay," Wendy swallowed, fighting the roughness in her throat. "If that's what it takes."

"Good." Iona rubbed her hands together. "Let's offer to drop the charges in exchange for a grade that won't hurt your GPA."

Wendy squeezed her head, hoping to stop the concussive pounding. What was she getting herself into?

Kisrie checked the f-stop setting and the ISO. There was no way she could take the shutter speed down any further without a tripod. But what a cool texture shot. And she wasn't gonna miss it. The metal poles of the flags rose from the center of the barrel creating a weird spiral.

Trumpets blared in the distance. Crud! She was late. But would the poles ever be oriented like this again? She had to try. Nope, take it down another stop. Can't quit now. Drummers were playing eight on a hand. Kisrie sighed and opened the aperture as far as it would go, but she couldn't get the exposure right. Too dark.

Kisrie shut off the camera and stowed it in its padded case. She yanked her flag from the bin and scooped up her rifle and sabre. The band was now playing "Ultimate Warm Up." Running cymbal laps would bite. Running by itself was painful enough; running while crashing cymbals every four beats was child abuse. And Gavin, her instructor, seemed to relish the latter.

Someone slapped her on the back. Kisrie spun around, hitting her head on a nearby shelf. "Jacque, I swear you're gonna kill me one of these days!"

"So, how'd it go with the 'rents last night? They sentence you to youth group?"

Youth group. One more place to feel like a dork.

Kisrie pressed her lips together and glared at Jacque.

"Sorry. Not funny. I know."

"I haven't told them yet."

"No!" Jacque's mouth rounded into a perfect oval, her hands pressed against her cheeks. "What about the twin sense? Your mom knows. I know she knows. You know she—"

"What am I supposed to do, Jack? Offer myself up for some sort of sick sacrifice? Subject myself to hearing about how much of a slacker I am or how I'd rather be glued to my camera than a textbook, then have her go on and on about how great Keri is and how I do nothing but embarrass her? I need a break from people pushing me. Plus, I'm afraid she might pull me out of photography." The venting relieved some of the pressure, but not much. No one would ever understand.

"Whoa. Anything else?"

Kisrie cradled her equipment. Thoughts of the conversation in the bathroom sprang into her mind. She shook her head. "We're so late. And I think I'll blame you." She took off toward the field ignoring Jacque's squeals and wait-for-me's while her conscience reminded her something very bad could happen.

The band formed a series of arcs on one end of the field and played through the ballad while Gavin gathered the color guard opposite the band. His pink-and-silver pinstriped shirt hugged the six-pack under his ribs, and leg muscles flexed under his white jeans as he stood with bare feet in a solid second position. He'd make for a great candid shot. Between his exaggerated facial expressions and postures—such an interesting subject for that upcoming photo contest.

"Ladies, we're going to start with spins and stops on sabre. Too many of you are letting your elbows stray out into space. And your catches make your arms look like worn-out rubber bands. Squeeze! Pull! Lift! I want to see you catch white tape. Set!"

Kisrie jerked to attention, abandoning her daydreams

about the perfect shot. Did Gavin notice her? She and Jacque stood side-by-side at the back of the block. Jacque twisted her mouth to the right to get Kisrie's attention. "Kiz, how'd you get a bad grade anyway?"

"And five, six... dutdutdutdutdutdutdut!" Gavin stopped mid-clap to move another guard member's sabre into the correct plane.

Kisrie gritted her teeth together, doing her best ventriloquist imitation while catching her sabre at port. "You know that contest for photography?"

Jacque's right elbow drifted away from her waist. The sabre rolled over her fingers and hit the ground. "Oh, I see. You got your eyeball stuck to your camera and couldn't stop shooting things. I was hoping you had a better reason than that. Like you suddenly got stupid like the rest of us."

"Gonzales and Kelley, give me twenty!" Gavin barked inches behind them. How'd he sneak up on them like that? Along the sidelines, the band stopped playing scales. Laughter rippled through the group.

Lowering herself onto the grass, Kisrie wished a hole would open up in the middle of the field and swallow her. Then she wouldn't be late. She wouldn't miss perfect shots. Gavin wouldn't be mad at her. She wouldn't be humiliated in front of the entire band and guard.

She wouldn't have to face her parents about The Grade.

And she wouldn't know about Wendy's plan.

Kisrie lay face-down and crushed her pillow over the top of her head. Nope, no better. Flinging it to the side, she flipped onto her back, letting her arm and pillow dangle over the side of the bed. She could barely make out the popcorn texture of the ceiling with the weak glow of her night light. "One hundred bottles of Sprite on the wall, one hundred bottles of Sprite. Take one down, pass it around—Ahhh, this isn't gonna work!" The conversation she'd overheard in the bathroom replayed itself in her head, drowning out all attempts to sleep.

She peeked at the glowing numbers on her alarm clock.

3:00 a.m. If she was lucky, she could get two and a half hours of sleep before getting up for school.

And then what?

Wendy was the kind of person to go ahead and spread nasty rumors. The girl could win some sort of red-carpet-trophyish award for her creativity and rumor-spreading prowess. And this rumor wasn't about some faceless man among thousands.

It was about Kisrie's uncle. Her mother's twin brother.

But what could *she* do? Go to the principal and say "Like, um, Dr. Martinez, there's probably gonna be some nasty rumor going around about Mr. Plank that he's selling grades for, um, inappropriate acts with a minor. None of it's true. Just so you know."

Like that's gonna fly.

Kisrie groaned. If she did tell, Dr. M. would want to know who was spreading the rumors. And where she heard it. And where was her proof?

If Wendy found out Kisrie ratted she'd get beaten up, shoved into a dumpster, or dunked into a toilet. Wendy had a thing for dunking her in a toilet. Her whole life would be ruined. Rumors about some sort of drug use and illicit activity would be thrown in for kicks. *That's* what she had to look forward to if she told on Wendy.

Maybe she could wear a disguise into the principal's office. Maybe she could leave an anonymous phone message from a payphone. But where could she find one of those? Everybody had a cell. Well, everyone but her.

Email from a computer in a public place? She wasn't even allowed to have her own private account! Had to use the *family* addy.

Or just keep her mouth shut and pray it all blew over, that nobody would believe Wendy. Yeah, like that was gonna happen.

3:15 a.m.

Anxiety gnawed at Kisrie's stomach. She pulled her knees into her chest and cradled them with her arms. The more she thought about not saying anything at all, the more uneasy she felt. Conviction? The Holy Spirit? A bad burrito? But wait, she'd had grilled chicken for dinner.

"Okay, okay. I'll go talk to Dr. Martinez tomorrow morning." Kisrie mashed her pillow against her face and screamed.

Kisrie twisted a curl of hair tighter around her finger. She looked down. The end of her finger was purple. She relaxed and let the curl slip through her fingers, but she still couldn't breathe. Why'd she ever think this was a good idea?

The secretary, Mrs. Hampden, sorted through papers while chatting into the phone cradled between her ear and left shoulder. Dr. Martinez swept into the office, a dark look on his face. Mrs. Hampden dropped the papers and pointed to Kisrie hunched in a chair.

"The police are in the student parking lot. Another break-in." He sucked in an ionosphere worth of air through his nose.

So. Now what? Wait? Wendy might catch her in here and just *know*.

With a nod, the principal looked at Kisrie and waved her into his office. She had to use both arms to lift her leaden body out of the chair.

"Mrs. Hampden!" The choir teacher jogged into the office out of breath, her gauzy skirt swirling like a cloud around her legs. "Dr. Martinez—"

"Can I help you, Amy?"

The choir teacher glanced around the office and stutter-stepped through the gap between Kisrie and Dr. Martinez. "This can't wait," she said with another timid look around, her eyes meeting Kisrie's before turning away. The teacher's voice morphed into a hoarse whisper—more like a stage whisper. "Some students came in this morning talking about a sexual assault between a staff member and some students."

Sounds faded. Tiny pricks of light danced around the periphery of Kisrie's vision. A massive, unseen force crushed into her chest making her gasp. All three adults stared at her.

"Do you need to see the nurse?" Mrs. Hampden asked.

Kisrie shook her head in slow motion. She was too late.

Kisrie's combination lock wouldn't budge. She dialed fast. Then slow. Of course it didn't help that her hands were shaking. A few tugs and a kick—nothing. Kisrie stared at the stupid dial. Out of the corner of her eye, she saw a flash of hot pink. Two girls sauntered by.

"Mr. Plank is such a perv," a Katy Perry look-alike flipped her hair out of her face.

"Like, yeah," Girl number two said.

"Can't believe he tanked that girl's grade after she gave him what he wanted." One of the girls bumped Kisrie, who pressed her forehead against the locker vents.

Kisrie bit down on her lip and blew air from the corner of her mouth. "It's not true." Her words sounded like they were stuck in thick pudding. It's not like it mattered anyway. Who would listen to her?

"Did she say something?" Girl number one paused their conversation.

Kisrie wished the locker door would swallow her whole. She pressed her head harder.

"Nah, looks like she's not feeling so hot. Anyway, it's all too freaky if you ask me. I hope he ends up on death row. My mom will, like, flip when she hears this." Something rustled then crinkled. "Want some gum?"

Peeling her forehead off the metal, Kisrie looked at the two girls who proceeded to ignore her.

"Duh! Let's go." Both girls interlocked arms and scurried down the hall like hamsters on speed.

This was happening way too fast. How could anyone believe a thing Wendy said?

Kisrie put a hand to her forehead. Oh, no. Her fingers stiffened. She rubbed. The grooves on her skin ran deep. She had to look. Hand gripping the dial, she spun it to the right, the left, and then the right. "Come on, come on." Kisrie shook the door and gave her locker a kick. The stubborn lock yielded. A small magnetic mirror confirmed her fears. Great. Vent head. Another thing to be teased about in addition to being fat.

The second bell rang. Kisrie rubbed her head again. This was where bangs would come in handy. She swept the next two block's worth of books into her backpack and slammed her locker. Her skin felt like a bajillion caterpillars were crawling all over it.

If only she'd gone from the bathroom to the office before Wendy opened her evil mouth.

If only.

"Why do the ancient Greeks have to be soooo boring?" Tammie Benton poked Kisrie while twenty-two students mashed toward freedom from the dark lecture hall reserved for AP Social Studies.

"It's not the Greeks who were boring. It's Mr. Odesto's teaching that sucks." Kisrie adjusted her pack onto her left shoulder. "If it weren't for the Greeks, we wouldn't have feta cheese."

"Oh. I had no clue."

"Now you do." Kisrie switched her pack to her right shoulder.

"Y'know, Kiz, my mom says it's real bad for your back to carry your pack on one shoulder like that. And you of all people, wanting to be a chiropractor."

"I don't *want* to be a chiropractor."

"I thought you did."

"Nuh-uh. My *mom* wants me to."

"Kisreeeeee!" Kisrie's head jerked up. Jacque shot into her vision. "I gotta talk to you. Like, now!" Jacque skidded to a halt, her sides heaving. "Hey, Tam."

"So, talk." Kisrie rolled her eyes. She didn't have time today for all the petty schemes of Jacque and Tammie. Didn't they know there were life-and-death situations at hand?

"Can we go somewhere"—Jacque looked up and down the hall—"more private?"

Tammie's face squinched. "Is it serious?"

"Uh-huh. Way serious. You should come too. I may need your brain."

"What about the guard closet?" Tammie pointed.

"Can't it wait until later? The late bell's gonna ring." Kisrie switched her bag to the other shoulder again.

"Noooo. Kiz, this is serious. It's about Mr. Plank, and that's all I'm gonna say here and now. Tam, help me move her."

Icy lace patterns skittered down Kisrie's spine. She knew what Jacque was going to say. But how to look surprised? Acting wasn't her thing.

Jacque and Tammie sandwiched Kisrie, grabbed her arms, and dragged her down the hallway to the guard room. Tammie's bony fingers bit deep into Kisrie's arms. Kisrie wished she could share some of her excess padding with her skeletal friend.

Jacque peeked around equipment and storage. "No one here."

The bell rang.

Jacque took a deep breath and waved her hands as if she were drying nail polish. "Someone is spreading rumors about Mr. Plank. Actually, Wendy is."

Kisrie fought to keep her mouth shut and leaned in for more.

"Kiz, she's saying Plank promised her he'd give her A's if she slept with him."

Tammie's hand flew over her mouth.

Kisrie blinked. Hard. Three times. This was not the same rumor she heard in the bathroom. At least she didn't have to feign surprise. Or horror. Horror was more like it.

"Bad stuff." Jacque paused.

"I . . . how . . ." Tammie backed away.

Kisrie slumped her shoulders. "This just . . ."

"So, what do we do? Tammie, any ideas?"

Kisrie shook her head, but it didn't erase all the images popping into it. "Let me get this straight. Wendy said *she* is sleeping with my uncle? She, as in Wendy? *Wendy*?"

"I heard her talking to some boys in the library."

"Well, you both know it's not true." Kisrie cracked her knuckles and pulled a rifle out of the bin and started spinning. Spinning helped her think.

"Well, yeah." Tammie grabbed a sabre.

"I had to tell you."

Kisrie puckered her lips and blew out a raspberry. "Yeah you did, Jack."

"So, what do we do?" Jacque pointed then flexed her feet.

Kisrie searched the old ceiling tiles. No answers written by the finger of God. "I don't know. Tammie?"

"I think Kiz should go to Dr. Martinez."

Been there, done that. Too late. "And say what?"

Tammie did three backhand spins on her left. "Tell him Wendy's spreading a rumor and say what it is."

Jacque slung an arm around Tammie's shoulders. "That's what I love about you, Tam, you're so black and white."

"It's not gonna make any difference." Kisrie slid the rifle back into the bin and looked Tammie and Jacque in the face. "I mean, don't you remember what happened last year when I told on Wendy for punching that guy who refused to take her to the dance?"

"She stole all the tampons from your bag, put your name on them, and handed them out like cigars." Jacque said.

"Oh, but don't forget about the time she—"

"Get to class!" Hall Nazi materialized in the doorway to the guard room. Jacque screamed and hid behind Tammie.

"Now." Hall Nazi's boot tap-tapped.

"We were just talking." Kisrie lunged for her bag. How did the Nazi sneak up on them like that? The woman was never quiet. Not with those heels.

"You need to be in class." More tapping.

"We're going. We're going." Jacque flashed her best flirty smile and did a small bow before pushing out of the room.

Kisrie swallowed hard. She'd have to go to class without a pass, which meant a phone call home from the teacher.

Wonderful.

Eat it, Keri." Mom pointed her fork at Kisrie's ten-year-old sister. The spoiled brat examined the inside of her burger bun as if it were the soiled sole of a shoe.

Kisrie bit into her burger, collapsing the corners of her mouth as the squishy green guacamole oozed onto her tongue. Mom had *the look*, making Kisrie's heart pound as if she were running laps in PE. She forced a swallow, then choked as a horrifying thought struck.

Did Mom know?

Kisrie pushed her plate away. Could Mom be laying a trap to see if Kisrie would come clean? A small groan escaped her lips.

"Mom, are you sure this won't kill me?" Keri laid the burger down.

"No one has died. Yet." Mom took a bite of her sandwich, taking her time to chew. "The omega-3 oils are good for bush babies too."

Why did Mom and Dad fall for that bush baby crapola? Her sister one day decided she was a bush baby. A clear sign of mental illness. No reason. Except for maybe voices in her head. If their parents really wanted to play into Keri's delusions, why not just send her to the zoo to live with the other bush babies?

Keri replaced the top bun. "If you say so, Mother."

Mother? What was up with the little freak? Come on, who was she trying to fool? When the parents weren't around . . .

"Kisrie," Mom picked up a napkin and poked at her ketchupy lips. "I'm wondering when you're going to tell us about that English paper your uncle returned to you *the other day.*" Mom's eyes narrowed. She leaned back in her chair and folded her arms.

Whew. The paper. Not the rumors. Or did Mom know about those too and was waiting for the right moment to bring that up?

Kisrie grabbed for her water glass and missed, knocking it over. Water spread across the table and poured into her lap.

Mom rolled her eyes, grabbed napkins, and handed them to Kisrie. "You can talk while you clean that up."

Kisrie opened her mouth, but no sound came out. Why didn't the words come? She had a litany of excuses from the other day.

"Do you need some water?" Dad sent her a crooked smile and headed to the fridge.

Less than fifteen seconds to remember her best excuse for the grade and keep Mom off the rumor topic.

But what if twin-sense expanded to mom-sense and Mom could tell what Kisrie knew?

Dad traded her a glass of water for her goopy napkins. Hands trembling, she raised the glass to her mouth. The glare from Mom caused Kisrie's insides to shrivel. Keri gnawed at her burger, a triumphant gleam in her eye.

"Oh." Gulp. "That."

Mom's eyebrows arched. Her frown hardened.

No way out but through. "I got a D."

"I heard."

Then why did you ask? she wanted to say. Talking back meant instant death in this family. "I . . . uh . . ."

"No chiropractic school is going to take you seriously with grades like that."

Here it comes—The Lecture.

"Kisrie," Dad cut in with a sideways glance at Mom. "Maybe you can tell us what some of the comments were. Did you not understand the assignment?"

"Well . . ."

"I bet she was out with her camera." Keri took a huge bite of burger and appeared to swallow it whole. "Actually, I know she was. I saw her burrowing under a pile of leaves in the backyard."

"Keri, stay out of this." Dad wiped up the remaining liquid.

Mom continued her drilling stare, waiting, like a hungry wolf hunting a fat rabbit.

"I was planning on doing it the week before, but I ended up spending more time on my algebra, and then there was this project for photography that is going to be entered in a county-wide contest . . ." Kisrie trailed off. It was no use.

Mom pushed to her feet, lips pressed into a thin white line. She thrust an open hand toward Kisrie's face. "I want the camera."

No. This could not be happening.

"Kisrie? Camera. Now."

"It's mine. I bought it with my own money."

"Tomorrow I will be calling the school and having your schedule changed. Obviously, photography is too much of a distraction."

"But, Mom!" Kisrie blinked and bit the inside of her cheeks. If Mom only knew just how much she loved that camera and dreamed of shooting for *National Geographic* or any magazine with glossy pages. But it probably wouldn't matter if one of her photos made the cover of *Newsweek*. Photography was nothing more than a quaint hobby in Mom's eyes. She'd be disappointed Kisrie wasn't cracking someone's spine into alignment or hunching over a microscope searching for a cure for cancer.

Mom's finger pointed between Kisrie's eyes. "Bring me the camera. You need to go to your room and rethink your priorities."

Sobs threatened to erupt from her chest. Holding them back, Kisrie slid off the chair and stalked to her room. And she didn't even have a cell phone to text Jacque or Tammie about this cataclysmic tragedy. What would she do now?

Her photography teacher thought she had a chance to win a caption in the competition for high school students. Kisrie had hoped such a victory would prove to her mom that she had exceptional talent, since *exceptional* seemed to be what mattered most to the head of the Department of Chemistry at the University of Denver and mother of a ten-year-old flute prodigy.

Bold yellow letters jumped out against the black background of the camera's strap. Kisrie picked up her well-loved Nikon D3300 and stroked the wide-angle lens. Two years of birthday and Christmas money and the de-pooping of a neighbor's yard went into this camera.

She hung it around her neck. Should she hide it? But what would she say to Mom? Mom would never believe the camera was lost or loaned to a friend.

Footsteps thudded up the stairs.

Smoke hung in a blue haze over the tiny living room. "You don't care if this sick habit kills us both, do you?" Wendy wrinkled her nose. Even exposed to nicotine in the womb, she never got used to the stuff. When she was finally out on her own, she vowed to breathe fresh, clean air.

But before that could happen, she had to make sure nothing got in the way of her becoming Colorado Teen Queen. She shot a confident look at Iona. "I got everyone talking."

Iona took a long drag on her cigarette then let it dangle from the corner of her lips.

"Hope you didn't spare any details. And if you're lucky, things will get embellished over time." The cigarette bobbed up and down.

"Even the rats in the dumpster will know about it."

"You know," Iona puffed her death stick probably with the intent to look thoughtful. Big fail. "You'll have to follow this up and make a visit to the principal." A smoky cough. "I'm sure he doesn't want any of his teachers messing with his students." Iona kicked off her heels and leaned back into her recliner. "I'd hate to see you disqualified from that pageant. You're gonna need all that money."

"I better not be." What if this stupid plot didn't work? There was a chance the old codger couldn't be bought. Wendy headed to the fridge. "So, you think Plank will actually change my grade?"

"It's either that or lose his job. We need to take the man to his breaking point and then offer to drop the charges."

Wendy winced at her mother's words. Revenge was one thing, but this plot was shaping itself into another. Rumors would've been enough.

"Your grades have to be near perfect. You need to make up for the fact that you don't attend private school or some place like Cherry Creek."

"I don't think that matters."

"You that naive? Money talks. Get that into your head now. You want out of this?" Iona gestured around the nasty room. Brown water spots stained the ancient dropped ceiling, and cigarette burns from previous tenants peppered the thread-bare carpet.

Wendy thought about the drunken idiot in the street who constantly grabbed at her backside. "Of course I want out." She leveled her gaze at her mother. "I don't want to end up like you."

"Then do as I say." Iona pulled a lipstick from the folds of her clothing and smeared it on her already-made-up lips.

Wendy opened the refrigerator and shuddered. What other option did she have?

Who uses algebra in real life? I mean get real.

Holed up in her room, Kisrie snarled, trying for the gazillionth time to solve for that nebulous x. Staring out the window, she rolled the pencil back and forth between her thumb and index finger. Banging her head on the desktop didn't help much, just gave her a nasty welt and a headache. No sudden revelation of algebraic prowess. Concentration dissolved when the phone rang. No use. Kisrie massaged her eyebrows. Time for the back of the book. Why do they only give answers to the odd-numbered problems? Miss Fabricatore assigned the *even* numbered ones. John Fielder probably doesn't use algebra when shooting those amazing Colorado landscapes.

"Solve. 5(-3x-2)-(x-3) = -4(4x+5)+13. Why?" Kisrie threw her pencil at the window and tangled her fingers in her hair, pulling and rocking. "This is so stupid! Who. Cares. About. Solving for x?" A knock on the doorframe caused her to squeal. She spun to see who interrupted her anti-algebra tantrum.

"Kisrie? Can you stop what you're doing to talk?" A hard edge in her voice, Mom leaned against the doorjamb, arms folded.

"I'm trying to figure out this"—Kisrie edited her thought —"algebra."

Mom pursed her lips again. "I just got off the phone with your uncle."

"I told him I'll redo the paper even though he won't change my grade." Kisrie ground her teeth and picked at a sliver on the back of her chair. This better be about the grade. Not the rumors. But then again, how could Uncle Evan or Mom know about Kisrie's connection?

"Tell me what you know about these rumors flying around the school." Mom picked her way over piles of clothes to the edge of Kisrie's bed, pushed aside a zoo of stuffed animals, and sat down.

"Rumors?"

"Kisrie."

Kisrie turned back to her desk and slammed her book shut. "They're just dumb ol' rumors!"

"Ah. So you *do* know about them."

"Nobody believes them."

"Rumors like this can get your uncle in a lot of trouble. He could lose his job."

"But they're not true!"

"You know that. I know that." Mom licked her lips. "I want to hear from your mouth what the kids are saying."

Awkward. Heat rose into Kisrie's cheeks at the thought of what she knew she had to tell her mother. "They are saying he's trading immoral, uh, acts for grades." There. The truth.

"What?" Mom dragged the word out.

Don't make me say that again. "They are saying he . . . they're saying if you want a good grade, then . . ."

Silence.

"I tell people that's stupid and he's not like that."

Kisrie and her mom sat in silence. More silence. An eternity of silence. Eternity and then some. Like, what could she do about it now?

Maybe everything was going to be okay. Maybe the kids weren't buying Wendy's crap. Maybe it would all go away and Kisrie could go back to being miserable about algebra and having to drop photography for a human geography class—whatever that is.

"About your grades . . ." Mom trailed off, crossing her legs.

"They need to go up?" Kisrie squeaked.

"That failing grade will require nothing but A's to bring you back to where you belong."

"I got a D on one paper. I didn't *fail.*"

Mom brushed tiny, white cat hairs off her pant leg. "Anything at or below a B is failure. And don't you talk back to me."

Tears slid from Kisrie's eyes. It wasn't like she didn't care. It was just that her mom expected her to care about the wrong things. Things she wasn't good at. Like math or human geography, things she struggled to understand.

"Colleges look at transcripts encompassing all your years of high school. Your grades last year were lackluster. You're a sophomore now. You don't have time to waste to raise that GPA." Mom folded her hands. "The best schools make decisions on who may or may not attend by picking the student with an A in English over the student with a B. Competition is fierce."

Heat flushed Kisrie's face as she pushed up from her desk. No way she could tell her mom how much she *didn't* want to go into pre-med or to a fancy school. All she wanted to learn had to do with aperture, f-stop, lighting, and composure. Not body parts, mathematical formulas, and science. But according to Mom, being a photographer wasn't a real job. "I'll try harder."

Best to say what Mom wants to hear.

"I need to see all your grades come up in the next few weeks before you can do something that is not school-related." Mom rocked to her feet.

"But what about guard?"

"You get academic credit for that. Therefore, it's school-related."

Uh oh. Photography was a club that met during study hall times. She'd rather scrub the grease off the garage floor than be told to drop out of the photography club.

"Okay." If only she could get a brain transplant from a math genius.

Mom's lips curled in a satisfied grin. "Thank you." She left the room.

The trembling started in Kisrie's chin and worked its way up her face, causing her eyes to blink through burning tears. She bolted for her bed and threw herself across it face-down. Mom didn't know about the C in Algebra. The teacher's note suggesting a tutor hid in the dark recesses of her gym locker with ripe tube socks.

Kisrie never had gotten straight A's. But not for lack of trying. It was her dad's buffering that protected her from the wrath of Mom come each report card. She wasn't like Keri the ten-year-old wonder whiz, who went to a special music school and studied eighth-grade stuff. The occasional B or C from her younger sister was received with a "Well, she's way ahead of her grade level" excuse from Mom. *So* not fair.

Kisrie rolled over to stare at the ceiling. Now, without photography, how could she prove to her mom she had talent?

Students milled around the room talking to one another after the tardy bell rang. Uncle Evan wasn't at his desk. Unusual. He was always in there before the students. It was rumored he never went to the bathroom, and he always ate lunch at his desk. Some of the goth kids even wondered aloud if he were a vampire.

Kisrie tugged her notebook from her backpack.

"Anyone see Becky this morning?" A student shouted from the rear of the room.

"Yeah, she was on the bus," someone answered.

Instigator boy pushed further. "Yeah, but she's never late for class and neither is Plank."

This was not headed in a good direction. Kisrie twisted to face the obnoxious kid in the back. "Would you shut up?"

"Ooh, we upset the fat cow."

The entire room burst into laughter.

In the midst of the teasing, Uncle Evan slipped into the classroom, straightening his bow tie. It was tilted by maybe a microscopic one-billionth of a degree. Everyone froze for a momentary stop-in-action like they do in the movies.

Glances were exchanged. Kisrie's spine tingled. Wendy's

rumors must be getting around. How could her classmates be stupid enough to believe them?

Moments later Becky wandered in, her face flushed bright red. Trotting across the room, she kept the back of her head toward the teacher.

Someone coughed.

Another cleared his throat.

Kisrie's heart beat faster and faster as her uncle fumbled with the cap on the dry-erase marker. The cap rolled off his fingers and onto the floor. Uncle Evan was no klutz.

Becky smoothed her rumpled skirt then sat with her hand shading her face.

What's up with these people? Everybody knew Becky and her Guamese boyfriend always got busted by the Hall Nazi for public displays of affection every single passing period. The girl *never* got to class on time. Ever.

"Pull out your copies of *The Crucible*." Uncle Evan's usually smooth voice cracked. He put a balled hand to his mouth and cleared his throat. The pressure and worry about these rumors must be freaking him out.

Chairs squeaked. Papers crinkled. Giggles trickled through the classroom.

"Is there a problem?" Mr. Plank faced the students, marker poised as if he were about to write a brilliant poem in the air.

"Mr. Plank," Jacque called from her seat, "is it a book?"

"Miss Gonzales . . ."

"We never got them," someone else said.

"Kisrie, Mike, and Juan, would you go to the back cabinet, retrieve the books, and hand each student a copy?"

Kisrie stared at her uncle as he turned to write on the board. His shoulders sagged toward the floor. Nothing about her uncle looked perverted. Could anyone really take this stuff seriously?

"Are you gonna help or not?" Mike stood by her desk. She wiggled out of the chair and navigated an obstacle course of backpacks and purses to the cabinet where the books were stored. But she was never good at obstacle courses. Her toe hooked into a ropey strap. She tried to shake it off while moving forward. It slithered up around her ankle. The forward motion was too much. All balancing efforts failed. Face met floor. Laughter exploded in surround sound.

What else could go wrong?

Ugly conversations about Uncle Evan and his alleged escapades saturated the air in the hallways. Avoidance was futile. Everybody, including the custodians, yammered on and on about The Plank Scandal. If only her parents had bought her an iPod for her birthday, Kisrie could've tuned it out.

With her spine against the wall, Kisrie slid down to a sitting position in the empty band room staring at the hummus and crackers in her lunch bag. A plain ol' peanut butter and jelly sandwich would've been a pleasant surprise.

As far back as she could remember, Kisrie was a target for her peers' taunts. In third grade, the art teacher had instructed the class on how to make red, heart-covered mailboxes for Valentine's Day cards. Kisrie maneuvered her scissors in a deep curve along the folded edge of the hot-pink construction paper. An extra large mailbox meant an extra large helping of cards, right?

On the morning of February fourteenth, all the students in room 17C plunked the mailboxes on their desktops. Kisrie buzzed around the room stuffing Sponge Bob cards in slots. Classmates sped around in a blur, some hoping not to be caught slipping a note to a secret crush. Kisrie danced in anticipation over tearing through the tiny envelopes.

Last card delivered, she skipped to her seat. All around her, kids dumped their boxes onto their desks. Kisrie slid into her seat and shook her box.

Nothing happened.

Peering into the slot, Kisrie saw glue spots and empty space. Her hand shot up.

"Kisrie?" The teacher asked.

"My box is empty." She blinked hard, forcing the tears back into her eye sockets.

"What do you mean?"

"I don't got cards."

The girl behind her snickered.

"Everyone was supposed to hand out cards to each member of the class." The teacher squeezed through a clump of gossiping girls on her way to Kisrie's empty box.

"But I didn't get any." Her eyelids lost their battle against her tears.

The teacher reached down and picked up Kisrie's mailbox. "Who took Kisrie's cards?" She scanned the room making circular motions with her neck.

Twenty-seven pairs of eyes honed in on the teacher.

"Nobody took them, Miss Smith," a boy with boxy hair said from the front of the room.

"Then where are they?"

Wendy Wetz held up a small, white envelope with her name in bubble letters. She slid her finger under the flap. "We didn't give her any." *Rip*!

"Wendy!" The teacher put Kisrie's box down.

"Well, it's the truth. My mom says I don't have to give cards to people I don't like."

Miss Smith looked around the room. "What about the rest of you?"

"She's too fat." A girl with a million braids said, cutting a glance at Wendy.

"Uglier—"

"Enough!" The teacher frowned. She bent her elbows and clenched and unclenched her hands. "Take your seats and give me your cards. Everyone gets cards or no one gets cards." Miss Smith stomped around the room snatching up the mailboxes and torn envelopes.

Cries of protest rang in Kisrie's ears while she bolted from her desk to the hallway. The principal found her curled up under the sink in the girls' room after Miss Smith had reported her missing.

And that was only one instance. The list of torment, torture, and teasing could wrap around the globe four times.

"Kisrie? Hellllloooo! Wake up from whatever dream you're

in. Unless, of course, it's about me." Long, tan fingers with fiery-red nails waved in front of Kisrie's face, attached to Jacque who squatted down for a second. "The bell rang, y'know."

Kisrie rubbed her eyes, wishing the rubbing would erase the painful memory her mind replayed. Jacque popped up and bounced on her toes. Members of the low brass section trickled in for jazz band.

"Girlfriend, you are so spacey. I've gotta stop by my locker, so I'll just meet you in the hall by the library, okay?" Jacque executed a perfect pirouette and skipped out of the room.

Trick was getting to class without being accosted by Hall Nazi. Kisrie prayed there'd be no delay.

So much for zero delay.

During the passing period after lunch, Kisrie had watched Wendy prance through the halls as if she were a model on a runway showing off a new pyro-inspired design. A kerosene can swinging from Wendy's hand would be all she needed to complete the picture. Kisrie imagined her nemesis pouring liquid onto the tiny sparks of gossip igniting them into flaming accusations.

"I heard his niece goes to this school."

"Isn't that his niece or something?" A beefy boy wearing a CSU T-shirt thrust his chin in her direction.

Did someone just pour lead in her sneakers? Kisrie's feet ground to a halt.

"Hey, you!" someone called from near the library doors. Kisrie rolled her shoulders forward and tucked her chin to her chest, wishing she could collapse into a ball and roll away. "Some uncle you got there."

"Will you visit him in prison?"

Comments shifted from rude to nasty. The crowd closed in on her. Shuffle to the left. No, the right. Duck under the arm of the kid with the smelly armpits.

"Cow Pie! Looks like you got yourself stuck in a bog."

Students peeled apart like zipper tracks, Wendy being the zipper walking through the crowd.

Six-inch stilettos stabbed at the tiles near Kisrie's feet. "So, I hear *Uncle* Plank has been a naughty boy." Wendy slipped a finger under Kisrie's chin, forcing her head up to level. No matter how hard she tried, Kisrie couldn't look The Queen of Mean in the eye.

"Gonna try and defend Uncie's innocence?" Wendy smiled at the crowd. "Here's your chance. All these kids wanna know their teacher isn't a perv."

Laughter tore through the group. Wendy flicked her hand away and strutted through the crowd, which dissipated as fast as it formed. Kisrie clenched all the muscles in her gut to quell the trembling. Light footsteps slapped the floor.

"Hey Kiz, I just saw what Wendy did to you." Tammie shifted the weight of her backpack across her shoulders.

Numb. Kisrie's brain was numb. What to say about what just happened?

"You okay?"

Sucking her lips in, Kisrie blinked hard and clenched her fists. Teachers droned instruction behind closed doors, which meant one thing—tardy.

Heat radiated off the fake grass at Littleton Stadium. At least the sun was directly above and not hovering over the press box where it could cause nuclear burns to everyone's eyeballs.

Multi-colored silk dragged on the turf as Kisrie ran to set up the closer flags to the right of the fifty-yard line. Other guard members stepped out and set down their assigned armfuls of equipment. The drum line warmed up with a funky cadence, drowning out the pedal tones of the low brass. Kisrie dropped her load, letting the poles clatter to the ground. Shaking her aching arms, she scanned the field, collecting her bearings.

Drat. Forty-five or forty? Can't remember the stupid yard line.

The timing and penalty judge yelled a one-minute warning. Little time to get the flags stripped, set, and her body into the opening form.

"Forty," she decided, saying it out loud, measuring out six-step intervals along the front sideline, then backfield on the thirty.

The loudspeaker crackled. "Mountain Ridge Miners, is your band ready?"

Musicians shifted forms and took their opening poses. The drum major saluted from the scaffold. Not *everyone* was ready.

Kisrie guesstimated the location of the last two poles, threw them down, and sprinted to her opening spot, grabbing the opener flag from her starting point. Everyone else was in place. The drum major raised his arms and rolled his eyes at her. Her chest pumped under the crimson-velvet stretch fabric of her costume.

"You may now take the field for competition!" The announcer's voice echoed through the stadium.

Fans and parents screamed as the drum major counted off the meter. Kisrie's body kicked into auto mode, allowing the music and form to carry her along like an aspen leaf in Bear Creek.

Midway through the opener, Kisrie and six others transitioned from flag to sabre. In the middle of the set, Kisrie cradled the sabre making a wide circle on her right side. She paused, lunged, and did a fishtail around her wrist. But she started too high on the blade and it flung away, bouncing on the turf into the path of another guard member. Kisrie lurched to the right to grab her weapon-gone-wild but was a second too late. The girl chasséd into the blade. It wedged between her shins, hurling her forward. She hit the turf with a thud and skidded an inch or two.

Kisrie yanked her blade from between the girl's legs. The girl, a mean chick named Chrissy, rolled to her knees and shot her a murderous look. Angry rug burns on her left cheek glared in the bright sunlight.

Kisrie pivoted away and ran to her open spot, trying to get back into the routine.

"Dip, release." Kisrie whispered to herself, launching a blade triple with the rest of the guard. The victim of her clumsy drop blended into set a beat later, releasing only a double. All six sabres landed with a sweet smack. Maybe the judges would credit them for the quick recovery?

Mountain Ridge's guard made it through the ballad without any more mishaps. But when the pit played their feature and the guard jazz-ran to their closer flags, all heck broke loose.

"Wrong yard line," ripped through the undulating scales from the vibes.

Girls skidded to a halt trying to figure out which way the form was skewed. Some ran to the left, others to the right. The band entered with a long chord that was supposed to be illustrated with a toss. Instead, the guard scrambled like rats escaping from a science lab.

"Someone's gonna die!" A senior section leader yelled, grabbing a pole out of Kisrie's hand. Feet planted in second position, Kisrie twisted from side to side looking for a pole. It was every girl for herself! There! She spotted one three yards in front of her. Three sets passed before the color guard caught up with the show.

The brass squealed out the final note punctuated by the battery. Guard members twisted, turned, tossed, and caught.

It was over.

Exposed skin sparkled. Chests expanded and contracted. Extended limbs trembled. Nothing happened. Kisrie squinted through the haze and glare. The audience sat still like a block of ice.

One clap, then another. The announcer cleared his throat into the mic. "Mountain Ridge Miner Marching Band!"

Four beats. Cadence. Time to go. Guard members scoured the field collecting all the sets of flags and weapons as the band marched off in parade lines. Kisrie, arms full of equipment, lingered toward the back of her section until the entire band arrived at the equipment trailer in the upper parking lot. Another band was on the field warming up.

Parents swooped in and started de-pluming the hats on the musicians' heads. Kisrie dropped her load of stuff and started sorting.

Gavin and the band director, Dr. Morgan, huddled in the shadows by the buses. Neither one looked happy. Actually, they both looked like they were in the mood to eat a student.

That student would be her.

A hand slammed into her shoulder, knocking her off balance. "What's the matter with you?" Chrissy, the girl who tripped over Kisrie's sabre, screamed in her face, adding another shove. Kisrie stuttered backwards. Where were Jacque and Tammie?

"I said, what is *wrong* with you?"

"It was an accident." Kisrie entwined her fingers behind her back. Zoë and Miranda, section leaders of the guard, stomped toward her. Their faces were twisted into hideous snarls.

"Brain, Kelley. What happened to your brain? You screwed us all up!" Zoë jabbed a pointer finger at her own head.

"How many times did we remind you to set up on the *forty-five*?" Miranda said.

"You better start praying to the universe that your stupidity won't tank our score. Miranda, hold me back. I'm feeling a little homicidal."

Miranda circled her arms around Zoë in mock restraint.

"Look what you did to my face!" Chrissy pointed, a purple bruise peeking out from behind an abrasion.

Zoë spit at Kisrie's feet. "We're sorry you had to go through that, Chrissy. She's gonna owe you big time."

Miranda hissed through clenched teeth, her lips pulled back, "Save us all the humiliation and don't even think about marching winter. Heck, spare us all and just quit now."

"Color guard, you need to load your equipment on the truck. The pit is waiting on you," Dr. Morgan smacked his hands together.

"You can just pack your poles and go home, Kelley." Miranda, Zoë, and Chrissy scooped up their belongings and tromped off.

In a corner of the parking lot on the north side of the field, Jacque and Tammie made a Kisrie sandwich. The rest of the band sat in a large group at the south end of the stands. All three girls curled their fingers through the chain-link fence. Finalists for the invitational were about to be announced.

"Wonder how bad our score will be," Jacque said.

"Don't know."

"Wait. There's that old dude with the trophies. Listen."

Chants and cheers rose from around the stadium. "Ladies and gentlemen, we are going to announce the finalists who will compete later this evening."

"I can't listen." Kisrie doubled over and grabbed at her stomach.

"It's gonna be okay," Jacque said with a grimace.

Tammie patted Kisrie on the back. "You don't sound so sure."

" . . . Columbine, Bear Creek, Green Mountain, Arapahoe."

"They haven't said our name yet."

"Maybe we're first."

"Jacque, you're delusional," Kisrie said.

"A girl can hope, can't she? It was obviously a simple mistake."

". . . Pomona, Rampart, Evergreen, and Air Academy!"

Kids and parents jumped and danced throughout the stands. Except for the group from Mountain Ridge.

"Oh Lord, it's my fault," Kisrie whispered in a half prayer.

"Did we ever not make finals at this competition?" Jacque asked Tammie, her face a few shades lighter than normal.

"I. Don't. Know."

By now, Miranda and Zoë had probably told the entire band it was Kisrie's fault they didn't make finals. She'd be committing suicide if she rode the bus home. Seemed like everything she tried to do ended in disaster. "Maybe I need to just quit now and spare you all from more embarrassment." Shoving off from her friends, Kisrie ran as fast as her stubby legs could carry her, ignoring her friends calling after her.

What were you thinking, running off like that?" Mom's eyes narrowed.

"Self preservation?"

"Don't get smart with me."

Kisrie raked her fingers through her hair. "Smart? That's a weird word, Mom. Most of the time you tell me I'm *not* smart." Kisrie slapped both hands over her mouth. Did she really just talk to Mom in a Wendy-like way?

Mom's eyes grew large. Her cheeks puffed out. Face boiled red.

"Hey, Kiz." Dad materialized between mother and daughter. He draped his arms across their shoulders. "Don't talk to your mother like that. We're upset because you took off. You scared us to death."

"But they were gonna kill me." Twisting hair around and through her fingers, Kisrie huffed. "I blew the whole competition because I'm so . . . stupid and clumsy."

"That's no excuse for running away and leaving the boosters and Dr. Morgan in a panic." Dad tightened his squeeze. "You're lucky Jacque called."

"What part of homicide do you not—"

"Don't take that tone with us." Dad dropped his arm to his side.

"I think you need to call Dr. Morgan and apologize for all the chaos you caused. And the booster president. She was dialing the police when Jacque, Tammie, and the clarinet section found you up on Windemere." Mom paused, probably to think of a nastier job than scrubbing the garage.

"You know, Kisrie, these kinds of things wouldn't happen if you paid attention to what you were doing." Mom planted her hands on her hips. "I get the impression you're unable to get your priorities straight."

"It's not like that! I just couldn't remember which yard line I was supposed to start at."

"Whoa. Let's refocus here." Dad moved backward away from Kisrie and her mom. "The issue at hand is you taking off from the band without permission. Running away, Kisrie. Your mother is right. You need to apologize to all the adults involved." Dad jabbed his index finger at the air above his head. "Add organizing and cleaning out the shed to your chore list."

The garage *and* shed? It would be Christmas before all that got done. What were they thinking? Kisrie stared at her shoes. The mismatched laces hung limp and untied. One set had little SLR cameras all over them in black and white; the other sported the Reece's logo. *Whatever.* Keri never had to scrub the greasy garage or do anything like this. So. Not. Fair.

"You've got time to spare before bed. I'll back the cars out, and you can start moving stuff from one bay to the next." Dad made it sound like he was gonna take her in the backyard and teach her to throw a football through a tire or some other quarterbacky-type thing.

What would life be like if she ran away and joined the circus?

Kisrie rolled to the left. Flipped right. Smashed her pillow overhead. Counted sheep. But the sheep were jumping the empty forty-five yard line. Not helping! Her stomach lurched and rolled at the thought of having to face anyone from the band, even Jacque and Tammie. She couldn't think of anyone she hadn't let down in the past few days.

And—because she feared Wendy—her uncle could go to prison, at least according to the stupid gossip. Jacque said she wouldn't be surprised if Aunt Zena left him. That would be devastating.

A soft meow pierced the silence as Squeaky, her black-and-white tuxedo cat jumped onto the bed. Grabbing the cat, Kisrie's mind wouldn't let go of Uncle Evan. He used to be more fun when Megyn was here.

An ache swelled in her chest at the memory of her favorite cousin.

Her only cousin.

Megyn, who had smuggled water balloons—in early March, no less—to Kisrie's tenth birthday party. Megyn, who told Kisrie she was "cooler than most of the kids in high school" because she had principles. Megyn, who always made Kisrie feel valuable.

Uncle Evan's eyes had twinkled with pride when Megyn announced she was going to study literature in college. Just like her dad.

Megyn died a hero. She'd intervened when some freak tried to rob a lady in a wheelchair at the light rail station. The guy pulled out a knife, a real knife. But Megyn fought for all she was worth. She died protecting someone she didn't even know.

Kisrie pulled the cat under the covers. Would she make that kind of choice? Lay aside her life?

When Megyn was killed, Uncle Evan aged half a century overnight. The weight of his grief cut deep crevasses across his face. He rarely smiled. No one would believe he and Mom were twins.

Now, what were these rumors doing to him? Could he stand to lose yet another part of his life?

A tear rolled down Kisrie's face. If she was more like Megyn, things wouldn't have gone so far in this Wendy fiasco.

Truth.

Gasping, she bolted upright. Deep inside her heart, the word echoed.

"Hello? Who's there?"

Squeaky popped her furry head out.

She glanced down at the cat. "Who's speaking to me?" She listened, waited. Nothing. Goose bumps danced up and down her arms. Every shadow looked alive, like hungry trolls hiding in the dark, waiting to devour her.

Several minutes passed before Kisrie picked up the cat and padded to her parent's bedroom door. She knocked. Dad invited her in. His voice sounded like he had sand in his larynx. The night light glowed yellow from alongside the bed. Her mother lay curled on her side, snoring like a renegade chain saw. Dad stretched and yawned.

"Did I wake you?"

Dad swept his arm toward Mom. "What do you think?"

"Oh."

"What's up, honey?"

"I'm not feeling too good right now. I think I'm hearing things."

"Like what?"

Mom rolled over with a groan.

"Let's go into your room to talk. Your mom's been working hard all day on her research project." He pushed back the covers and climbed out of bed.

Kisrie followed him, hugging the cat to her chest. Squeaky hissed and leapt from her arms. She needed something else to squeeze. A pillow would have to do. Moments later, they sat on Kisrie's bed.

"You're gonna think I'm losing my mind." Maybe she was.

"Honey, I knew that about you a long time ago."

"What?"

"That you lost your mind."

How could Dad joke around at a time like this?

"Da-aaad."

"I'm sorry, Kiz. Just couldn't resist." Dad patted her knee.

"I heard something."

"What did you hear?"

"A voice." She fidgeted with the edge of her pillow.

"A voice?"

"Yeah." A cough covered the nervous crack in her throat. "A voice."

Who was she kidding? Best to just spill it. Get it out there and let Dad decide whether she was hearing things or not. "It sounded like . . ." Kisrie let out a long sigh and waved one arm in a circle above her head. "It came from somewhere in my room, but then it was louder in my head, if that makes any sense."

Dad nodded. "What did this voice say?"

So far so good. "Only one word."

"What?"

"It said, 'Truth.'"

"That's it?"

"Uh-huh."

"Okay. What do you think it means?"

Kisrie rolled her eyes. "That's what I'm asking you, Dad." Then another horrible thought struck. "I haven't told any lies lately."

"All right." Dad stood and started pacing. "Is someone else lying?"

"I . . . I'm not sure. I mean, like, I was thinking about . . . stuff . . . and it was like someone was in the room talking to me, but I didn't hear it with my ears, or maybe I did. It was really weird."

Dad stopped walking and turned to face her. Kisrie's mind raced. If anyone needed a dose of truth it was Wendy, not her.

"What's gonna happen to Uncle Evan?"

"Is that what's bugging you? Not the guard thing?"

"They both are. Dad, I'm so scared, I can't think straight. Mom is really angry with me, and Wendy can spreads lies like butter on . . . on hot corn. And she always gets away with it."

"Does she have to?"

"Have to what?"

"Get away with it. You know your uncle. Call it what it is."

Kisrie flung the pillow across the room. "What? You want

me to say, 'Hey everybody, listen up. Wendy's a big, fat liar. Mr. Plank is not doing what she says he is.' Yeah, right."

Dad retrieved the pillow. "Look Kisrie, I'm not asking you to make a public announcement. Challenge kids on the source of the rumor. Find the inconsistencies. Play detective. You've read *how* many Brandilyn Collins novels?"

"I don't know, Dad." Kisrie balled her fist and pressed it into the mattress.

"Now let's go back to the voice. Any ideas?"

Oh, she had ideas all right. But if she acknowledged what it really was, wouldn't she be responsible to do what Dad just said? Was there a way to expose Wendy's lie without setting herself up to be a murder victim? An anonymous ad in the *Denver Post?*

Dad failed at hiding a yawn.

Kisrie licked her lips. She couldn't tell Dad about the bathroom. If her parents knew she knew about the rumors beforehand, Mom would probably evoke the Old Testament and have her stoned. "This whole thing rots."

"I'm sure you'll do the right thing." Dad moved in and kissed her temple. "Go to sleep. Church in the morning." And he was gone.

Wendy glanced at the clock and cursed. Time to get up. Not like she ever fell asleep in the first place.

Today was the day she would shatter what little dignity she had left. But it would be worth it, right? If this worked the way she hoped, she could get out of this crappy life.

Flipping on the light switch in her bathroom, Wendy tripped over the rug and muttered another curse. Dollar-store rugs didn't have the no-skid padding on the back. Dollar store and discount retailers would be nothing but a painful memory with a big-time career. No more living in seedy apartments with curling linoleum floors and moldy ceilings. She'd have marble. Marble and granite. And thick, padded bath mats. Wendy stepped over to the sink and slammed a fist on the edge. What was up with the crooked mirror? She caught her reflection. And what was she about to do to herself, to her reputation? Could this cause her to lose the position of power she now enjoyed at school? Would it be worth it in the end?

Wendy dug her fingers into her scalp, tangled them in the dark tresses, and pulled. Her soul shrieked. She didn't dare let out a sound. Iona might not be alone. Shouldn't she be worrying about a history quiz or an algebra test? That'd be *normal.*

Her hands fell to her sides then gripped the edges of the sink. She stared in the mirror. "Hello. My name is Wendy Wetz, and I'm here to solve the problem of world hunger in my role as Miss America." The whispered words didn't match what she saw looking back at her.

Dark circles rimmed her eyes. Hair hung limp, mouth pulled down into a permafrown. The farthest thing from a beauty queen. However, this look could work for her when she talked to the principal.

Scuffling to her dresser, she pulled out some torn sweats and a mismatched T-shirt. Dressing like Kisrie would complete her loser look.

Running to catch an early RTD bus, Wendy vowed public transportation would be a thing of the past once she made it big. An Audi or BMW was more her style.

At the bus stop, she checked her cell for the hundredth time. Bus was running late. She'd better make it to school to catch Dr. Martinez before he got busy. The hiss of brakes caught her attention. The door folded open, and she climbed aboard.

Sliding on dark sunglasses, Wendy made her way down the aisle to the back of the bus. She dropped into an empty seat and ran through some ideas of what to say to the principal. How should she act, telling her tale? It's not like she was a stranger to faking it. Years ago, survival dictated she pack her feelings and emotions behind a wall thick enough to withstand a nuclear holocaust. She tried to feel something other than a simmering rage. Rage wouldn't help her sell her story. Dr. Martinez needed to feel sorry for her.

Sadness or shame? Shame was a good one. Mr. Plank was an old geezer she would say took advantage of her need for a 4.0.

And that meant tears.

Wendy tried to remember the last time she cried. Problem was, she hadn't cried in years. Tears only made the abuse from Iona's clients more loathsome. Poking herself in the eye would have to do.

"Mountain Range." The driver's voice cracked over the speakers.

After crossing the street toward school, Wendy looked around. Too early for students. She was alone.

Here goes nothing. She pulled the sunglasses away from her face and poked herself good and hard in the eye. "Ow!" Tears welled up in both eyes. For as much as it hurt, it better look nasty.

Older-than-the-Rocky-Mountains Mrs. Hampden sat at the reception desk sipping what looked like motor oil. Phone crooked between her shoulder and cheek, she chatted about admission prices to football games. The moment she saw Wendy, she hung up.

Wendy kept her eyes down. Breaths shallow. The smell of Mrs. Hampden's coffee turned her stomach. Wendy gave a loud sniff. Time to put on an Emmy-winning performance. Her eye still stung from the firm poke.

"Can I help you with something?" Mrs. Hampden asked. She set down her coffee mug. Her fingernails tapped on the handle.

With one hand, Wendy lifted her sunglasses with a dramatic flair. The other hand shook as she rubbed her eyes, making sure each action was noted by the ever-watchful secretary. She choked out the words "I need to talk to Dr. Martinez."

"He's reviewing his phone messages, but"—she leaned forward—"if this is important, I'll buzz him."

Mrs. Hampden took the bait. Wendy forced the tears to flow and swallowed. "I have to talk to him. It's about . . . about . . . Mr. P . . . Plank." Wendy let out a loud wail and fell into a chair. She hoped a distraught girl would wail like this. The homecoming queen sure had when her date dumped her at the dance for Wendy.

"Oh, my. Let me buzz him." The secretary jabbed a button on her phone. "Dr. Martinez, we have an issue."

In a matter of seconds, Dr. Martinez popped his head out of his doorway.

"Wendy . . . come on in." He motioned with his hand.

Wendy made sure her legs wobbled as she stood up. She fell back into the chair once, then weaved toward the principal's office like she'd had a gallon of margaritas for breakfast. Mrs. Hampden followed.

"Wendy, what's the matter?" Dr. Martinez asked. He stripped the wire-rimmed glasses from his face and set them on the desk. Wendy steeled herself and stared at Mrs. Hampden.

"I need her here. School policy."

Time for a deep sob. "I . . . I . . . didn't want to do this. I . . . don't know if I can . . ." Bury face in hand. Let them pull it out of her.

Dr. Martinez didn't say a word. He sat like he was waiting for something.

Maybe she wasn't sobbing hard enough. How to get him to dig deeper? Another wail? Too close to the first one. Bigger sobs and more snot would have to do. Wendy sucked in a stuttering breath and did the hyperventilation-style sob Sabrina used on her parents when she needed money.

"Wendy, I can't help you if you don't tell me what's going on."

There! It worked! But, man, this process was gross. Leak a little more. "B . . . but I don't want anyone to . . . to get into trouble!" Wendy pulled the *l* at the end of trouble like taffy, increasing in volume before breaking off into more choking cries.

"Tissue?" Mrs. Hampden held out a box.

Wendy grabbed a handful and blew her nose while she planned her next statement. Go for the kill? Both adults appeared riveted to her dramatics. Eh, why not? All these tears were giving her a headache.

"Mr. Plank. He knew they were important to me."

Dr. Martinez leaned forward. A deep crease cut into his forehead. "What was important?"

"My . . . my grades. He . . . he told me that if I wanted A's"—pregnant pause—"I had to . . . had to sl . . . sleep with him. S . . . so I did!"

The color drained from the principal's face, so much so that he no longer looked Mexican. If not for the brown eyes, he could have passed for a Swedish zombie. He and his secretary exchanged worried glances. Mrs. Hampden hovered near the phone.

Yeah! They were buying it. Hook, line, and sinker, to be cliché. Which Mr. Plank despised.

Wendy described how Mr. Plank had caught on to how important the Colorado Teen Queen pageant was to her and had first lured her into the cafeteria storage room after school. Mrs. Hampden's eyes grew large. Dr. Martinez took on a greenish tint.

"Sooo," Dr. Martinez rubbed his chin, "there was more than one incident?"

"I don't remember how many times with me, but when things began to go weirder, I told him no more, and that's when he failed my project." Wendy lowered her face into a handful of tissues.

"Is that all?"

Looking up to meet his gaze, Wendy whispered, "There were others."

Dr. Martinez nodded to Mrs. Hampden. Her fingers hopped over the buttons of the phone.

It worked. They were calling it in. No turning back now. Wendy's hands shook. Why didn't she feel like celebrating?

~12~

The cacophony of teenaged voices grew as time passed and Mr. Plank had yet to make an appearance in class. A paper airplane embedded itself in Kisrie's curls as Dr. Martinez marched into the classroom. Everyone froze for a few heartbeats.

Dr. Martinez cleared his throat. "Due to some rather unfortunate circumstances, Mr. Plank will be out until further notice. I've put in a call for a substitute who should be here before the end of class. Mr. Plank gave me his lesson plans for the day, therefore, I would like you to pull out your copies of *The Crucible* and begin reading from Chapter One." The principal wrote the assignment on the board.

Cell phones slid out of who-knows-where underneath desktops. Fingers flew while students feigned interest in the lesson. How did they do that, not even looking?

A shudder worked its way up Kisrie's spine. What were they saying?

Weirdness permeated the atmosphere. Dr. M. never taught. Her uncle *never* missed class.

"Excuse me, Dr. M.?" a timid voice from the middle of the room called out.

Mid-marker-stroke, Dr. Martinez twisted to face the class. "Yes, Lau?"

All cell phones disappeared.

"Is Mr. Plank going to jail?"

"I'm not at liberty to discuss the situation. Get to work."

Jail? Uncle Evan could end up in jail? Of course he could. The writing on the board wiggled and squirmed before Kisrie's eyes. A T. rex stomped on her heart. This was all her fault for keeping her stupid mouth shut.

Silence lay like a heavy blanket of snow on the room for the remainder of the block. Kisrie's mind raced with every possible worst-case scenario—Uncle Evan in shackles; Uncle Evan's face on the front page of the *Denver Post*; Uncle Evan being strapped to that lethal injection table. All because she didn't come forward with what she knew. Was that a crime? Her mom would disown her for sure. Maybe she needed to find that Island of Patmos where John wrote the book of Revelation.

Phones reappeared, and everyone texted like mad under their desks. More speculation. Somebody had probably already created a Facebook page defaming her uncle.

An iPhone clattered to the floor. The whole class inhaled as one. Dr. Martinez took long, sustained steps to the spot where the offending phone lay.

The phone's owner writhed in her seat.

"All phones on Mr. Plank's desk. I'll give you thirty seconds." He bent then picked up the phone. "Your parents may retrieve the phones after school at their convenience."

But the damage was done.

And there wasn't a thing her phoneless self could do about it.

Kisrie left English class feeling like her breakfast was about to make an encore appearance. The whole world, from Denver to Singapore, believed her uncle was a vile criminal.

It was amazing how kids could spend entire class periods texting and not get caught. If a teacher took away a phone, the kid would show up with a new one the next day. How to turn all this around?

Leaning on lockers, Lau bragged about how her parents were prosecutors. Her mom worked for the district attorney's office and could lock Mr. Plank away for eternity.

Prosecutor, persecutor . . . was there a difference? Pressure squeezed Kisrie's brain until tiny points of light swirled through her field of vision. All this, because Wendy's mad about a grade? Why would anyone believe Wendy? She lied all the time. Kisrie's mind drifted back to that awful day in the bathroom.

She, Kisrie Kelley, knew the truth. She'd heard Wendy and Sabrina dream up their dumb little plot. But what did she do? She shied away after an obstacle arose and let the thing blow up into this nightmare.

Dr. Martinez seemed to be a reasonable man. Principals had to be reasonable to do their job, right? He also knew Uncle Evan really well and would listen to Kisrie's story. He had to. Her uncle's whole reputation depended on it.

Not bothering to go to her locker, she dragged her lead-filled body to the office. Several policemen sat in the waiting area. Mrs. Hampden's usually-smooth bun hung limp. A silver strand stuck to her sweaty forehead. Kisrie stood at the desk sucking her cheeks into her mouth.

Mrs. Hampden looked up. "Can it wait, or is it an emergency?"

Kisrie's teeth chomped down on her cheeks. "Um, it's really important. It has to do with my uncle."

Mrs. Hampden swiped the stray hair into place. She patted her bun, pulling and tugging it back into place. "I'm sorry, the principal is very busy right now. I can see if one of the guidance counselors has an opening."

Rockets of pain tore through Kisrie's stomach. "My uncle is Mr. Plank. I have to talk to Doc M. Something bad's happening."

Mrs. Hampden leaned to her left and picked up the phone. Her eyes never left Kisrie. "Sir, I have another one here to see you."

The policemen standing in the corner of the office turned

their attention to Kisrie. Dr. Martinez emerged from his office, his tie off. A student peeked out from the copy room.

"Come on in, Kisrie." Dr. Martinez led her to a leather chair and motioned for her to sit down. "Mrs. Hampden informed me you are here to talk about Mr. Plank. You're his niece." He sat down and passed his hand over his face.

Kisrie dug her toe into the rug and rolled her ankle in circles. "Mr. Plank didn't do any of that stuff the other kids are accusing him of."

The principal leaned over the blotter on his desk. "Would you care to elaborate?"

Great. Like the principal was gonna believe her. But it was now or never. Her uncle's fate rested in her hands. She took a deep breath before plunging in. "Dr. Martinez, there's something you need to know. Last week, I was in the bathroom because I choked on some peanut butter cups at lunch when my friend Jacque scared me. Anyway, while I was in the stall I heard some kids talking about him."

"Go on."

"They were mad because he gave them bad grades on this English thing, and one said Mr. Plank was going to pay." Kisrie stopped to take a breath and let this revelation of truth sink into the principal's mind.

Dr. Martinez shifted back in his chair, forming a steeple with the tips of his fingers. "So you're telling me you overheard some girls discussing the demise of your uncle while they were in the bathroom?"

"Yes. It's nothing but a nasty rumor. The kids are just saying mean things to get him in trouble because they are mad at him for failing them. I mean, he made this assignment worth half our semester grade!" Oops. Could've left off that last comment.

"What leads you to believe these girls are making this up?"

"Uncle Evan . . . he would never . . . you know him. It's not like him."

"And these girls?"

"Liars. All of them."

"Who are these girls, Kisrie? I need you to tell me exactly what they said."

"Um, they said they were going to spread rumors about my uncle giving passing grades for . . . sleeping with him." Ew. How does one follow through on the verse "whatever is lovely, pure, yada yada, think on these things" in a situation like this?

"*Who* said this, Kisrie?"

Kisrie's body shook. Dr. Martinez's eyes widened. Did she really have to answer that? Would it hurt not to say? "I . . . uh, I was in the stall and I . . . didn't see who they were."

"You didn't recognize their voices?"

On cue, the word *truth* paraded through her mind. "No." *Now* who was the liar?

"How about you tell me how many different voices you heard talking in the bathroom."

"Three."

"Who were they?"

"I . . . I was in the . . ."

"Give me your best guess." The principal folded his hands.

Kisrie jammed her fists under her knees. "Um . . ."

"Kisrie," Dr. Martinez narrowed his eyes under bushy brows. His nose wrinkled as if he could smell the stench of her dishonesty. "I think you know exactly who said these things."

All of a sudden, the freckle on the back of her hand became the most fascinating object in the whole world. Dr. Martinez slammed both of his palms on his desk and practically launched out of his chair over his desk. Kisrie cringed, expecting a brain-shattering head butt.

"You *know* who these girls are. You're more worried about your reputation than that of this school and your own uncle!" Foamy spit collected in the corners of his mouth. "Withholding evidence is a serious crime, and I'll make sure you feel the full penalty of it if you don't tell me who said this."

Fear ripped through Kisrie's veins. She'd made a ghastly mistake. Now she was trapped in her lie.

Truth!

"Names. Now."

Licking her dry lips, Kisrie attempted to swallow, but there was no saliva in her mouth. "W . . . Wendy . . . Sabrina, B... Brittany."

Now she was going to die. Might as well throw herself in front of an RTD bus. It would probably be less painful than what Wendy would do.

Dr. M. didn't look up. His jaw shifted from side to side. He drew in a deep, shuddering breath and sat down.

Now what? Suspension? Expulsion? Prison for obstruction of justice? Death by hanging?

The principal pushed a button on his phone. "Mrs. Hampden, would you please come in?" His eyes snapped up and bore into hers.

"Don't think you're getting off easy, Kisrie. Your failure to speak out from the beginning has allowed this thing to blow up. I will find appropriate consequences for your actions. Be sure of it." He looked down and picked up a pen, then poked the end into his blotter. "Get back to class."

Kisrie slinked out of the office, scanning the hallways for potentially problematic people. Dr. Martinez's threats didn't scare her as much as what Wendy would do. Discombobulated, Kisrie gathered her belongings and stumbled out of the principal's office. The copier room was empty. Mrs. Hampden shuffled through a heap of mail. Kisrie took it all in. Who knew how long before Wendy figured it was Kisrie who ratted her out?

Wendy gathered with her friends in a tight circle behind the school buses.

" . . . and the best part was that Dr. Martinez let me stay in the counselor's office all day instead of going to class!"

"Now what?" Sabrina asked.

Wendy motioned for the circle to squeeze tighter until each girl was head-to-head. "There's not much to do. We sit back and watch him take his fall. Then I make a move to negotiate my grades."

Wendy and Sabrina burst into fits of laughter.

"Hey, Wen?" Brittany twisted the strap on her backpack. "Listen . . ."

"S'up, Britt? You not finding this as funny as the rest of us?" Wendy patted her on the shoulder.

"I saw Kisrie Kelley talking to Dr. Martinez this morning while I was copying the attendance thingies for Mrs. Hampden."

Wendy hopped backwards. "What?" A string of curses followed.

Sabrina and Brittany looked at each other then at Wendy.

"Why's that a surprise?" Sabrina rolled lip gloss around her mouth. "She was probably tattling on some kid who used a bad word. I've seen her rat on kids for using nasty words."

"That wasn't it." Brittany tossed her head. "As I was sayin', I heard ol' Cow Pie tell Doc M. she overheard our conversation in the bathroom."

"You're freakin' kidding me. I hope you're kidding." Wendy flicked Brittany on the back of the head. "Punch line?"

"No punch line. I'm not joking."

"Did she name names?" Sabrina asked, her voice a little shaky.

"No, she told him she heard about it in the bathroom but didn't recognize the voices."

"The heck she didn't." Wendy smacked a fist into her hand. "She knows it was us."

The threesome remained silent for a few moments. Brittany hummed some dumb song from a Disney movie. Wendy gazed into the blue Colorado sky.

Wendy spoke first. "At least she had enough sense to know her big fat life would be in jeopardy by naming us." Wendy lowered her voice and put her arms around the shoulders of her friends, drawing them nearer. "However, she needs some incentive to make sure she keeps her flabby trap shut."

13

Dishes clattered and silverware rattled as the dishwasher door slammed into place. Zena Plank swallowed hard, forced her trembling face to be still, and then turned to face her husband. "It's protocol. They have to put you on leave."

Evan Plank twisted the dish towel and stared past his wife through the window above the sink. "This process is so unjust."

Zena closed the distance between them and put her hand on his back. "Social workers and the police will conduct an investigation. They'll see right through the lies. You'll be back in the classroom."

Lord, let that be the case.

"Is that so? Remember what happened to Crystal Sims four years ago when those football players accused her of impropriety?"

"She was found not guilty." Zena dragged her fingertips back and forth across the top of Evan's shoulders.

"Parents didn't trust her. Rumors continued." Evan's voice broke. He put a fist to his mouth and coughed. "She lost control of her classroom and was forced to resign." Another cough. "Now she's holding traffic signs on I-25 for CDOT."

Zena knew that anything other than the classroom would be devastating for Evan. He lived and breathed for his students. "Crystal was new. She didn't have a history. Evan, you've been there for *thirty years*. I bet it won't even go to trial." She wished she could really believe the words coming out of her mouth. The justice system was becoming more biased against adults in authority.

"It is highly improbable the authorities can prove I didn't touch those girls. It's my word against theirs." He smoothed out the towel and then folded it in a perfect accordion pattern. Setting the towel on the table, he moved to the pantry, opened the door, and started moving cans around.

Zena sidled up to him. He appeared to be putting the cans in alphabetical order. A sob climbed up her throat. Evan's OCD ways were one of the things that endeared him to her. "Listen to me. The investigators have lots of techniques for discerning the truth. I know the forensic psychologist for the county. He's handled a lot of these cases. He's a good man. Fair."

Evan pulled away and rotated a can of Kroger-brand tomato sauce in his palm. "Maybe this is a sign I need to retire. I should have retired a year ago after Megyn's funeral."

"Oh, no, no, no, no." Within a few long strides Zena stood in front of her husband. She cupped his face in her hands and lifted his head so she could look into his eyes. "Evan, you offer those kids so much. They *adore* you."

A tear rolled down his cheek.

"Evan, not a year goes by in which you don't receive an email from a former student thanking you for holding him or her to such a high standard. Remember Anthony? How he ran into you at the bookstore and apologized for raising a fist to you?"

Evan nodded.

"Anthony went on to tell you how he found Christ and is now the lead drummer in a Christian punk band. All because you wouldn't back down and you told Anthony you loved him too much to let him wreck his life." Zena pressed her lips together to gather control over her quivering mouth. Her husband was too great a man to be taken down by such ridiculous accusations. He had to fight. *Had* to!

Evan slipped from her grip.

"I need to go lie down." He turned and slumped away.

Zena slapped her hand over her mouth to muffle the cry that escaped her lips. She fled to the dark study and flung herself facedown on the floor.

Dear Lord, please help my husband! Don't let me lose him! Please!

Iona punched the buttons on her TV remote with one of her nasty, purple fingernails. "So Mr. Plank is on administrative leave."

Wendy looked up from her history homework. "He should be locked up for what he did."

"I'm impressed. You're playing the role so well you're believing your own lies." A cackle stuttered through Iona's dark, red lips.

"They want me to see a shrink."

"We can't risk that. I'll call the social worker tomorrow and see what I can do." Iona turned the TV off.

"Iona?"

"What?"

Wendy tapped her pen on the table. "Kisrie Kelley told the principal she overheard us talking in the bathroom."

Iona's upper lip curled in disgust. Wendy felt as if worms crawled over the surface of her skin.

"Now, *there's* a problem. How're you gonna fix it?"

Wendy slammed her book shut. Wood splintered. The table crashed to the floor. Neither of them moved. "I have my ways."

"And they are?"

"Why should I tell you?" Maybe this whole thing was a bad idea. Maybe she should come clean.

"You're such a wuss." Iona's hand shot out and Wendy's head snapped back.

"What was that for?"

"Screwing up."

Wendy rubbed her face. "She didn't give names."

"How do you know?"

"I just do." What was she thinking, bringing up Kisrie?

"Kisrie's a nobody." Iona patted her pocket. She pulled out a pack of cigarettes. "What does she care?"

Wendy gritted her teeth. Normal kids would not be having this kind of conversation with their normal mothers. "She's Plank's niece."

"So? If you have enough of your friends come out with stories, she'll be brushed off as a little girl trying to stick up for her relative."

"Already happening, Iona."

"Good. Well, if you screw this up . . ."

"This conversation's over." Wendy grabbed her schoolwork and sashayed to her room.

Kisrie kicked her feet onto the coffee table and allowed her muscles to relax. Bill O'Reilly's "Talking Points" had started when a shrill whistling noise ripped through the silence.

"What the—" Kisrie slammed her hands over her ears. How a human could emit such horrid sounds without help was a mystery.

"I'm telling Mom you're not doing your homework!"

"Keri, you turtle turd, what are you doing?"

"I'm a bush baby. Bush babies are nocturnal primates and need to be in the dark. You don't. You're polluting my habitat. Get out!"

"I thought you were a giraffe."

"I'm a bush baby!" Keri scampered to the foot of the stairs. "Oh, Mother?"

Great. There goes my last hope for relaxation.

Footsteps echoed off the hardwood floor. Kisrie tried to catch what Bill was saying about some stupid celebrity wearing a dress made of raw broccoli sprouts. Keri stood in front of her, stretching her eyelids wide open with her fingers and blocking the view of the screen.

"That's gross. Quit it."

Kisrie hit the pause button on the remote.

"I'm nocturnal," Keri said. "I'm stretching my eyes to see better."

"What's going on down here?" Mom pressed herself between Kisrie and Keri.

Forcing her eyes wider, Keri said in a near-British accent, "She's invading my habitat."

"Am not."

"Keri, was your sister down here first?"

Keri shook her head like a wet dog fresh out of a pond.

"Keri, enough of the dramatics. Now. Kisrie, why aren't you doing homework?"

"I wanted to watch O'Reilly."

"Your grades don't warrant TV time. March yourself up to your room and get busy."

Keri ambled by Kisrie, plucking the remote from Kisrie's hand. Smiling like a drunk muppet, she turned off the TV, bathing the room in darkness.

"Keri, turn a light on and go to your room. I know you have new music to memorize."

"Yes, Mother."

Keri sauntered away and hopped up the stairs.

Mom leveled her gaze at Kisrie. "Homework?"

"Can't I do it later?"

"Absolutely not. Until you bring home straight A's, I don't want to see you anywhere near the TV."

Kisrie rose to her feet. "How come Keri can hide in the dark pretending she's some rabid animal? How come you don't make her do homework all the time?"

Mom shook her head. Red curls swung around her face. "Your sister is not a rabid animal. She's just . . . expressing her imagination."

"Mom, she's not imaginative." Kisrie broke the last word into stretchy syllables. "She's crazy!"

"You can go ahead and add the upstairs bathroom to your list of chores." Mom scrunched her forehead. "And that includes scrubbing the mildew out of the grout."

I'm sorry I'm at grade level and not so imaginative.

Kisrie clenched and unclenched her fists and ran up to her room.

"Upstairs bathroom!" Mom called after her.

What, Mom can read minds? Kisrie leapt from the doorway onto her bed. Plush animals flopped to the floor moments after Kisrie made meteoric impact on the surface of her bed. No way was she going to spend a Friday night writing a paper about the Visigoths sacking Rome. There were bigger things to worry about. Like what Wendy would pull next. And did Kisrie have anyone she could call to chat it out?

Nooooooooo. Jacque was on some date with her latest flavor of the month. Tammie had some family shindig.

Like, didn't anyone care this was a crisis? Wendy could be plotting a slow, gruesome death like the Spanish Inquisition! Draw and quarter. The Rack. Kisrie's mind wandered into places that gave her nightmares.

15

Ew. The dude across the bus aisle hung halfway off his seat, mouth agape, and a slim line of drool snaked from the corner of his mouth. Kisrie shuddered.

Quiet. No one bothered her. No one talked about the mess with her uncle. She wished this reprieve would stretch on forever. But then again, an iPod would be nice. Or an iPhone with an app that would keep her brain from wandering into Wendy-inhabited territory.

But a forever reprieve wasn't meant to be. When the students poured from the buses to change in the stadium bathrooms, the rumors swirled once again.

"What's up with these stalls?" someone shouted from behind a doorless partition.

"The toilets are tin!"

"Good thing Plank isn't here. Not much to keep him out!"

Kisrie let her uniform fall to the floor. She planted her hands on her hips. "Would you guys just stop?"

"What's this? Kelley's defending the perv?" A senior guard member hopped over with one leg in her uniform.

"He's not a perv." Kisrie picked up her costume.

Something pushed hard against Kisrie's backside. Arms

windmilling, Kisrie fought for balance but instead ended up in a puddle on the floor. A snaky trail of water streamed from one of the toilet stalls. Her guard uniform was wet with *toilet* water.

"Kelley, isn't the Plankster your uncle?" A bare foot attached to the antagonizing senior held Kisrie to the floor.

"Yeah, he is. Oooops!" Jacque slapped her hand over her mouth. "Sorry, Kiz."

Kisrie clenched her teeth and growled. "Jaq-eee." A gaggle of half-dressed high schoolers surrounded the unfolding drama.

"What's he like?" Chrissy, the girl she tripped with her sabre at Littleton, said with an exaggerated wink.

Twisting the fabric, Kisrie wrung the dirty water from her costume. Did Chrissy really ask that? Really?

"You gonna answer me or what?" Chrissy squatted down. Eyeball-to-eyeball.

Tammie pushed into the circle, rubbing deodorant under her arm. "Hey gang, would you just leave her alone?"

All eyes zeroed in on Tammie. Chrissy coughed. "What? Are you her bodyguard, you little twerp?"

"Twerp? I haven't heard that one in like, forever," Jacque said, forcing a laugh. No one joined in. "Okay, not so funny."

"Mr. Plank is a decent man, and he would never do any of the stuff you idiots are saying." Kisrie gritted her teeth and pulled back her lips, hoping to appear more ferocious than she felt.

"Ladies!" A breathless band mom ran into the bathroom. "Gavin is waiting." She turned to Kisrie. "Why aren't you dressed yet? The band is headed to warmup now." With a quick about-face, she turned and jogged out of the bathroom.

Everyone snapped into action. Jacque and Tammie pulled Kisrie to her feet.

"Sorry, Kiz," Jacque said.

"They're stupid. That's what they are. Here." Kisrie handed Jacque her leotard. "I need to get my hair up first."

Intervals for warmup block were supposed to be at six steps. To Kisrie, they felt more like sixteen. Kisrie's left hand closed around air on the last flip of the spin medley. Her pole clattered on the ground. Gavin froze mid-clap and the girls around her turned to stare. It wasn't like she was the only one to drop during the exercise. She bent down to pick up the flag.

Miranda snorted. "I think we need to make Kisrie *Plank* do the exercise again on both sides. No mistakes, or she runs after the show."

The section leaders, Miranda and Zoe, were out to get her.

"No time. We need to work on the weapon feature in the closer." Gavin waved the guard out of block to switch equipment.

During the show, Kisrie fought hard for composure. Everyone in the whole wide world knew she was Plank's niece.

Yep, she was doomed.

In their eyes, she was now the molester.

16

Pastor Dan looked like that Spock dude from the old Star Trek series. Kisrie'd seen the show a few times with her dad. As if on cue, Jacque snickered then breathed, "Live long and prosper," into Kisrie's ear. Creepy.

Heads dipped in prayer.

"You say that every week," Kisrie mouthed.

"What? It fits."

Whack! All of a sudden, Jacque jerked upright and rubbed her head.

"Some cranky old lady just hit me with a bulletin."

"Shut up and pray." Kisrie pulled Jacque's head down by the bangs.

Pastor Dan said, "Amen," and the drummer rocked out an intro to a song Kisrie had never heard before. All around, people stood. A claw-like hand with glittery talons bit into Kisrie's arm, and she was yanked to her feet.

"Look over there. It's a swayer." Jacque said over the singing, pointing.

Kisrie turned her neck. A blue-haired elderly woman at the end of a pew near the front held her arms toward heaven and rocked back and forth. Her eyes were closed. "And there's a jumper. Boing. Boing." Jacque sandwiched Kisrie's face with her hands and rotated her head.

A man with salt-and-pepper hair shot hairy eyeballs at them from a few seats down.

"Jack, quit touching me and sing."

"You're not singing."

"I'm not disturbing anyone like someone I know."

"Who?"

"Eye roll."

"That's a funny name."

Both girls squared off. "Here's me," Kisrie pointed to her eyes, "rolling my eyes." Kisrie rolled her eyes in a most exaggerated manner then turned her wrist and stabbed her fingers toward Jacque. "At you."

"Oh."

"Will you two either get with the program or leave the sanctuary?" It was one of those wanna-be-secret-service-type guys thinking he was cool and all that because he could stand at the back doors through the entire service.

Kisrie and Jacque sat down.

"If I need to talk to you two again, you'll be sitting with your parents."

"What crawled down his throat, got stuck, and died?" Jacque plunged her hand into her purse.

"Gross. Besides, *you* got us in trouble."

Music softened. A prayer was said from the stage. Jacque opened her cell phone. Her thumbs were all over the screen like popcorn kernels in a hot pan of oil.

After the last song, the sanctuary door creaked open. A dozen heads swiveled. Kisrie gasped. Uncle Evan and Aunt Zena headed down the aisle.

Oh, no. This can't be good.

Uncle Evan was a mere shadow of his usual self. He and Aunt Zena looked like they had both aged twenty years.

"What's he doing here?" Jacque's eyebrows arched upward.

"You *are* from Planet Stupid. He goes to church here."

"Oh. Forgot."

Horror ripped through Kisrie's body as her aunt and uncle approached the stage. They stood stone-still while Pastor Dan adjusted his mic.

"One thing I love about this church is its willingness to abandon structure and respond to the Holy Spirit." Pastor motioned for the Planks to join him front and center. Where everybody could see.

Kisrie put a hymnal over her head.

"Folks, we have a family in need. I'm asking for prayer warriors to come forward and pray over this couple. The rest of you, please pray as the Spirit leads while you remain in your seats. We will take as much time as needed." Pastor Dan lowered his head, draping his arms across the shoulders of Aunt Zena and Uncle Evan.

Mom, Dad, and Keri were the first to join the pastor's prayer circle. Standing on her toes, Mom scanned the crowd.

"Jacque, hide me!" Kisrie fell to her knees on the hard, tile floor.

"You make a good foot rest, Kiz."

Feet by the dozens scampered down the aisles to pray. The place was emptying fast.

"Maybe you should go up there and pray for him. Like, that might get your mom off your back."

The tile smelled like old coffee. It was sticky where Kisrie's hand rested. "I don't want to go up there, okay?"

"It's not like many kids from our school go here."

Going up there meant more pressure from her mom to be a public advocate for her uncle. How could people believe Wendy's dumb ol' lie? How could anyone believe her uncle could do . . . those kinds of things?

"I can't, Jack. I just can't." 'Course, this created a whole new terror. Forget what Wendy might do; what would *Mom* do, since practically all the chores in the house and around the yard were already assigned? Death and dismemberment didn't seem so out of the question.

17

The salsa bowl in the middle of the table called her name. Who cared about calories at a time like this? Kisrie was destined to be stocky for the rest of her life anyway. She stabbed a tortilla chip into the bowl and fisted another.

"I can't eat any of this stuff," Keri said, laying the laminated menu on the side of her chair.

"And why not?" Dad asked.

"They don't have caterpillars or dung beetles."

"Excuse me?" Mom asked, the menu hovering below her eyes.

"I'm a bush baby. We don't eat burritos or tacos." Keri said it with the air of royalty.

Another chip. And one more. The salty jalapeno kick did nothing to deaden the dread building in her gut.

"Kisrie, would you knock it off?" Mom clamped her hand shut like a clam. A waiter stopped at the table with a note pad. "You folks ready to order?"

"Why yes, of course." Mom flashed a stiff smile.

Keri piped up with her Queen-Victoria accent. "He wants the number four. She'll have the organic Tex-Mex salad." She paused, scrunching up her face and looking down at Kisrie. "I don't know about that one. She'll eat just about anything, and do you have dung beetles?"

"Thanks Keri, but we can order for ourselves." Dad scanned his menu.

"Yes, Father."

"Dung beetles?" The waiter scratched his head with the end of his pen.

"Don't mind her. She's our creative child." Dad grabbed the menu out of Keri's hands.

Waiter Boy dropped his hands to his sides. "Well, I know we don't carry insects. Problems passing health inspection."

Keri crossed her arms and slumped in her seat. "Then I'll have the number four combo plate please."

What was wrong with this family? Kisrie grabbed a handful of chips and shoved them in her mouth, skipping the salsa.

"About your orders?"

"I'll have the chicken enchiladas with black beans, please," Mom said.

"Kisrie?" Dan waved his hand in front of her face.

Silence equals invisibility. Kisrie scooted the bowl of chips closer to her and scooped up as many as she could hold.

Dad grabbed the chips out of her hand. Several fell onto the table. "It's your turn to order."

The waiter dropped his pad and bent to pick it up.

"Kisrie, you order what you want, or I'll do it for you. I know how much you love bean sprouts." Dad winked.

Order? Where was she? "Oh. Uh, can I have spaghetti?" Silence fell over the table. The waiter's mouth opened and closed like that of a dummy on a ventriloquist's knee.

"This is a *Mexican* restaurant," Her mom said, strangling a water glass. Good thing it was plastic.

"She'll have the blue plate special. Extra green chili. No pork."

Waiter Man nodded and hurried to the kitchen.

Dad cleared this throat. "What's going on here?"

"I want to go back to Africa." Snatching a chip, Keri dunked it in the salsa and popped it into her mouth.

"You've never been to Africa," Kisrie mumbled.

"She speaks!" Dad pinched a tiny tortilla crumb from the now-empty basket.

Mom took a sip of water and set down her glass. "I would like to know where Kisrie was this morning."

Keri puckered her lips and sipped her water like a dainty old lady.

"I was in church."

"I didn't see you when we prayed for your aunt and uncle."

"Got lost in the crowd."

Keri swallowed. "I saw Jacque sitting on her."

"Jacque wasn't sitting on me, gnat breath," Kisrie whispered out of the side of her mouth to her sister and resumed her chip dipping. Why was lying easier than telling the truth when she knew darn well the truth was what she was supposed to be telling?

Might as well eat the chip pieces that fell on the table.

Mom turned to face Dad and crossed her arms. "I never liked the idea of teens sitting with friends instead of their families."

"Kisrie doesn't like church."

"Shut up, Keri."

"You don't. You and Jacque sit back there texting *boys*." Keri drug out the word for several beats.

Now that was funny. Texting boys. Her? Yeah, right. "Ooh yeah, I was asking Nick from the drum line to help me sneak out of my bedroom at midnight so we could go hook up." Too bad that wasn't true, nor would it ever be.

"If you two don't start behaving, we will pay for our chips and salsa and leave without lunch."

"My office needs some organization . . ." Dad let the end of the sentence dangle on his breath.

Kisrie dunked a chip into the salsa. It broke in half. "I prayed in my seat."

"But I saw . . ." Keri wriggled under the hand Dad pressed over her mouth.

"Enough, Keri. One more word out of you and *you'll* clean my office."

"It doesn't look good." Mom said.

Really? This was about looking good to the church people? About peoples' perception of the Kelley family? "I . . . I don't know what to say." No more chips! Not even crumbs! The world was gonna end.

"How about apologizing for your insensitivity for starters? Your uncle needs people to stand with him now more than ever, and to think his own niece is more concerned about what her peers think . . ." Mom trailed off and looked away. The veins bulged in her neck as she sawed her jaw.

"But . . ." No. No more lies. Jacque did sit on her. It was a ploy to remain unseen, to disconnect from the painful circumstances Kisrie could have *prevented* if she'd had the guts to come out with the truth the moment she knew what was going down.

No, Mom, it's not so much about who I think will see me; it's about not wanting anyone to find out that this whole mess is my fault.

18

Back at the house, Kisrie made a beeline for her bedroom. She thought about slamming the door, but the consequences deterred her. She pulled it shut behind her. A backwards flop landed her in the center of her plush zoo. She stared at her ceiling.

Lord, my life is such a mess! Her prayer was interrupted by a soft knock at her door. Her father poked his head through the crack between the door and its frame.

"Come in," Kisrie mumbled, cradling her head with her hands. Dad sat next to her on the bed. He placed a large hand on Kisrie's leg.

"It's such a beautiful day, I find myself unable to fight the urge to head over to Mt. Falcon and do some hiking. Wanna come?"

Kisrie rolled onto her stomach. "What about the Broncos game?"

"Ah, I spend all week in an office in front of a screen. I need some fresh mountain air."

"I need a new life."

Ignoring her comment, Dad scanned the room, looking for something. He leaned toward her desk where a pair of hiking boots rested on top of one another under her chair. Next thing she knew, they were on top of her.

"What about Mom?"

"What about her?"

"She wanted a piece of me too."

"No one wants 'a piece' of you, Kiz." Dad scratched his nose.

"She was mad after church."

"You and I are going to talk, okay?" A sly grin pushed his cheeks upward. "And take some killer pictures."

Kisrie's heart skipped a beat. Pictures? Dad was gonna let her use his Nikon D800? *The* Camera? She shook with excitement.

"Your mom is working on her research article. The photography thing will be our secret. Okay?"

About an hour later, Kisrie and her father climbed up the pine-scented path to Eagle's Nest lookout. From what used to be an old summer cabin, a spectacular panoramic view of the Highway 285 corridor into the southwestern Rocky Mountains stunned the eyes.

Kisrie and her father reached the overlook. Kisrie's sides heaved in and out. The camera bag was open in seconds and she perched on the railing, checking the f-stop settings and framing shots. Her father's breathing was as easy as if he was sitting in his recliner. Reaching under his windbreaker, he grabbed something that crinkled.

"Peanut butter cup?"

"Are you kidding?" Kisrie lowered the camera, letting it hang from her neck. She hopped down from the railing and tore the bag from his hands.

"It's a special treat. Don't say a word to anyone."

"Dad, you know you can trust me when it comes to chocolate." Kisrie felt her face stretch into a smile.

Popping a candy in her mouth, Kisrie leaned over the brown pipe railing and breathed through her nose. So peaceful here. She tried to imagine herself as the owner of the Eagle's Nest overlook back when it was a tiny cabin rather than a picnic shelter.

How cool would it be to wake up to that awesome view! Her reverie was interrupted by her father's voice.

"Kiz, we need to talk." He sidestepped next to Kisrie, his muscular left arm draped across her shoulders.

Kisrie stared at the concrete patio. "About what?" She dipped her hand into the bag for another.

"How 'bout you tell me how these rumors at school started. About your uncle."

"If they're just rumors, why talk about them?"

Dad removed his arm from her shoulders and wandered to the other side of the concrete observation deck. "Well, the school administration is taking this seriously. For now, they aren't buying the whole rumor thing."

"I know. It makes me so mad that Wendy would—"

"Wendy?" Her dad rolled a foil wrapper into a tiny ball and pushed it into the back pocket of his jeans.

Kisrie's hands flew to her mouth. Her dad pivoted to face her. He cocked his head and stared, waiting—no, daring her to continue.

In one and a half steps he latched onto her hand and pulled her away from the railing. "Let's take the Tower Trail, and you tell me about Wendy."

"I can't." Isn't there something to the whole reliving trauma thing?

"Can't or won't?"

A family with a herd of toddlers swarmed the lookout area. Dad let go of her hand. "Walk. And talk."

The autumn leaves crunched under each footfall. Kisrie tripped over an erosion bar and slammed her knee into an exposed tree root. It felt like a fiery sword stabbed her kneecap. Rolling onto her bottom, she let out a loud wail. Her dad rushed to her side and sat on the path next to her. A mountain biker appeared around the corner, legs churning in low gear, his breath in short, regular bursts.

"Kiz, you're going to get run over." Her dad put his hands in her armpits and dragged her underneath a large Ponderosa pine. A dark stain swelled on the knee of her jeans.

"Pull your pant leg up so I can take a look." Kisrie obeyed.

Her dad fished around in his CamelBak for a first-aid kit. Moments later, the wound on her knee was bound in a clean bandage.

Her dad pulled her up. "Think you can walk, or do we need to go back home?"

"I can walk," she replied.

Father and daughter traveled in silence to the tower. It was unoccupied. They climbed up the stairs and gazed over the treetops at the whole Denver Metro area. Kisrie experimented with different manual settings and closeup texture shots of pine needles and tree bark.

Spicy and clean, Dad's aftershave mixed nicely with the woodsy scent of the pine trees. A gentle breeze tickled her nose with his scent.

"Back to Wendy. She doesn't have anything to do with this accusation, does she?"

Truth!

Kisrie rolled her eyes toward the sky. *Okay, okay.* She retold the entire story, choking incident and all.

"You did tell Dr. Martinez it was Wendy and Sabrina, didn't you?"

Kisrie nodded. "But I didn't want to."

"Even after your 'truth' experience?"

"Dad, I . . . she . . . Wendy hates me. Remember that little fact? If she knew I knew the truth, I'd be swallowing my teeth. I didn't wanna get involved." A pine cone lay at her feet. She picked it up and tossed it from hand to hand. "I just want my high school life to be like normal. Okay, better yet—over."

"What's not normal about it?" His voice softened.

Kisrie swiped her hands up and down the length of her body. "Look at me! Do I look like any of the other kids? Look at this . . ." Kisrie grabbed a handful of muffin top that rolled over the waistband of her pants. "I'm . . . I'm fat! I'm a big, fat, ugly cow! Why do you think the kids moo at me in the halls? Why do you think boys gag when someone teases them about getting stuck with me on a date, huh?"

"Sweetie, I'm so sorry they think that. You aren't fat—"

"I am! You only say that 'cause you're my dad. You *have*

to say nice things about me." Kisrie turned away and let her tears fall the long distance to the ground.

"I had no idea it was so bad."

She sent the pine cone sailed over the railing. "It's always been this bad." Kisrie buried her face in her arms. "I just stopped telling you and Mom about it in middle school because I didn't want to be pulled from any more classes for counseling.

"Dad," Kisrie wiped her nose on her sleeve. "That counseling Mom made me do with Aunt Zena didn't help. Nobody gives a rip about that inner-beauty junk. They totally care about how you look. Big chest, tiny butt, straight teeth, dark skin, exotic eyes. All stuff I don't have."

Her memory stirred up the incident last week when dumb ol' Jacque had decided to ask Clay if he'd go to Homecoming with Kisrie. It was during homeroom when Jacque inquired, and Clay had doubled over laughing. A few of his friends came over to see what was up. He practically shouted to the whole world that Jacque asked *him* to take Kisrie to the dance. The teacher couldn't get the class under control. Ugly names and mooing sounds bounced off the walls until the bell rang an eternity later. Inner beauty—what a joke.

Light breezes blew her curls around her face, some sticking to the shiny tear tracks running down her cheeks. Every now and then, her father reached over to wipe her face.

Being ugly hurts.

The tears kept coming. Dad hung on to her as they descended the stairs of the tower. They trudged in silence to the foundation of the Summer White House. Dad walked over to the stone wall of the unfinished foundation and leaned toward the mountain ranges as if seeking their age-old wisdom. Kisrie stayed back, etching circles in the dirt with the toe of her boot. Hikers mingled around the site, reading the historical information about how Colorado school children had collected pennies to fund Walker's dream of bringing U.S. presidents to scenic Colorado each summer.

After forever, a day and a half, and then some, Kisrie's dad came back to her. He nodded to the trail leading toward the castle ruins on the opposite ridge. "Dad, my leg hurts. Can't we just go home?"

"We're not done yet. Rather, you're not done yet. I know you know what I mean." His long legs carried him away from her.

Kisrie had to jog to catch up with him. After following the Ponderosa pine-covered ridge a ways, Kisrie plopped on a bench overlooking the foothills. Shades of red, yellow, and orange brush created a mosaic on the meadow below them.

"She'll kill me."

"You sure?"

"Are you senile already? Old football injury wiping out your memory? Dad, she shoved my head into a toilet in seventh grade and slammed my fingers in a desk in sixth. Oh, and she shoved me on the kickball court in fifth, then kicked me in the—"

"I get your point. But the threat of being beaten up shouldn't keep you from doing the right thing."

"Easy for you to say. You never had to deal with any of this stuff. I saw your yearbook pictures. You were popular. Hot *and* big. No one could've wanted to mess with you."

"I'll concede I don't know what it's like to be picked on by peers, but I did lose a job because I was honest."

"So what? A job isn't the same thing. You can get another one."

Dad rolled a stick in his hand. His eyes seemed unfocused, far away. "In college, I worked at the campus bookstore. A football scholarship only goes so far. Anyway, when I was a junior I was assigned to close out the registers. Transactions and receipts didn't match up night after night. I finally figured out the manager was stealing money."

"So he said if you told, he'd fire you."

"That, and his dad was the football coach." The color drained from his face. He turned and locked eyes with her. "I started for the Buffs as a freshman. We ranked at the top of the conference. NFL recruiters were paying attention. I'd dreamed of going pro since my little-boy hands could fit around a football."

Shock waves prickled the surface of Kisrie's skin. She knew Dad had played football. Knew he loved the game as much as she loved peanut butter. But she never knew he'd wanted to play professionally. Had no idea such a dream was within his grasp. He'd never said anything about it before. "You were kicked off the team?"

"No, I chose to leave the team. Coach would've kept me as long as I kept my mouth shut. I told the truth and paid a hefty price."

"Do you regret it?"

Dad lifted his eyes to the sinking sun. A golden glow washed over his face, erasing all the lines. "No way. Not at all."

Kisrie retrieved the bag of peanut butter cups and poured herself a handful, then dumped them on her lap. She didn't have Dad's strength and character. Plus, he was a guy. *And* he had a choice. He didn't have to quit. The choice to live out his dream was there. She didn't even know if she'd live through this ordeal.

19

"Let's see." Wendy bit into a strawberry Twizzler. "Britt, you have PE class with her?"

Brittany pulled her phone out of her jeans and jabbed the screen. "Mmmm, hmmmm."

"Put the stinkin' phone down and listen to Wendy." Sabrina karate-chopped the phone out of Brittany's hand. "Haven't you heard you can get brain cancer from using a cell phone all the time?"

"Pshh, that's just some line cooked up by adults trying to get teens away from their phones."

Wendy shuddered. "Listen Britt, if you help me with a little something, I think I can hook you up with Warren."

That should get her attention.

Sabrina let out a squeal and danced in a tight circle. "He's hot."

Brittany's face pinked. "You got it, Wen. Whatcha need?"

Score! "A picture."

"No way!" Sabrina grinned.

"I need you to take a picture of Cow Pie in the locker room and text it to me. I'll make sure it gets around." Wendy planted her hands on her hips and sashayed around her friends.

"Bonus points if either one of you can get some good incriminating pictures of her weird little friends."

"Can I get in trouble for this?"

"Only if you're caught."

"I don't know, Wen, Ms. Glisp hangs out in there and takes away cell phones if she sees them. Britt could get suspended."

Wendy snapped her head around, locking eyes with Sabrina. How dare she challenge this brilliant plan? It was foolproof! "Not if she's smart. Remember that time at the coffee shop when I got Kelsey and Luke lip-locked near the restrooms? Thousands of hits on YouTube."

"The best part was when Kelsey's boyfriend turned Luke into a mashed potato." Sabrina threw a few punches into the air.

"This is just a still, right?" Brittany pressed her thumb into the side of her phone and held it pointing toward her face at arm's length. The phone made that pathetic fake shutter noise.

"Make sure it'll embarrass her if the whole school sees it." Wendy tossed out the idea to her hungry pack of wolves. Laughter erupted. Just as she planned, this was gonna be good.

"Kinda like anti-porn." Sabrina laughed.

"I sure wouldn't want to look at *that.*"

Wendy grabbed the bag of Twizzlers just as the bell rang. "Okay. Send it to me as soon as you get it." Sliding one out of the bag, Wendy skipped down the hall. Cow Pie and her herd had *no* idea who they were dealing with.

Two days later, it was clear something wasn't right. Sharp pains pierced Kisrie's gut as she quickened her pace toward the crowd gathered in front of her locker. Kids were shoving tighter and tighter like bees on a soda spill straining to look at something.

"Dude, that's wrong on so many levels." A senior brass player popped out of the melee shaking his head. What was wrong? Was her door smashed in? Did someone scrawl a death threat in Sharpie? Kisrie hefted her backpack onto both shoulders and teetered on tippy toes to catch a glimpse of whatever it was.

She saw it.

In full color.

An eight-by-ten image of her bending over in the process of getting dressed or undressed in the locker room. The left side of her briefs were wedged where the sun don't shine. Dimples of cellulite appeared deeper than the craters on the moon from the harsh exposure of what had to be a cell-phone camera. She didn't remember anyone in there with a phone. Ms. Glisp always—

"Hey look, someone just texted me a link to more pictures." Some kid in a Dallas Cowboys hoodie shoved his cell phone under the nose of a neighbor.

"There's more? Sick!"

More. Not just one, many. Showing what all over the internet?

"Whoa! Now that's more like it. Check this one out." A phone was held up and dozens of hands competed for the prize.

Kisrie tried to squeeze sideways through the dense crowd. Have. To. Tear. Down. Picture. But the crowd wouldn't let her through. Pressure increased inside her skull. Pulsing, pounding. The hallway tilted. She heard her name from far away. "Kiz! Kiz? Where are you? There she is, Jacque!"

"Oh my word, she's tipping over!"

"Well, grab her arms."

A scrawny kid with a CSU football jersey called out, "Nice bra, Jacque!"

"Jacque? Me?" Jacque stood up, ramrod straight. "Tammie, how does he know what my bra—"

"Grab Kisrie! She's falling!"

"My arms are full."

"Don't let her fall. We'll figure out the bra thing in a minute."

A thud on the floor. Something fell against Kisrie's feet.

Someone grabbed Kisrie from behind, arms circling around her chest from underneath her armpits. The haze cleared. Anger stirred. *Try again.* She tore from the grasp and clawed through the crowd, elbowing anyone in her way. Arms outstretched, she raked the air snagging the top of the picture and tearing it from the upper vent.

"Hey, leave that there!"

"Wait. Guys, here's a better one." An iPad rose above the crowd. A dripping wet Tammie was sloughing out of her swimsuit in the locker room.

Kisrie's heart stopped beating. This whole disaster wasn't limited to her anymore. Wendy was now out to destroy her friends. Her only friends! She spun to face the roiling mass. "Go away! All of you!"

"Nice butt."

"Teacher! We need a teacher!" Jacque jumped up and down, fingers cupped around her mouth.

Bell.

Clicking. Faster and faster.

Students constricted into little clusters around cell phones, now ignoring the hard copy Kisrie clutched.

"Break it up."

Clumps of students parted like water in front of a boat.

"Oh, yay, a teacher." Jacque raked her hair into a glossy, black pony tail and twisted. And twisted. Her mouth was in a tight, flat line.

"Will somebody please tell me what's going on here?"

Silence.

Kisrie's body trembled. She had to concentrate so hard on breathing, words failed her.

"Somebody's passing around pictures of her in her underwear." Tammie stepped forward to meet up with the teacher, finger pointed.

"You might want to check the phones too." Kisrie said looking directly at Tammie who seemed unaware of her own public humiliation.

The teacher narrowed his eyes and let out a deep sigh. He made eye contact with Kisrie; then his eyes fixed on the crumpled paper in her hand.

Arm shaking, she held it out to him. He uncurled it and

looked away. "Nobody goes anywhere until you give me your cell phones."

"You can't take our phones!" Cries of protest popcorned and echoed off the hard surfaces in the hall. Kids took off in all directions.

It looked like a bomb exploded, scattering bodies everywhere. Others stood rooted in place, poking at screens. More teachers appeared and made failed attempts at corralling the kids to confiscate their phones.

The first teacher on the scene tapped Tammie on the shoulder and nodded at Kisrie and Jacque. "Come on, let's get to the office."

Dr. Martinez paced while Kisrie stared at the impressions his feet left in the plush carpet.

"Wendy Wetz?" He asked, marching back and forth with his arms behind his back.

Who else? Obviously the Queen of Mean had discovered that Kisrie had ratted her out about the bathroom conversation and was getting even, but nobody could blame Kisrie if she ratted out Wendy for the sexting. Dr. M. had guessed it all on his own anyway.

"Kisrie?" The principal stopped and stared at her.

Wendy, Wendy, Wendy, Wendy. "I . . . I don't know . . . I mean, a lot of kids don't like me. It could be anyone." Kisrie kept her face pointed toward the floor.

Truth.

The word screamed like a passenger jet taking off in her mind. She grabbed her head with both hands. Wendy was not in her gym class, but she knew Wendy's slimy fingerprints were all over the deed. That girl held a power over everyone in the school, it seemed. And she always got away with murder!

"It looks like the gym locker room."

Truth.

Kisrie gritted her teeth. It made sense. The evil looks in the hallway. Nasty comments and names whispered in Kisrie's ear when the teacher was a distance away.

Wendy was not in the locker room, so who? Brittany! Brittany had PE with her yesterday.

"Kisrie, are you familiar with sexting?"

"Yes." Dad was a Fox News junkie. Some kids in Pennsylvania had had to register as sex offenders for the next ten years, and the state police did phone checks to make sure images were erased. If it came to that, Wendy would hunt her down for the rest of her life.

"Are either Brittany or Sabrina in your PE class?"

Jacque and Tammie's reactions to their images haunted Kisrie. Tammie had crumpled to the floor. The girl who wore long skirts and freaked out over changing on the bus at band competitions was as exposed in those pics as any human could be. The high school counselor had needed to call Aunt Zena in for backup, because Tammie was in a catatonic state.

Jacque looked paler than those vampires in the *Twilight* movies when she saw the profile shot of her, shirtless and stepping out of her sweats.

Fear shot barbs into her throat when Kisrie choked out Brittany's name.

Dr. Martinez massaged his jaw.

"Is Jacque in your PE class too?"

"Yes."

"Did you see Brittany hovering nearby while you were changing?"

Who had time to notice? Ms. Glisp gave them exactly ninety seconds to change in and out of their gym clothes under the threat of ten laps around the three-court-wide gymnasium. "No."

"Kisrie, I need you to talk to me. This whole thing will be resolved faster if you tell me what you know. It will also help me to keep you and your friends safe."

The glass on the door rattled. Mrs. Hampden poked her head in. "Excuse me, Dr. Martinez. Jacque Gonzales is here to speak with you and Kisrie."

The principal swung his arms behind his back. "Bring her in."

"Kiz, I found this on the floor by your locker." Jacque

pushed a small piece of paper into Kisrie's hand without looking at Kisrie's face. "Hey, Doc M."

Kisrie smoothed it out. "Keep it shut." was all it said.

Dr. Martinez held his hand up, waiting. Kisrie passed it to him. His eyes rolled back and forth. He pushed his glasses up higher on his nose.

"Keep it shut?"

How could Jacque be so stupid as to bring that here, in front of Dr. Martinez? This now created more questions to which Kisrie knew the answer. Wendy. Somehow Wendy *knew* she knew what went down in the bathroom. If these pictures were just the warning, what would the punishment be? What if her parents saw the pictures? What if Keri found them online?

"Kisrie, answer me please."

Her head snapped up. "Wh-what was the question?"

Dr. Martinez folded his arms and glared over the rim of his spectacles.

"I . . . I don't know what this is about. Um . . ."

Jacque, help me!

Kisrie made large, oogley eyes at her friend. Jacque turned her face away.

No. You can't abandon me now!

The principal's eyes softened. "You're afraid. I understand."

Tears bit the inside corners of her eyes as Kisrie nodded. Scared to death, and for good reason. Wendy was successfully taking away the one thing Kisrie couldn't bear to lose—her friends. Jacque stood hunched over, hands crammed into the tiny front pocket of her low-rise jeans, not looking at Kisrie.

"It's not my fault!"

Jacque's head snapped up. Her eyes were, what? Angry? Hurt? It was an emotion Kisrie had never seen before on her friend's face.

"Look, ladies. I know this is hard, but I need your help." Dr. Martinez sank into his chair and leaned back, motioning for the girls to sit in the chairs opposite his desk. They sat. "Let me say this up front. I will do everything in my power to keep you safe. Tammie included. But if we are to stop this kind of thing, I need you to cooperate with the police and me. We need to send a message that sexting will not be tolerated at Mountain Ridge High."

Kisrie looked to her friend, hoping for a supportive glance. Nothing. Jacque stared into space.

Bile rose in Kisrie's throat. Her heart pounded and air pushed and squeezed, struggling to get to her lungs. She wanted to run away. To Antarctica. No people there, only penguins.

"Can I transfer schools?" Jacque's voice was flat. Her eyes looked dead.

She wasn't serious, was she?

"Tammie couldn't even handle staying to talk now. Can't you put her in that protection thing where she gets a new life?" Jacque turned her head and stared at Kisrie.

It wouldn't be a stretch to add the words *and new friends* to the end of Jacque's statement.

One thing was clear. Her friends were bailing on her. She couldn't blame them. Their reputations had just been destroyed.

But there was no way she could face this alone.

Hiding was impossible. Why didn't Dr. M. just send her home and spare her the horrible comments and jokes?

"Get some new granny panties!"

"My phone doesn't have enough pixels for your butt!"

"Victoria Secret called. They're recalling their barnyard campaign due to misrepresentation of cattle."

Why did she have to stumble through the halls as kids pointed at her and laughed, or worse yet, showed her images on Facebook from their phones? The photos of her and Jacque were bad, but Tammie's were far worse. Nothing was left to the imagination.

In bio, Kisrie slid a note to Jacque apologizing for everything, but her friend acted like Kisrie was the spore of some deadly infectious disease like Ebola. Let the note sit on the table in the open. So anybody could grab it.

In the office, nobody would tell Kisrie how Tammie was

doing. Something about confidentiality. Who was the real criminal here? Kisrie for doing what everyone else was doing, dressing out for gym? Or Brittany for bringing a banned cell phone into the locker room and posting the horrid pictures?

Shame lowered Kisrie's shoulders a few inches. Mom had to know. If the faculty was treating her like she did something wrong, how much worse would it be at home? Stuff like this never happened to perfect little Keri. Stuff like this probably never would either.

Kisrie threw her flag bag down on the porch and fumbled with the door latch. At least guard had been sufferable. It was a miracle no one bothered her during rehearsal, probably because Gavin was on the warpath, intent on redeeming their abominable performance at Littleton.

Pueblo didn't quite do it for him. The guard was second in their caption even though the overall score had put Mountain Ridge's band in first place. Anyone who opened their mouth was doomed to cymbal laps.

Jacque stayed as far away from Kisrie as she could, and Tammie never showed.

Wendy Wetz deserved to be fed to a swarm of hungry alligators swimming in hydrochloric acid for all the havoc she'd wreaked over the years! Kisrie would love nothing more than being the person to shove the Queen of Mean into the pit, but what if Wendy survived? Escaped? She'd have Kisrie's throat slit like those terrorists from al-Qaeda do to Americans and Christian converts.

The door opened and Dad stuck his head out. "There you are. Your mom and I are in the living room ready to talk when you get your stuff put away."

They knew. She shook her head. Of course they knew. Dr. Martinez probably called them hours ago. She wasn't prepared for this, just scared for this. No time to call for advice . . . and who would she call? Her friends had abandoned her.

Would her parents blow up at her for the choices she made? Blame her for this mess, alienating her even further? There was no way out but through, and it looked like she had to go through alone.

"My students rarely pull out their phones in my classes, because they are paying vast amounts of money to be there. That's the problem with free education. It's taken for granted." Mom paced back and forth. Her face pulled tight with fear and disgust. "And why do they allow those phones in locker rooms?"

Kisrie pinched the bridge of her nose. "Mom. Cell phones are not allowed in the locker room. I didn't know someone had one."

"You could be more aware of your surroundings. You seem to be lost in your own little world most of the—"

"Gwyn." Dad shot Mom one of his silencing looks.

Kisrie flung her hands down to her sides. "I'm guessing you got a call from the principal."

"He called when your mother was picking up the phone to call him. When she went into work late this morning, she had a friend request from you on Facebook. The profile picture…"

Kisrie's muscles stiffened. "Profile? I don't have a Facebook profile."

"We know. That's why your mother was calling the school when the home phone rang."

Facebook, Instagram, probably Snapchat, and of course, Twitter and whatever new social network thingie was out there. Her rear, hanging out for the whole world to see. Tammie . . . oh, no. This whole thing was way worse than she thought.

Dad let out a sigh. "Dr. Martinez is talking to the police. There's no real precedent in Colorado for sexting, especially of images taken without the subject's knowledge."

"When they find out who did this, I want to press charges." Mom clenched and unclenched her fists.

Great. A mongo, serious problem the adults didn't know how to solve because it hadn't happened before? That meant pinning the crime on Wendy would take time. Time enough for Wendy to find out Kisrie had talked to the principal *again*. Time for Wendy to plot something worse.

Keri jumped off the fourth stair from the bottom with one of her bush-baby squeals. "Everything okay in here?"

Everyone jumped. How could the brat sit quiet and eavesdrop that long?

"Keri, go up to your room," Dad said.

"Yes, Father."

Mom and Dad watched Keri slink up the stairs. A slug coated in salt could move faster. Days passed. Dad drew in a deep breath.

Mom punched her fist into her palm. "What I don't understand is why someone would do this to our daughter."

Kisrie stared at the floor. "It wasn't just me."

"What?" Mom and Dad stared at her.

"They took pictures of Jacque and Tammie . . ." A sob bubbled up from her chest. "They . . . Tammie . . . she'd been swimming."

Understanding washed across Dad's face, then horror. Mom grabbed his arm and hissed, "Call the police. Now. Do it, Bern."

"Did someone follow you to the principal's office when you went to refute the accusations against your uncle?"

"Bern, this isn't time to play detective!" Mom pulled away. "I'll get the phone myself."

Kisrie wrapped her arms around herself, trying to squish the overwhelming emotions back in. "No. No one followed me."

Mom assaulted the keypad on the phone.

"Wendy's behind this." Dad was way too observant. Kisrie nodded. But so what? She made sure someone else was set up to take the fall for her. That's how it always worked. Wendy'd get some dirt on someone and call in a favor, threatening to reveal some ugly secret or worse. Fear of what Wendy could do to her clotted her throat.

"Hello? Yes. Yes. My name is Gwyn Kelley, and I'd like to report a crime against my daughter."

Mom's breathing was heavy as she either waited on the phone or listened to some spiel. Dad looked like he needed a week's worth of sleep, and Kisrie felt like a steamroller hit her.

Then anger flooded in. Kisrie stomped her right foot. Why did Wendy keep getting away with all this, and why had she been part of allowing that trend to continue?

"Yes. Oh, hello. Yes. Wendy Wetz has posted—"

Okay, but not like this. "Mom!"

"Hold on," Mom said into the phone then covered the talk-in end with her hand. "Kisrie, what?"

"No! Not like this! She'll kill me. She wasn't the one with the camera."

"Kisrie, if she's behind it, the police need to know. You must do the right thing."

"I don't need a stinking sermon!" Kisrie picked up a magazine, rolled it into a tube, and slammed it on the coffee table.

"I'm sorry." Mom said into the phone. "This is difficult for my daughter. May I call . . . what's that? Send someone out? No, not yet. I'll call later."

"Kiz," her dad tried to break in.

"You guys don't understand what I'm going through! You keep telling me to do the right thing. Well, I have news for you—doing the right thing sucks! This 'the Bible says' rot is ruining my life!" Kisrie's throat ached as she bolted past her parents and thundered up the stairs.

"Maybe we should pull her out of Mountain Ridge." Mom's voice cracked.

Kisrie stopped mid-stomp. "No! If I leave, Wendy wins."

Going to a Wendyless school had been a dream since kindergarten. So, where did *that* come from? What did she just commit herself to?

If he didn't know it was chicken, Evan Plank's throat was so dry he would have believed he was swallowing a gnarled tree trunk. Zena placed a steaming mug of coffee next to his plate. New lines had appeared on her face since this debacle began.

Dr. Martinez had called that morning to inform him police reports had been filed against him. The school board was meeting now to determine a course of action. Evan dropped his fork on his plate and buried his face in his hands.

"Evan, they can't prove you did anything."

Evan pulled his hands off his face, causing a friction burn on his fingers. His mouth opened and closed, but no sound came out at first. "Neither can they prove I didn't."

"You've been in this district for thirty years. No incident reports filed. Ever."

"To be cliché, when it rains it pours. At least seven students have come forward with stories. Word against word. No way out."

Zena twisted the diamond on her left finger. "Those girls are going to be grilled incessantly. They're going to have to tell their stories again and again from all different angles. The details won't line up. Give it time."

Evan pushed his plate away and massaged his eyebrows.

"I can't do this, Zena. After . . ."

"Having no closure makes it harder."

Evan snapped his head up. "You are speaking as though all of this tragedy were happening to someone else."

"You're depressed."

Zena's eyes bore into his like green lasers. He looked back at his plate. "You are not my psychiatrist. You're my wife!"

Rubbing his face, Evan rose. Maybe a hot shower would do him some good.

Steam clouded the bathroom. Scalding water beat down on his back, yet he felt nothing but raw emptiness. Shrugging into his clothes without bothering to dry off, he walked out the back door and into the moonless September night.

Shivers knocked his teeth together as a chilling wind tore through his damp skin deep to his bones. He'd been in education long enough to see the cultural shift from personal responsibility to entitlement. And the entitled always won. Or at least it appeared to be so.

Maybe it was time to get out before the next disgruntled parent or student made another ridiculously false claim, further damaging his painstakingly-built reputation.

Even though the accusations were all lies, the shame was real. Shame that anyone questioned his integrity.

Integrity was a value that had defined the professional and personal life of Evan Plank for half a century, a value passed down through generations of Planks.

It was time to put an end to this madness.

22

Uncle Evan's problem was no longer a secret. Jogging up the front walkway to the school, Kisrie brushed past a notepad-clasping man interrogating a tall boy in a football jersey. The reporter's head jerked to follow her movements. "Isn't that..."

Kisrie sucked in her gut and sprinted for the door.

Tammie shuffled down the hall like she was searching for the meaning of the universe in the grout.

"Tammie!" Kisrie skittered to a halt.

"I don't feel like talking." Tammie moved on.

"You're not okay, are you?"

A blast of air blew out Tammie's lips. She pulled her feet together, straightened her spine, and faced Kisrie. "What do you think?"

"I . . . I don't know." Kisrie hung her head. What do you say to a friend whose entire reputation had been ruined because of you?

"I swear, if I hear one more word about my bra—"

Kisrie's head snapped up. Jacque positioned herself alongside Tammie and slung her arm over Tammie's rigid shoulders.

Both girls stared unblinking at Kisrie. Awkward didn't begin to describe how that made her feel. "Um."

"Why didn't you just go say something, Kiz?" Obsidian eyes shot cold waves through Kisrie's heart.

"Say something?"

"Yeah, after Wendy laid out her plan. You were so afraid for your own backside, you let it go. Now look who's butt is all over the internet!" Jacque squeezed Tammie to her. "Let's just say it's not only yours, and at least yours is somewhat covered."

Stinging tears forced themselves from behind Kisrie's eyes. "I had no idea she would . . . I mean, I don't even have a cell phone to think about something—"

"We're talkin' *Wendy* here."

"You're treating me like I'm the one who took the pictures! I'm a victim here too."

"Victim. That's the problem, Kiz. You've embraced that label since kindergarten when Wendy picked you out as her favorite chew toy. It's time you shake it off and grow up."

Was what she suddenly felt shock? Horror? Realization? Whatever the emotion was, it was too powerful for Kisrie to process. Flinging her hands in front of her, she charged forward. Jacque and Tammie split apart like a log under an axe as Kisrie burst through them. Pain saturated her from the inside out. Her vision blurred. Was it too late to transfer to another school? Bear Creek, Pomona? Both had really good color guards, and without friends, what did it matter if Wendy won?

23

Wendy tasted victory. It was the end of the second half, and she was ahead in the tonsil-hockey match with her new boyfriend, Gabe. She pushed him against his locker, her lips locked in position for the final goal.

"Wen! Wen! Wen!" Sabrina squealed. Wendy startled. Sabrina baby-step-ran toward Wendy and Gabe the best she could in her four-inch platform sandals. That girl sure could use a walking coach. Awkward!

"Can't you see I'm busy?"

"I, uh, see that, but Wen, this is life and, like, death!"

"Yeah, right."

"Oh, it is. It is. You see, Francesca told me that Willy overheard Sammy tell Brooke that Carmen heard Cow Pie telling her low-life friends that she knows who took those pictures." Sabrina let out a gasp and took a deep breath. "Brittany could be in some serious trouble."

Wendy sent Gabe away, blowing him a kiss. "Whoa, come again?"

"Uh, Cow Pie, uh, supposedly told Martinez that Brittany took those pictures."

"So, she's not as dumb as I thought." Maybe leaving

behind the note was too obvious. Waiting a few days would have made the note more random. It wouldn't take long for Martinez or the police to connect Brittany to Wendy, and Plank. That would be disastrous. Like, going to jail disastrous. Wendy massaged her head.

"Yeah, I hear the police are getting involved, because it's some new phone crime thing." Sabrina kicked off her shoes and shoved them against the lockers.

"You don't think he can take Britt's phone, do you? I don't think teachers can search phones." But the police can. Wendy felt a vice tightening against her temples.

"How would I know, Wen? You're the smart one."

"We need to make sure she erases her photo files and her texts."

"Uh-huh. I also hear Cow Pie's blaming you, Wendy."

"Blaming . . ." The note. Wendy had underestimated that fat slab of meat. "Well, I guess we need to figure out what will motivate her to stop talking." Kisrie was messing with her one chance to win a hopeful future. "Sabs, text Brittany and tell her we need to see her right away. It's urgent."

Pictures of ending up like Iona in dark rooms with nameless men slithered through Wendy's mind. She blinked. Hard.

She needed that scholarship. Kisrie was poised to ruin it all.

All Kisrie had ever wanted was to make it through high school unscathed. To be in guard, take photography classes. Get her credits and graduate. Then she could go to college far away from anyone who ever heard the horrid nickname, Cow Pie. But no, she had to have a Wicked Wendy in her life from kindergarten until now.

Getting her head shoved into a toilet paled in comparison to this sexting thing, and that paled in comparison to the pain of losing her two best friends. Her *only* friends. Kisrie stomped down the band hall.

"Kisrie!" Someone said in a cross between a shout and a whisper.

"Where are you?"

Was she going crazy to the point that the lockers were talking to her?

"In the guard room."

The voice was so distorted from the bad attempt to whisper that Kisrie couldn't identify it. "How do I know if you're friend or foe?"

"Hey Tam, what's a foe?"

Jacque. Last she knew, Jacque wasn't talking to her.

Tammie's head popped out of the guard room. Her eyes were red and swollen. "Just get in here. We need to talk."

Tammie and Jacque stood waiting with their arms crossed.

Fear squeezed Kisrie's gut into a ball of pain. "Okay." Did she really want another lecture on how she needed to grow up?

"Kisrie, Tam and I've been talking." Jacque paused to search Tammie's face for the go-ahead look. "Anyway, I think—I mean, we think it's best if we all kind of keep our distance."

Silence.

"D . . . distance?"

"Yeah, as in . . ." Another look at Tammie. "Tam, I can't do this." Jacque's lower lip trembled.

Tammie stepped closer and picked up a sabre, giving it a little flip as if to help focus her thoughts. Cheeks shiny and eyes red, Tammie forced a half-smile. "Right now there are almost ten thousand likes on that stupid Facebook image."

A semi-truck slammed into Kisrie's chest. She blinked, swallowed. Her lips opened and closed, but no sound came out.

"Yeah, ten thousand. And the elders of our church have called me and my parents in for a meeting to talk about my…uh . . ."—Tammie made quotey fingers—"indecent exposure and the fact that I was in a swimming class with boys."

Tammie went to one of those churches where they frowned upon women wearing pants and really had issues with any kind of modern fashion or teenage behavior. Kinda old-fashioned.

"But I didn't—"

"We know it wasn't you, Kiz. It was Brittany and Sabrina, most likely blackmailed by Ol' Wetbottom."

"So why . . . why cut me off?"

Now's not the time to get all hysterical. Breathe, Kisrie. In. Out. In. Out.

"What's it gonna be next? My parents are practically locking me in my room to protect me from all the weirdos out there who are seeking me out because of the picture." Tammie practically spat out that last word. "My mom had to call the phone company to change our number. Dad's in the process of changing our email addresses, and I can't touch a computer or a cell phone!"

"But . . . but you didn't *do* this; it was done *to* you."

"Someone created profiles making it look like we posted as ourselves." Jacque swiped away a trail of mascara from under her eyes.

"And not everyone knows the truth or is willing to believe it."

"All because you were my friends." Kisrie hung her head.

"Look. We're still your friends, but it has to be from a distance." Tammie pulled a tissue from Jacque's bra and blew her nose."Until this clears up. You do understand?"

No. This is not fair!

Kisrie's knees turned to warm Jello. She slumped onto the edge of a storage bin. The tears flowed unhindered.

Jacque nodded. "Remember what I said about the whole victim thing."

Hooking arms, Tammie and Jacque left. The sabre dropped to the floor, skidding to a stop at Kisrie's feet. She picked it up and held it in a left flat. From a seated position she tossed a hilt single then a double. Ceiling was too low for a triple. Now what?

Another wave of pain washed through her. Kisrie lay the sabre in her lap and rested her head in her hands, crying what Oprah calls the ugly cry.

Wendy had won. She'd ruined Uncle Evan's life. She'd ruined Kisrie's life and now the lives of her friends and their families. The kind of humiliation that went along with sexting was worse than she could have imagined. So. Not. Fair. If only—

Kisrie sat up straight. Did Wendy have to get away with this? Seriously.

She stood and threw a low, buzzy single. The blunt steel blade bit her hand. The pain felt good.

Was it possible for someone to go through life as evil and mean as Wendy and *never* get caught? Ever?

Spin, spin, spin . . . smack! Ow.

Anger bubbled and boiled in Kisrie's chest. Evil needed to be stopped! What was the worst thing Wendy could do beyond what she'd already done? The school was on alert, making sure Kisrie and Wendy didn't cross paths.

Resolve was building inside her. What did Kisrie have to lose if she went to the principal right now and connected all the dots? Would that be getting past the victim thing?

The blade whistled in the air. Kisrie's triple was barely higher than her head.

White tape!

She threw the sabre into the bin and stomped out of the storage room no longer a victim.

Cool air rushing against Kisrie's burning eyes felt good as she ran to the main office to speak with Dr. Martinez. All the time, she was on the lookout for any of Wendy's gang. Mrs. Hampden sat behind her desk, phone plastered to her ear. Her mouth opened and snapped shut.

"I'll be right with you," she mouthed.

Sharp pains impaled Kisrie's stomach while she waited. And waited.

"Mrs. Harding, five dollars and seventy-five cents is a great value for a school lunch . . . No, we won't be serving steak… I'm sorry, but we don't negotiate price." Mrs. Hampden hung up with a huff and looked Kisrie in the eyes. "Well?"

Kisrie stepped forward. "I need to talk to Dr. Martinez. It's urgent."

"I'm afraid you will have to schedule an appointment for tomorrow afternoon. Dr. Martinez is in a conference with another student at the moment."

"Mrs. Hampden, this can't wait."

"I'm sure it can." Mrs. Hampden poked at the keys on her computer.

"No, it's about my uncle, Mr. Plank." Kisrie leaned over

the desk toward the now-pale secretary. "I need to talk to him about the kids who are behind this icky plot." Kisrie was amazed at how bold she was being. Never in her life had she felt such confidence. It was as if the warm sun had broken through the cold clouds in her heart.

Reaching for the intercom, Mrs. Hampden nodded. "Dr. Martinez, I have Kisrie Kelley here who would like to speak with you about the *situation*."

"I really think Wendy had Brittany take those pictures of me to make me keep my mouth shut," Kisrie said. "Is there any way this all can prove my uncle, Mr. Plank, is innocent? Can you make sure Wendy doesn't know I talked to you today?"

"Kisrie, I will not tell Wendy you came to me, and this whole case has been turned over to the police." Dr. Martinez crossed his arms over his chest.

"But what if she *does* find out? She's gonna bury a dissection tool deep in my gizzard or shove my neck under a band saw in the wood shop!" Might as well make him aware of the danger she was in.

Dr. Martinez put a hand on Kisrie's shoulder. "Kisrie, I need you to calm down and listen to me. The police are aware of the possible connection between the accusations against your uncle and the sexting incident. They are analyzing the note in the lab and tracing links on phones. What I need from you is to trust the authorities and to stay calm." He paused and wiped his forehead with the back of his free hand. "We're looking at your schedule to see if any changes can be made. Do your best to stay far away from Wendy and her friends."

Dr. Martinez sighed, his arms swinging down to his side. "Kisrie, I appreciate your efforts to defend your uncle."

Kisrie lifted her head and looked the principal in the eye. "Will he get fired? I mean, I've seen stories on the news where teachers are accused, and even if it was all a big, fat, honkin' lie, they can't teach anymore."

"If he's innocent, all charges will be dropped. His official record will be clean."

"But that doesn't stop the rumors, the whispers." Was there any way to erase these lies?

"Again, all I ask is that you trust me and the authorities who are handling this case. Take a seat in the waiting area of the office, and I'll let Mrs. Hampden know you need to see the guidance counselor to go over your schedule." The principal sat down behind his desk. "If you need to talk, I'm here. Okay?"

Kisrie cocked her head and studied his face. He and Uncle Evan were close friends outside of work. Peace swelled inside her chest. Dr. Martinez would do what it took to make things right. He was on her side. She wasn't alone. Wendy better watch out. Kisrie was gonna tell that queen of mean what she could do with her stories.

25

Kisrie headed to her locker. Her water bottle was in there, and it was hot for a late fall afternoon. Doubt invaded her moment of peace. She hoped she hadn't made a mistake convincing Dr. M. about Wendy's involvement in the whole mess.

A sharp pain exploded in the middle of her back. Her feet scuttled to keep balance. "Hey!" She spun to see what hit her. *Crunch!* Kisrie's nose collapsed like an accordion into her face. She blinked in surprise, staring into the grinning faces of a trio of very large girls.

Her nose ached. She felt something warm flow over her upper lip.

The one who smashed her face laughed, pink and silver barbells wiggling in her tongue and lips.

"What'd you do that for?" A pool of blood formed in Kisrie's hand, now cupped under her nose. She was way too mad to be scared. Yet.

"We hear you have a big mouth," a shorter girl with a tattoo of a marijuana plant on her neck said with a voice like an oil-starved lawn mower engine. Kisrie's scalp burned. Her body slid backwards. Someone was dragging her by the hair. She thrashed her legs, trying to get her sneakers to stick to the tiles.

Fear vibrated through every cell in her body.

What did she hear only minutes ago? Trust the administration and the police?

Clumps of hair tore from her head. Swinging her right arm up over her shoulder, Kisrie made solid contact with her attacker then fought to stand straight and face the thug.

The attacker stepped back. Chunks of blondish curls floated to the floor from a hand with weird pentagram things tattooed onto the knuckles. *Kisrie's* hair!

"You gonna keep your mouth glued shut?" The girl with enough facial piercings to set off metal detectors at Denver International Airport asked, sinking a heel into Kisrie's solar plexus.

Kisrie collapsed forward. "I don't know what you're talking about!" The words barely had enough air behind them to be heard. Her lungs were frozen.

Breathe in! Why can't I breathe?

She needed to straighten up. But that didn't happen either. Was she paralyzed?

Lord, help me! Kisrie screamed out in her mind.

A gasp.

Oxygen.

Air.

The she-thugs stood waiting. Through the pain, Kisrie's mind cleared a little.

She wondered what was next. This had Wendy's stench all over it. How did Wendy always seem to be one step ahead of her? What was she, a freaking spy?

The pack of gangbangers pounced. Air rushed out of Kisrie's lungs like a rifle shot. She exploded into a tornado of whirling limbs, but she was outnumbered.

Oh God, help!

"Cat fight!" A voice shouted from somewhere down the hall. Rapid footfalls beat a staccato on the hard floor.

"Help." Kisrie crossed her arms over her face. She had to break away. Her body struggled to obey her brain. Her fingers wiggled a little bit. She wanted to fight back, but it hurt so much to move.

Her legs whipped out from underneath her. Her hip slammed into the floor.

The three girls laughed while she lay in a growing pool of blood. A denim-clad leg hovered over Kisrie's fingers. While the she-thugs shouted at the crowd, Kisrie saw an opportunity. Her hand crept closer . . . closer . . . closer. Kisrie grabbed the ankle and yanked it toward her. A girl landed on the tile floor with a loud *whump*. Kisrie didn't have time to revel in her tiny victory. A rubber sole with the brand name *Vans* flew at the left side of her head.

Kisrie tried to block the blow with her arm, but the kick found its mark.

The attack stopped as fast as it started. Someone shouted "Martinez!" and the thugs seemed to vanish.

Kisrie prayed for unconsciousness to overtake her, but it never came.

26

Dr. Martinez stared at his phone. Evan Plank wasn't returning his calls. That was not good. Last year after Evan's daughter was murdered at the light rail station, he and Zena had to take Evan to the emergency room for being catatonic. It took psychiatrists several weeks to find the right drug cocktail to bring his friend back.

A silver Starbucks coffee mug sat on the corner of his desk. Giving it a shake to see if there was anything in it, he remembered it had been a Christmas gift from Evan. Something swirled inside. Tossing his head back, mug against his lips, he took a swig of cold, bitter coffee. His eyes screwed shut in reaction to the awful taste. He was awake.

Wendy Wetz and Kisrie Kelley had been plaguing each other since grade school. Wendy had a history of antagonizing other students but somehow always found a way out of it. It was as if the girl knew just when to stop. Until now.

"Dr. Martinez! Dr. Martinez!" A small, hunchbacked custodian burst into the office. A crack appeared on the glass panel in the door. The coffee cup rocked out of his hands, and a dark stain spread across his tweed trousers.

"What is it, Alfonso?"

"Oh, Dr. M.! Them kids—they're beating some poor girl to death out there!" The old man spun on his heels and scuttled out the damaged door. Dr. Martinez jumped to his feet.

"Call 911!" Dr. Martinez shouted to Mrs. Hampden.

Sprinting down the hall to the left, he saw and heard an undulating mass of humanity. "Break it up!" He picked up speed.

Student bodies mashed into one another. Cheers and shouts worked them into a frenzy. Voices bounced off the metal lockers. Dr. Martinez shouted again but was unheard. He lurched into a small space that opened between two students and found himself being tossed about like a ship on a rough sea.

Kids who looked up to identify the person pressing in tried to allow him through the best they could. He squeezed the shoulder of a tall boy.

"What the—hey, Dr. M., whasssup?"

The idea that students could find this kind of violence entertaining sickened him. "Back away. Now."

"Martinez!" Someone screamed.

"Principal! Principal! Martinez!"

The students seemed to shrink an inch or two. A handful backed out of the mob, knocking others over in their efforts to escape.

"Run! Martinez!"

A group of girls in the center of the mob stopped mid-strike then bolted, slamming into a wall of human flesh. Altercations broke out as the girls tried to claw their way free. They looked like Carmelita and some of her gang members. Good thing the police were on their way. Martinez had dreamed of a gang-free school. "Everybody freeze."

The crowd peeled back for the gang members.

Dr. Martinez leapt toward them but didn't get very far. "Somebody stop them!" Asking was futile, but you never could tell if there was someone in the crowd who might try to help. Nobody did.

The crowd thinned, letting him pass. Arriving in the center, he saw a crumpled, bloody form on the ground. There was so much blood, he couldn't tell who it was. He knelt beside the body. Blood-matted curls. "Kisrie!" He pressed his fingers on her throat, checking for a pulse.

A low moan dribbled from her swollen mouth.

Students backed farther and farther away. The sound of running feet slapped the tiles.

"Kisrie? An ambulance is on its way." He didn't dare move her in case of a spinal injury. A huge gash stretched across her forehead. Her nose was at an odd angle, gushing blood like a faucet. Tears etched white paths over her bloodstained cheeks. Anger at this senseless violence boiled through his arteries.

"Who did this?" Dr. Martinez called the question out to the remaining onlookers while stroking her matted hair.

Everyone started talking at once.

"You." He pointed to a knobby-kneed boy. "Give me your shirt." The boy grabbed the bottom seam of his sweatshirt, pulled it over his head, and handed it over. Silence fell over the crowd like a lead curtain as he pressed the sweatshirt over the wounds on Kisrie's head.

Sirens blared outside.

Time seemed to slow before four police officers and three paramedics appeared at his side. It was fortunate both stations were down the street.

Spasms gripped his chest. Violence was not going to be tolerated in *his* high school.

He knew who was behind this. Wendy Wetz. That girl had flirted with trouble since the day she entered kindergarten. He had heard the stories. Zena Plank had warned him. But public schools cannot turn students away. She was *his* problem now. He had to find a solution.

27

Pain. Big, bad, ugly pain. There was no other sensation. Kisrie concentrated, trying to find *something* on her body that didn't hurt, but everything did. Her tongue felt seven hundred times bigger than normal and like it was made out of wood. If only she could have something to drink. Her lips peeled back from her teeth—or at least that's what her brain commanded them to do. "Bbbb . . ." Her face must really be messed up if her voice couldn't get past her lips. She crawled her arm up to her face and let her fingertips sweep over her mouth. Her lips were the size of watermelons! It felt like if she didn't get something to drink, her tongue would smother her.

"Bwwaaaahhh." Pushing out that one syllable left her feeling drained.

"Kisrie. Honey." Mom's cool hand wrapped around the one Kisrie used to probe her lips.

"She's awake." Dad said from nearby.

"This is so awful. I hope the police have caught those kids."

"Gwyn, they're working on it. We have to be patient."

"Where's the supervision?"

What was the deal about the debate over school safety?

Kisrie was about to die from desert mouth. "Bwaaaa . . ." This wasn't working.

"Is the water pitcher full, Gwyn?"

Thank you, Dad.

"Oh. That's what she . . . sure. I'll pour her some."

"There's a straw over here. She'll need it."

Kisrie's eyes felt like they were full of broken glass. Her brain willed for them to open, but nothing happened. While Mom was pouring the water, she felt her face again. Swollen lips. Whoa, what was that metal thingy on her nose? She could feel that her eyelids were so swollen it felt like she had tennis balls for eyes. At least her eyes were still there.

"Kisrie, do you need more pain medicine?" A straw poked at her lips. It hurt. "Open up a little so I can put this in."

It felt like hours passed before her jaw yielded enough for the straw to push into her mouth. She took a small suck. Cool, soothing water rolled over her tongue. It seemed to shrink to half its size. Oh man, that felt good. She drank more.

"I'm so glad to see her drink something."

A herd of cows with paper hoofs stampeded into her room.

"Mr. and Mrs. Kelley, I'm Dr. Winston, neurologist."

"Nice to meet you, Dr. Winston." Dad cleared this throat. He sounded choked up.

"With your permission, I'll have my interns look her over and determine if she's ready to go home. After that, we'll draw up the release instructions and go over them with you."

"Wait. Release? My daughter was beaten to within an inch of her life! She's not even been here twenty-four hours. What if a complication manifests itself in the middle of the night?" Mom's voice rose in pitch. "Are we supposed to keep watch over her? What do we look for? How will we know if there's—"

"Gwyn, let the doctor run his tests. He'll let us know what we're supposed to do."

"Folks, I'm not suspecting anything serious, but I want confirmation. Be assured I will provide you with very detailed aftercare instructions and a way to contact me directly."

"All right." Mom exhaled long. "Go ahead."

Go ahead? I don't want a billion interns poking at me! What about me? Don't I get any say? This is so. Not. Fair. "Nnnnnnnaaaaaw-www."

"What's she trying to say?" The doctor asked.

"Gwyn, is her cup empty?"

"I think she wants more water."

"Give her another sip and we'll get started."

If the mere act of breathing didn't hurt so much, Kisrie would have slapped away every pressing hand and poking finger.

Stop touching me!

Hot tears cut through the pain in her eyes and rolled down her cheeks into her ears. Every time she tried to speak someone shoved a straw in her mouth and encouraged her to take a drink. Great. Now she had to pee.

All of a sudden, no one was touching her or talking about her like she was a corpse. Her bladder felt like it had been struck by lightening. "Eeeeeee." Someone had to be able to figure it out. "Eeeeeeee."

"She needs more water?"

No! No more water.

"Eeeeeeee." Kisrie jerked back and forth on the bed. Spasms tore through her body. Her bladder shuddered.

Oh, no.

"I think she needs to use the bathroom." Mom. "How do we . . . ?"

Someone grabbed her arm, pulled her forward a bit, and supported her back. "Can you walk?" a male voice asked.

A man? Oh, no. Oh, no.

"Are you sure about that?" Mom asked. Good ol' Mom!

"He'll escort her in with the IV pole and monitor. When she's situated, he'll step out."

"Okaaaay." Mom's voice reflected the wariness hammering in Kisrie's chest.

"Liability, Gwyn."

"Yeah, I know. But still, she is a girl."

"Point taken."

A few steps away from her bed and Kisrie felt as if the

floor fell out from underneath her. She was thankful for the strong arms that caught her and held her steady. Too bad she couldn't open her eyes. Jacque was sure to ask if he was cute. Or maybe not. Pain of a different kind roared through her.

"I think we need some more of the pain meds. She's hurting." The man escorting her to the potty called out.

Too bad the pain meds didn't numb her from the inside out.

"She has a broken nose, three stitches in the head, two cracked ribs, and a lot of bruising. No surgery needed. Surprisingly, no brain injury," The doctor said. "We'll keep her overnight for observation and pain management. If she's doing well in the morning, she can go home."

"Thank you, Doctor." Dad's voice sounded raw and raspy.

"You're welcome."

"Excuse me, Doctor." A new voice entered the room. What now? Kisrie wished they would take the cooling mask off her face so she could at least see what was going on around her… that is, if her eyes could open.

Footsteps clonked near her bed.

"The police were here earlier wanting to talk. They'll be back tomorrow as you're getting ready to leave, I'm sure." A deep voice said. The mask came off and Deep Voice's hand tugged at her left eyelid. A flash of light stabbed her injured eye. Kisrie snapped it shut. She hated being poked and prodded.

"You guys going to file assault charges?" The man asked while wrestling with Kisrie's eyelid.

Leave. My. Eyeball. Alone.

"Absolutely." Mom's anger colored her voice.

Kisrie lost the battle with the eyeball torturer. Her eye felt like it was bleeding from the light. She tried to go to her happy place but couldn't remember how to get there.

"Pupils look normal."

Okay, at least she could sort of see now.

"Someone beat you up so badly you ended up in the

hospital. That's a crime." Eyeball Torturer continued with his sermon. At least he was talking *to* her, not about her or at her.

"Uh huh."

Wendy should be locked up and the key thrown away. But again, Wendy hadn't physically touched her. Kisrie shuddered. How much power did that girl truly hold? Was it better to count her losses and wave a white flag? Give in?

Justice.

Aw, rats. Not that still small voice thing again. How much was too much? How far did God really expect her to go in doing the right thing? Kisrie had already lost just about everything dear to her.

You still have Me. I'm Enough.

Kisrie groaned.

"Kiz? Are you trying to say something?" Dad was at her side, stroking the little space of unbandaged skin on her forehead.

A nurse came in and wheeled some funky machine out of the room. Kisrie gingerly touched her face. The cooling mask and drugs must have worked. Her face didn't feel as large as a rhino's butt anymore. But could she talk? "Do . . . do the right . . . thing."

Do the right thing.

The words tasted bitter in her mouth. Her jaw popped. She jiggled it side to side to loosen it a bit more before speaking again. "I love . . . how God rewards me for doing the right thing."

"Kisrie, that's not how it—"

"Mom, I did the right thing and someone freakin' beat me up!" Okay, so talking wasn't a problem anymore.

"Language." Mom pursed her lips.

Dad took hold of her hand. "Honey, now's not the time for this discussion. You need to focus on getting better."

"They promised they'd protect me from her." Kisrie's conversation with the principal echoed in her memory. "He told me they were keeping an eye . . . " Stinging tears pooled in her eyes and rolled down her face, wetting the pillow. In a weird way, she felt betrayed by Those in Charge. High school life wasn't supposed to be this way. It sure wasn't this way on the Disney Channel.

"Look. The police and school administrators are doing everything they can to find out who did this to you, but you need to stop worrying about it now."

"I can't, Dad."

"Kisrie, your father and I are asking you to rest now. We'll talk later."

Later? *Later?* Later would be too late! Wendy had somehow managed to stay on top. She really must have spies everywhere. Was it possible to catch paranoid schizophrenia in a hospital?

"Bern? Can we ask the nurse if they can give her a sedative? She's getting worked up."

Mom could be so weird sometimes.

Kisrie wanted to rip all the tubes out of her body and hunt Wendy down. What she did when she found her was yet to be decided, but it would involve pain. A lot of it.

"She's been quiet for the past minute or so. I don't think sedatives are necessary."

"Would you please stop talking about me like I'm not here?"

Dad patted her hand. "Are you ready to get some rest?"

Rolling her eyes, Kisrie replied, "Whatever." Maybe her dreams would help her come up with a plan for revenge.

Vengeance is Mine.

Oh, no. Not the Voice again. Besides, personally doling out justice to Wendy would be more satisfying than waiting for God to do it. He didn't do things like rain fire and brimstone down on people anymore. Kisrie knew God wouldn't smite Wendy in the middle of one of her dog-and-pony pageants.

If opportunity presented itself, Kisrie needed a plan.

Popcorn! Git yer fresh popcorn!" Wendy sang, dancing into Sabrina's basement home theater. Must be nice to live in a real home with real parents who worked real jobs.

Sabrina grabbed the buttery treat from Wendy's hand and slapped Brittany's wrist every time she tried to snatch a fistful.

Still humming, Wendy skipped to the far wall and pulled the remote from a hanging basket. "Are you guys ready? I bet Cow Pie will never dare open her trap again!"

Brittany yanked the bowl out of Sabrina's hands and nodded with a full mouth. Bits of wet popcorn stuck to her chin.

Wendy's stomach lurched. Gross.

Executing a perfect pirouette in front of her friends, Wendy settled into the plush microfiber cushion with a diva-like sigh. She tossed the remote into the air, caught it, and pressed the On button with a freshly-manicured nail.

A Channel 9 News anchor's face filled the jumbo screen. "We have some breaking news. Violence erupted today after school let out at Mountain Ridge High School, the same high school investigating a sexual harassment case involving English teacher, Evan Plank. Live at the scene, we have reporter

Cassidy Bellanski. Cassidy?" The cameras focused on a petite auburn-haired reporter in front of the school's entrance.

"I heard they were airing the story while I was watching *Duck Dynasty*."

"Since when do you watch *Duck Dynasty*, Wen?" Brittany asked, spewing pieces of popcorn through the air. "I mean, like, come on. That's a redneck show!"

"Um, have you seen John Luke Robertson? Hello? Now, shut up. I wanna hear this."

Sabrina and Brittany stared open-mouthed. Those two really needed to learn how to appreciate fine specimens of maleness. Sheesh.

Cassidy looked at the camera and spoke to the anchor. "Thank you, Sierra. Police were called in shortly after school let out after members of a female gang beat up a freshman girl. The name of the victim, as well as the names of potential suspects, are being withheld at this time. No one is sure what the motivation was behind the attack, but sources tell us the victim is at Children's Hospital in stable condition." Grainy cell phone photos of the fight marched across the TV screen. "Back to you, Sierra."

All three girls celebrated by cheering, dancing, and throwing popcorn around the room. An unfamiliar emotion oozed through Wendy's chest, a heavy feeling. Kinda made her feel bad. Hold on. Guilt? She would not feel guilty about this. She ignored it and switched the channel to Style.

"Man, they beat her good." Sabrina sighed, closing her eyes and rolling her head back and forth in a ridiculous manner.

"I'm sure Kelley got the message. She's not gonna want any more of that."

"How'd you do it?" Brittany rescued some untrampled popcorn from the floor.

"Why would I divulge my secrets? I may need them for you two someday."

Sabrina and Brittany looked at each other. Sabrina said, "That's not very comforting."

"Well, you know not to cross me." Wendy rubbed her lower back.

"But what if those girls get caught and say you made them do it?"

"Sabs, trust me. They won't be telling. My connections run deeper than either of you know. Know what? I'm in the mood for some partying." Wendy pulled a tiny silver key from her pocket. How dumb for Sabrina's parents to leave it on the key ring with a label. She skipped to the liquor cabinet.

Sabrina's jaw dropped.

"Who wants a drink?"

29

Despite Evan's protests, Zena had pressed him to seek counseling from the team at church. It had been a complete waste of his time. All the psychological probing in the world couldn't bring his daughter back, nor could it undo the unwarranted damage to his character. He was over it. Evan Plank had nothing more to say.

But upon his arrival home, Zena quizzed him.

"Unresolved issues over Megyn's death are making it impossible for you to handle this. You act guilty when you mope around the house and refuse to talk to your friends . . . and to me."

"She was murdered."

"I—"

"He's still out there somewhere."

Tears pooled in Zena's eyes. "Evan, I don't want to lose you." She stepped toward him, lowering herself to meet his gaze. "You need to get help."

He moved out of reach. "Nobody can help me. No one has the ability to bring Megyn back to this world, and it looks like I will not be exonerated in this abuse case." He walked out of the house. Zena's cries became fainter as he gained distance.

He walked and walked for what felt like hours until he found himself along the intersection of Kipling and Alameda. Far from Littleton. Longtime friend, Raeford Smith, drove by in his Land Rover. He pulled onto the shoulder of the road and invited Evan into the car.

Evan ended up holed up in a spare room above the Smith's garage, bathed in the bluish glow of the TV screen. He didn't want Zena to see him like this. It pained him too much to see how he was hurting her.

Channel 4's news team preceded the weather with a report about a fight at the high school. Cell phone footage captured from YouTube drew the voyeuristic public into the fight. The cell phone user was recording from behind the victim. Blood-caked curls stuck to her neck. Evan's stomach heaved. "Kisrie!" He bolted from his chair and took a swing at the TV, knocking it from the stand. Hitting the floor, the screen shattered, shrouding him in total darkness.

Dr. Martinez had called him earlier to tell him about Kisrie's attempts to clear his name. She claimed to have overheard Wendy Wetz and a few others plotting to spread a rumor as revenge for the grades they had earned on their essays. Now this. Kisrie had a penchant for becoming the focus of some social rioting. She had tried to do the right thing. He wasn't about to ask any more of her.

Evan balled his fingers into tight fists, raising them toward the ceiling. His soul cried out. Or was that his voice? Tears flooded his face. He sank to the floor. He tried to recall the details of Megyn's face but it blurred with Kisrie's. They did look alike.

Evan had no idea how long he lay on the old, smelly carpet, but when he got up, he knew what he was going to do. What he *must* do.

Kisrie's head throbbed. Her throat felt like a porcupine was stuck inside. Groaning, she stooped to pick up the big plastic bag that held her street clothes. Keri was in the bathroom flushing the toilet. She gritched about how the water swirled the wrong way.

"You're not in Australia," Kisrie said, trying to peer under the bed for her sneakers.

"Africa, bone breath."

Kisrie opened the bag and peered in. Her favorite sweats with *Mountain Ridge Color Guard* in block letters down the leg. Good-bye, hospital gown! Those things should be banned. Talk about indecent exposure.

"I'm going to check out the gift shop while your mom helps you get dressed. You're coming with me, Ker."

"I can't, Dad. I'm nocturnal. The light is too bright out there."

"Keri. Come," he commanded, giving her arm a tug.

"Yes, Father."

Ugh. How can they be fooled by that brat? Kisrie watched her father leave the room hand-in-hand with Keri.

Her mom sat at the foot of the bed. Kisrie sensed Mom

wanted a mother-daughter moment but wasn't quite sure how to fix the awkward tension in their relationship. Kisrie wasn't Keri, after all.

Mom toyed with the hem of her shirt. "Kisrie?"

"Yeah?"

"Are you able to talk to me while I help you get dressed?"

Kisrie's heartbeat fluttered. Was her mother gonna take this opportunity to blame the whole mess with Uncle Evan on her? Could she pretend to faint from a stroke in her gizzard or press the red button thingy on the cord wrapped around the rail of her hospital bed?

Mom glanced up.

Okay, here goes. "Yes, Mom?"

"I want you to know I understand how hard this is for you. Confusing even."

Hard? Getting the snot beat out of you was merely hard? Kisrie grunted as a signal to go on.

"I also know things have been . . . how do I put this?" Mom's eyes searched the ceiling for an answer to her question. "Strained between us."

No argument there.

"What I'm trying to say is that I love you."

Whoa. Stop the trucks! Did Mom just use the *L* word? Out loud? To her, *Kisrie?* Something shifted in the brick wall around her heart. "Mom?"

"Wait. I'm not done." Mom reached toward her, arm shaking, and rested it on Kisrie's hands which were now folded in her lap.

Kisrie blinked back tears and bobbed her head.

"I spoke with your Aunt Zena this morning. Things are not going to get easier. A number of students have come forward accusing your uncle of . . . crimes."

Horror ripped through her. "A n—number? I thought it was only Wendy. How can they . . . I don't—"

"We need to talk about options."

Options?

"I'm concerned about how dangerous things are for you right now. These kids aren't messing around, and it seems like there's little any one can"—Mom's voice cracked—"can or *will* do."

Kisrie's mind reeled. So. What was Mom getting at? What was gonna happen to Uncle Evan? What was *really* going on here?

"I'm sure we could enroll you at Bear Creek or Columbine. I wish I could just homeschool you."

Starting over would be nice. There were a few kids from church who went to those other schools. But Kisrie didn't like them, nor did they like her. But what did that matter? It's not like she had friends at Mountain Ridge anymore.

On the bright side, she could be anonymous. Maybe she could get plastic surgery and change her appearance a bit so no one would recognize her.

But . . . where would that leave Uncle Evan?

And what about Jacque's accusations . . . okay, *true* statements about Kisrie always playing the victim?

"I . . . I'm not sure I should leave."

Mom blinked. She wiped her eyes and stared for a moment before speaking. "Kisrie, what's it going to be next? First the sexting, now this. You do understand that if this goes to trial, you'll have to be involved. Testify?"

Where was the nurse with the pain meds? Kisrie hurt inside and out. And she wanted to get dressed. "Mom, can you please help me get dressed? I can't move very well."

Mom grabbed the color guard sweats and seemed to regain a little composure as she pulled the legs over Kisrie's feet. "No matter what we decide about school, we need to make sure it's the right thing."

Kisrie bent her knees, and Mom hiked the pants higher. Why does the conversation always have to come back around to doing the right thing?

"We're gonna have to stand you up to get these on."

Good thing the bed could raise and bend. But even with all that mechanical help, the pain was intolerable. She cried out several times, which brought two nurses into the room. It took three adults to get her out of the heinous hospital gown and in decent clothing.

The nurses left. Mom paced up and down the length of the bed, muttering to herself. "If she stays at Mountain Ridge, she can dispel the rumors . . . but at what cost? I can't quit my job and homeschool her, at least not right away . . . always seems to be a target for bullies."

Mixed emotions of shock and anger roiled in Kisrie's belly. If her ribs hadn't been wrapped so darn tight she'd gasp. Do the right thing? What *exactly* did her mother want her to do? Mom was so confusing in her traumatized state. How was she, a mere sophomore, supposed to stop the other kids from talking bad about Uncle Evan? Alone?

It wasn't a question of whether she loved her uncle. She did. And she had tried to help. She really had.

Kisrie lassoed her thoughts. "Mom, I've done everything I can do, and look where it got me!"

Mom stopped pacing and stared. "Just hang in there and hang on to what you know is true. I guess that's what I'm asking."

Keri hopped into the room, a huge grin plastered on her sickeningly-cherubic face. "I picked out a really cool sweatshirt for you." She winked at Dad. "Huh, Dad?"

Keri tossed the bag on the bed.

Kisrie opened it and peeked in. A sweatshirt with a blue boy holding three balloons was folded in the bag. Corny. But it looked comfy for sleeping in. When no one was around, that is. At least her sister had made an attempt to be nice. Kisrie tried to smile, but the ache in her face caused her to stop short of a grimace.

"Did you know there's no cure for being nocturnal?" Keri chattered on and on about some conversation she had with a zoologist she ran into at the gift shop.

Kisrie nodded, pretending to listen. But what plagued her thoughts was how awful it was going to be to go back home and face all the nasty ick that was swirling around Mountain Ridge High School.

31

A man who introduced himself as Detective Arbuckle leaned across his desk in her direction. Embarrassment heated her face—she knew she looked like a bruised banana. Not much shape and very disturbing colors. Kisrie wrung her hands, avoiding eye contact.

"Kisrie. That how you say it?"

"Um, yeah," she muttered, twisting her thumb to an unnatural angle.

"Interesting name. Never heard it before."

"I think my dad was trying to be creative." Did names really impact the way your life turned out? If so, maybe she'd legally change it from Kisrie to Jane. See Jane run. Wait, she *hated* running.

"Can you tell me what happened the other day?"

Didn't police care about retraumatization? "Some girls beat me up."

"Got names?"

"Uh, no. I don't know their names. I've only seen them around school maybe once before."

"Why'd someone want to hurt you?"

Kisrie lifted her chin, turning her head toward the door

where her parents waited. How come they had to wait outside and leave her alone in here with this guy?

"Kisrie, you with me?"

"Sure. Whatever." Her fingers tangled in her hair and pulled. Happy place. Photography. Taking pictures of baby elephants at the Denver Zoo.

"I just asked you about motive. You listening?"

Kisrie shrugged her shoulders and rocked back and forth. Breathing didn't come easy with all the tape around her middle. "Why bother telling the truth when number one, it doesn't help my uncle, and number two, I get pummeled? Ask someone else about it."

"I'm interested in what you heard in the bathroom and who said it."

"I told Dr. Martinez. Let him tell you. I'm done with this." She gasped. Was she, in some sick sort of way, protecting Wendy?

The detective shifted his weight to the back of his office chair, the kind with wheels. "Wendy Wetz. That name mean anything to you?"

Kisrie's blood chilled. Hatred squeezed her soul. "Seems like you already know who, what, when, where, and how."

"I'm an old guy. My brain gets a little foggy this time of day, so I want to hear it from you."

Thoughts of Megyn drifted into her mind. Megyn fighting even though her attacker kept plunging a knife into her body. All for the sake of someone else. Megyn was a hero.

Shallow breath. Another. The pain in her ribs dulled. No other way out than to tell the truth. Again. The first time may have been too late for her sake, but she suddenly realized she didn't want to to make that mistake twice. Kisrie told him everything she knew.

Cupping her swollen face in her hands, Kisrie watched the detective scribble notes on a legal pad. That would make an interesting photo—low angle, long shutter, let the hand blur.

His head popped up. "May I ask you a question?"

"Why not?"

Really, there was nothing more she could say.

"Why'd you wait so long to go to the principal? You gotta know how serious this kind of stuff is."

Kisrie's eyes widened as far as the swelling would allow. I didn't want my head shoved in a dirty toilet probably wouldn't fly with the detective.

"You know, Miss Kelley, a lot of people could've been spared a lot of trouble had you come forward in the first place—including you." A sausage-link finger pointed at her face.

"I was afraid of what she'd do to me."

"Who?"

"Wendy."

"Why?"

For Pete's snakes, this was a bit much. He asked for it.

"Well . . ." Kisrie tried to breathe. "There was the time in kindergarten when she pulled up my dress, exposing my thighs to the boys to prove I was a fatso. Then every time I entered a place where she was, I'd be called all kinds of names. There was the valentine incident when she went around and told everybody not to give me cards. Then in middle school—I think it was middle school—she hit me in the face with a Hello Kitty backpack."

The detective's pen hung suspended from his fingers over his notepad. His mouth hung open. His eyes met hers during her brief pause, and he nodded. More? He wanted more? Well she had it.

"Toilets. Don't even bother to ask me how many times I had my head stuffed into a toilet! Wendy and her stupid friends made it a competition to see who could come up with the most creative reason to shove my head in a toilet." More heat rushed into her head. Her fists clenched against her legs. Pressure built. She popped to her feet. "And the toilets were *not* clean! Would you believe they stuffed my head into a potty full of poo because they did not like my shoelaces? Shoelaces! And do you think anybody did anything about it? Noooooo. No one seemed to give a stinkin' rip then, and do you really think anybody would give a care now? You wonder why the heck I didn't go to the principal?"

The pen dropped from Arbuckle's fingers, and Kisrie could count the fillings in his bottom teeth.

He asked for it.

32

Wendy sat in her third-block algebra class, working hard to flatten the upturned corners of her mouth. Several days had passed since the "incident," and Kisrie's chair remained empty. Maybe those girls had been a little hard on Kisrie, but sometimes the best learned lessons are the ones beaten into you.

Think C.P. will come back? Wendy scribbled on the corner of her notebook with looping letters. Tearing off the edge, she coughed and dropped the paper to the floor. Sabrina stared at the teacher in the front of the room, knocked her pencil off the desktop, and reached to pick up the note. Wendy waited.

Minutes later, Sabrina faked a sneeze and dropped the paper again. It glided back and forth in a flurry of sneeze droplets. Nasty. Wendy pulled a tissue from her bag and scooped up the note. There was an allure to going "old school" when passing notes. Texting was too easy. And expected.

What's a CP? Sabrina had written.

Wendy rolled her eyes and scratched a fast response.

Cow Pie, you dork.

The teacher never looked in their direction. She was too busy writing something boring on the white board.

Wendy slipped the paper onto Sabrina's desk and waited. And waited. She hissed, hoping Sabrina would look at her. Sabrina swiveled her head. Wendy frowned and waved her hands, palms up. Sabrina pointed to her head to signify she was still thinking.

"For the love of—"

The teacher twisted away from the board, the marker leaving a long blue streak after a partial quadratic equation.

"You have a comment, Wendy?"

"Uh, no, just yawned." Wendy opened her mouth and arched her arms over her head. "Late night studying." Snickers peppered the room.

"Would Miss Wendy Wetz please report to the office? Miss Wendy Wetz." Mrs. Hampden's voice crackled over the PA system.

"Go," the teacher said, erasing the smear.

Standing and adjusting her clothes so they fell just right on her body, Wendy sauntered to the door, winking at Sabrina. Twenty-four sets of eyes pleaded with her to take them along.

"You called me?" Wendy asked the old hag at the front desk.

"Dr. Martinez would like to see you in his office."

"Hope he's going to apologize for the mix-up at homecoming. We all know the voting was fixed. Empathy vote, if you ask me. Just because she's in a wheelchair doesn't mean she's queen material." Did she sound confident enough? Like, what else could there possibly be that the principal wants to chat about? Surely, no one was on to her little plot.

Wendy took long steps toward the principal's office. Dr. M.'s door was open, and he was speaking in a low voice to a middle-aged man with a bad comb-over. She stopped at the threshold. The batty old secretary crashed into her. Martinez spotted her.

"Come on in, Wendy. There's someone I'd like you to meet."

She put on her brightest smile, ran her hands through her hair, and approached the weird-looking man. Her arm glided away from her body. She was onstage at the Colorado Teen Queen pageant. "Hi, I'm Wendy." Forget Homecoming.

"Detective Arbuckle. Nice to meet ya, Wendy," he said. His hand was as rough as a piece of busted-up asphalt. Pain shot through her fingers as they were mashed into a compact mass. She pulled back. He didn't let go. So not cool.

"You're probably wondering why you've been called in today," he said as a statement rather than a question.

Mrs. Hampden took a seat in the corner. What was this, some kind of sick high school drama show?

"Oh, I don't know," Wendy paused for dramatic effect. "Homecoming? You're here to investigate the fixing of votes toward what's politically correct rather than fair?" She gave a nervous giggle.

Arbuckle's lips curved. The guy needed to invest in some lip balm. Wendy forced herself to hold her pasted-on smile.

"I'm here to talk about Plank."

Wendy blinked her eyes. Her mascara felt like it was made of tar.

"I've already spoken with the police, and I really don't want to have to talk about it again." Wendy fished in her pocket for a wrinkled tissue and dabbed at her eyes, being careful not to smudge her eyeliner.

"It's my job to talk to everyone involved again and again until someone tells me the truth." The detective crossed his arms and breathed out through his nose. Wendy shuddered.

"Truth? I mean, Mr. Plank molested me and some other girls. Slap on the cuffs and lock him away, right?"

"Principal here tells me you're a smart girl."

Wendy licked her lips. "Four-point-oh."

"Until your last English project, right?"

"Wh-what does that have to do with anything?" Where did *that* come from? Was she that transparent?

Detective Arbuckle pierced her with his hazel-gold eyes. "Answer the question, Wendy."

"I don't exactly track my GPA every time I take a test or get a project back."

"What was your grade on your English project?"

Why was this guy asking her questions he already knew the answers to? Rumblings rose up in Wendy's chest. Her eyes fell on a folder under the detective's notepad. "Looks like you have my records. See for yourself."

"Wendy, please. Cooperate." Dr. Martinez pinched the bridge of his nose.

"Fine. I got a freakin' F. And yes, that would hurt my four-point-oh."

The detective never looked up from his pad as she spat out her answer. "Tell me about your relationship with Mr. Plank."

A giant fist squeezed the air out of Wendy's lungs. Darkness crept in on the edge of her vision. This interview was not going as she planned. Who did he think was the victim here? She had to convince him *she* was.

She was the victim. At home. All the time.

She locked eyes with the detective. He'd better stay out of her personal life.

Game on.

33

Wendy wiped her eyes with the back of her hand. "He took advantage of my dreams. It was do him a favor and get an A."

Closing a file folder, Detective Arbuckle leaned forward. "I need you to write down all the dates, times, and places of the alleged crimes."

Specifics? "Um, what if I'm not sure of, like, the specific date or time?"

"Do the best you can." A blank sheet of yellow legal paper appeared in front of her, then a pen.

Wendy tapped the pen on the table. What had she told Martinez? One week ago? Two? One and a half covers the final incident.

How many times? Putting down a high number exposed her to deeper investigation and too many details to recall. Three times seemed believable.

Twenty minutes later, Wendy folded the paper and handed it to the detective. Her details were consistent. After school, cafeteria janitor closet. No witnesses around to see.

"About the fight."

"Fight?"

"Kisrie Kelley. She got banged up pretty good on Tuesday."

"How terrible!" Wendy hoped wringing her hands and staring down would come across as authentic. Or should she look up?

"You didn't see it?"

"No, I have to catch the bus three blocks away. I never hang around here after school."

Detective Arbuckle shot a glance at Martinez and Hampden.

"What do you know about the girls who beat her up?"

"Who exactly did the beating again?"

"Tell me what you heard."

"Um, they're in some sort of gang, I guess. They like to pick on random kids for fun."

"You're saying Kisrie was a random pick?"

Wendy sighed. "It's awful, isn't it? I have no idea why they'd pick her. Must've been in the wrong place at the wrong time."

The detective crossed his right leg over his left, cupping his knee with both hands. "Kisrie seems like a nice, normal-looking girl to me. What do you think of her?"

Looking up at him, Wendy grabbed the metal arms on her chair. Oops. Wrong body language message. She pulled her arms in, then splayed them on the table. Pageant smile. "She's so . . . sweet." Sweet? Gag. More like addicted *to* sweets. "What I mean is I just *love* Kisrie Kelley."

The detective cocked his head, and his mouth hung open a little. Seemed like he wasn't buying it.

"Kisrie? She's authentic. You know, real." Good, good. Back up the false claim.

"How long have you known her?"

"We've been best friends since kindergarten."

Arbuckle tapped a finger on his notepad. "You were such great friends you stuffed her head in a toilet? Hit her with a backpack?"

"Well, even the best of friends can get into arguments." Wendy curled her fingers under her palms and studied the backs of her hands.

"Did you know Plank was her uncle?" Bad Comb-over licked a finger and flipped to a clean page.

How to answer that? Everyone who was in classes with Kisrie during elementary school knew the relation. Arbuckle wasn't going to interview all Cow Pie's former classmates. "Um, not really."

"Interesting. You didn't know your *best friend's uncle* was a teacher in the same school district you attended?"

The chair felt hot. Too hot. It made her squirm. "Well, we didn't, like, talk about family that much. I think she was embarrassed by him." Hopefully, that will feed into the whole molester theme.

Arbuckle grilled her, asking the same questions over and over again as if he were deliberately trying to catch her in a lie. Mid-sentence, his phone beeped.

He glanced at the number and stabbed the screen. "Oh, that reminds me . . ."

Respond or play dumb? Wendy sucked in her top lip. Play dumb.

"We've collected crates of cell phones from students in this school."

Did the temperature just rise a hundred degrees? He hadn't asked her a question. Maybe he didn't expect an answer. Wendy waited.

"Did you know that our lab can retrieve erased files from cell phones and computers?"

That was a question. Better answer. "Um, no. I thought erased meant erased." Is this where she should plead the fifth and ask for a lawyer?

"You're dying to know what we found, aren't you?"

"Um, not really."

"Not even if I tell you that mass texts were sent out from your number?"

Maybe she did need a lawyer. At least that's what happened on those crime shows like *Dateline.*

"Do I need to get a lawyer or something?"

"Feeling guilty, Wendy?"

Anger snapped through her nerves. "No, of course not.

But I don't like being questioned like this without . . . without my mom here."

Detective Comb-over shut his notebook. "Alrighty. Tell you what—you talk to your mother. I'll be back tomorrow so we can continue."

Picking up the cell phone, he nodded and strutted out of the room.

Electric-bootied bugs scurried over every surface of Wendy's skin. She cursed under her breath. How was she supposed to talk her way out of this one?

Kisrie rested her head on the doorframe of the school's main entrance.

"You're blockin' the door," a deep voice growled, knocking her aside. Kisrie craned her neck to see her parents' Nissan Rogue driving away. Only a big yellow bus idled by the curb. Streams of students flowed toward her.

Wiping her clammy palms on her jeans, Kisrie sucked in a painful breath and stepped inside the building. She tucked her chin to her chest and headed to her locker, hips rocking. Students passed without pause.

Invisible. Invisible. I'm wearing Harry Potter's invisibility cloak and no one can see me. If only.

Anxiety accelerated her heart rate. Medical tape still compressed her rib cage, causing her to feel like she was breathing through a shoelace. So far, no sign of Wendy. Maybe she was already in Mount View Detention Center.

Hands trembling, she fidgeted with the dial on her locker. Kisrie spun the lock one way, then the next. Five, twenty-five. Start over. Five. A glance at her watch told her the bell was about to ring. The final number of her combination eluded her. A lazy stream of sweat meandered down the left side of her face. Sixteen! The door popped open, and an avalanche of books tumbled onto her feet.

Kisrie stared at the pile on the floor. She couldn't bend. Students looked away. The bell rang. Not knowing what else to do, Kisrie bent her knees, dropping her arm down from the shoulder.

"Auuugh!"

About a foot of space separated her middle finger from the books. She was *so* gonna be late.

Flexing her right foot, she raised her knee in hope of flipping the books from the tile floor to the bottom of her locker. The high-pitched squeal of the tardy bell bit through the clamor of thoughts in her brain. "Can someone help me?"

A mouse-faced girl from gym class stared at her with big gray eyes before shrugging her shoulders and disappearing into a nearby classroom. A weight settled on her heart. Even the other freaks of nature refused to associate with her.

Kisrie repositioned her foot under her history book. Before she could flex her shin, the book slid to the floor. She imagined she could hear her heart beating in the empty hall. Or did she really hear something? A steady rhythm of clicks grew louder and quicker. Crap. It was Hall Nazi.

"Why aren't you in class?"

Kisrie looked over her shoulder. "Uh, my books fell out of my locker."

Hall Nazi tapped a finger against her cheek. "And you expect the books to pick themselves up?"

"I can't bend over. My ribs are broken."

"You had five minutes to ask for help."

Was this woman for real? She had as much compassion as a starving alligator. "I asked for help, and everyone kept walking."

Hall Nazi took a wide stance, placing her hands on her hips. Her fingers curled into her black skirt. She blinked. And stared.

"Could you help me pick my books up?" Kisrie tucked her chin to her chest, squeezing her eyes closed.

Silence.

Kisrie popped one eye open, then the other.

The left corner of Hall Nazi's lip curved up. Kisrie wondered if the expression was a smile or a hungry grimace.

Two clicks, and Hall Nazi was kneeling on the floor scooping fallen books into her arms. Using her head, she motioned for Kisrie to step away from the locker. Books slid onto the top shelf, spines out in alphabetical order.

"Uh, thanks." It was weird seeing Hall Nazi do something kind.

The Nazi gave a wave of her hand and a curt nod. Her feet snapped together. She crossed behind, did an about-face, and then marched away.

"Excuse me . . ." Calling the woman a Nazi just didn't feel right anymore. "What's your name?" Kisrie shuffled after her. The tall, thin woman stopped but remained silent. "What do you want to be called instead of—"

"Mrs. Stepanski."

"Mrs. Stepanski. Thanks for your help." Kisrie's face burned. Was anyone looking?

"I'll let your teacher know why you are late," Mrs. Stepanski said, a new softness in her voice.

35

"Why don't you buy a ticket and come see me in the freak show when the circus comes to town!" Kisrie elbowed her way to the door of the guard room. It was only lunch, and she was weary of the stares and nasty comments. Maybe trying to stick it out here was a bad idea. If she transferred, she could start over. Maybe even go into witness protection and create a new identity. She doubted her situation would warrant that.

Rats.

Musty fabric odors wrapped her senses in a comfortable cocoon. Bright jewel-toned fabrics peeked out of a bin in the back corner. If she wedged herself between the guard equipment and the wall, she wouldn't be seen by anyone who might wander in, and that would be perfect.

Sloughing off her backpack like an old snakeskin, Kisrie allowed herself to be transfixed by a shiny object.

"So shiny." Okay, so that's kinda weird, talking to oneself in a storage closet. Kisrie rummaged through the sabres until she found hers. She turned the steel blade over and over in her hand.

Most people had no idea the blade was blunt. Her thumb bloodlessly traced the edge. Weren't there people who actually played with honed blades? Better catch it right or lose a limb. Gavin'd love that idea.

"Hey. You're back."

Kisrie's head snapped up and pain streaked through her torso. Jacque stood in the doorway, arms limp at her sides then twisted behind her back.

Kisrie forced all emotion off her face. "What's up?" Last she heard, Jacque and Tammie were committed to keeping a healthy distance from her. "What if someone sees you talking to me?" She looked away.

"Nobody can see us in here." Jacque turned her head and glanced toward the doorway.

"Jacque?" Tammie whispered and tip-toed through the door. "Oh." Her eyes scanned Kisrie's face and drifted to the dirty floor.

"So, what are you doing in here?" Jacque swept her arm in an arc over her head.

"The whole point of me sitting in a closet that smells like moldy flags and dirty socks is so no one would bother me."

"We're not here to bother you."

"Then what are you here for? Last time I talked to you, I was deemed a threat to your personal security." Come up with a good retort to that.

"Look, we were wrong. Okay—" Jacque stopped mid-sentence when Tammie grabbed her arm.

"What are you doing, Jack?"

Jacque slapped Tammie's hand away and glared at her. "The right thing, for once." She looked at Kisrie. "Anyway, after you got beat up we realized . . . we realized this whole thing is bigger than just us."

Tammie's head dipped ever so slightly as if in agreement.

"We both walked away from you when you probably needed us most."

Silence.

Yeah, they sure had walked away. And she, Kisrie, had walked into a brawl and been almost killed. Things weren't gonna get any easier, either. In fact, things could get worse. What's to say Jack and Tam wouldn't turn tail and run *again?*

"Y'know Jack, I tried to take what you said about being a victim seriously, and I ended up in the hospital. Oh, and don't forget, pictures of my rear end are swirling all around cyber-space too. If only that was *all* I had to deal with right now."

The tip of the sabre made a smacking sound when Kisrie slammed it into the floor. Her grip tightened around the hilt. "I don't know what your motives are, nor do I care. Real friends of mine would see I'm not in the best of moods and give me the space I need."

Tammie sank to the floor, her bottom on Kisrie's toes. "I hate this." Her whole body rolled forward and her shoulders shook.

Kisrie pulled her toe away. No. Tears weren't gonna work. Not now.

"Come on, Tam. She's not gonna talk to us."

"Why should I?"

"Because we are your friends."

"Friends aren't friends from a distance." Kisrie cradled the sabre and crossed her arms, pulling her shoulders back.

"We made a mistake." Jacque's voice sounded like the whiney motor of one of those wanna-be motorbike things.

Pressing her teeth together until her head throbbed, Kisrie hissed, "You're not the one who got the snot beat out of her and landed in the hospital. You're not watching your uncle shrivel before your eyes, his twin sister, my *mom*, crying over cut vegetables." She closed the gap between herself and Jacque. "Don't give me that 'we made a bad decision' crud!"

Tammie rocked her head back and let out a loud wail. This was pathetic. If they didn't have the guts to stand with her in the open, she didn't want them near her in a closet. "I'm outta here." Kisrie pinched the upper third on the blade between the thumb and pointer finger of her left hand, tossed a double, and caught it by the hilt in her right hand.

If no one was gutsy enough to stand by her, she'd stand by herself.

36

Naked fetal pigs formed a grisly queue on the front lab table. Their pruned little bodies boasted blue and red lines like those on a map. Mrs. O'Neill explained how blue takes oxygen-starved blood into the heart and red takes it out.

"I'm calling those PETA people to come and protest." Jacque lowered herself onto a wobbly stool next to Kisrie.

Kisrie's pleas for a new lab partner had failed.

"People eating tasty animals?" Kisrie shrugged her shoulders.

"Ew. Don't say that."

"Would lab leaders please come to the front of the room to pick up your safety goggles and pigs?" The biology teacher glanced down her long, pointy nose through tiny glasses. Jacque shoved her stool back with a sigh.

Tammie sat across the glossy, black table from Kisrie, scratching notes on paper. Without looking up she said, "You gonna perform a show for us?"

"What?"

"The sabre. Why'd you go and bring your sabre to class?"

"What's it to you, Tammie?"

"You're not afraid of getting beat up again, are you?"

Apparently the little talk in the closet hadn't taken effect.

"No, of course not." Kisrie watched Jacque reaching toward Mrs. O'Neill's desk as if she had expandable arms like Mrs. Incredible.

The silly girl shuffled forward inch by inch until her fingers touched the end of the tray. Kids in line behind Jacque rolled their eyes.

"Ugh, this stinks!" Jacque stepped back, took a deep breath, and then pulled what little neckline she had over her nose. Her chin was buried in her cleavage. With swift motions, she lunged at the desk, grabbed the tray, and ran on her toes to the lab station.

Jerking her chin out of her top, Jacque set the fetal pig on the table and slid the tray toward Tammie.

"Oh, sick!" Tammie threw her hands up in front of her face to ward off the slimy, formaldehyde-scented beastie splayed on the foam board.

"Great. Are you two going to focus? I want a good grade on this." Kisrie fumed and flipped through the instructions.

"I understand you're mad, but you don't have to be mean." Tammie pulled on gloves.

The pig stared at the ceiling with an unblinking eye. Jacque turned away. "Let's do a walk-out thingy to protest. I don't care about my grade." Jacque stood up. "Anyone else bothered by this?"

Other kids in the lab turned, waiting for the expected Jacque drama.

Mrs. O'Neill tugged on her lab coat. "Sit down, Jacque."

"Give it to me." This was going to be so much fun. Not! Stretching her arm across the table, Kisrie hooked a finger over the edge of the metal tray. She slid it in front of her. "Where's the scalpel?"

Tammie shoved a pair of smeared lab goggles onto her face. "I ain't giving you a scalpel. Your obsession with sharp objects is starting to creep me out."

"Don't look at me! I'm not coming near that thing." Jacque shielded her eyes with her hands. "See? I won't even look at it."

"You guys don't have all day." Mrs. O'Neill waved a scalpel at Kisrie then carried it over.

Scalpel in hand, Kisrie studied the instruction sheet. "Kidney. Liver. Spleen. Stomach. Bladder." She picked up the dissection tool then looked up. Tammie and Jacque huddled over Jacque's cell phone. "Why am I doing all the work?" The dissection tool clattered on the table.

Tammie and Jacque squeaked and jumped back.

Jacque poked the Home button on her iPhone and shoved it in her bra.

"Like, nobody's gonna notice you have a square—" How annoying. And disgusting. Jacque kept *everything* in her bra. Kisrie slapped the table. Bits of pig took flight. A chunk of something gross landed on the exposed skin in Jacque's perfect hair part.

"Contamination!" Shrieking, Tammie shoved Jacque away.

Jacque's hands flew to her head, fingers crawling across her scalp.

"What is going on over there?" Mrs. O'Neill hopped off her stool.

"A freak show." Kisrie said to the teacher. Then to her lab distractions, "Can I just do this by myself?"

Jacque's fingers found the gore. "Get if off me! Get it off me!"

"I will if you hold still." Tammie jumped, swiping the air to catch frantic Jacque arms.

An amused smile tugged at Mrs. O'Neill's right cheek. How could the teacher think this is funny? "Part of your grade is group participation."

Tearing the goggles from her face, Kisrie said, "I'm done. Just give me an F. I don't care." She grabbed her stuff off the adjacent stool. "I need to go to the bathroom." Or another planet.

Tammie and Jacque stopped their gross-fest and blocked her in by the stool.

"We try to be nice to you and all you can do is get madder." Tammie shook her head.

Kisrie tightened her grip on her belongings and took a step

toward her two used-to-be friends. "Everyone is staring at us. Let. Me. Go."

"Just let her go, Tam. If she wants to be crabby, let her be." Jacque opened up a gap between her and Tammie.

Kisrie stepped through and didn't look back.

37

Kisrie slipped into American history class during attendance. Her stomach ached from downing an entire bag of peanut butter cups in the bathroom during biology. Tammie and Jacque were a couple of dorks. And traitors.

History class crawled by in a boring fog. Kisrie's eyes slid to half-mast until the bell jerked her back to the present.

Avoiding elbows and book corners took more agility than that of a mountain goat as she threaded her way through the hallway. Her injuries made evasion tactics impossible to execute.

"Hey, Cow Pie, what's the matter? You mistake door knobs for your contacts?"

"Face looks like a rotting potato!"

Kisrie kept moving, ignoring her tormentors. She clenched her molars, biting her cheek. The metallic taste of blood rolled over her tongue. More insults crashed to her eardrums. She kept her eyes focused on the tile floor.

Two hands slammed into her chest. It exploded with pain. She tried to yell, but the tape wouldn't allow her lungs room for expansion. She looked up. Wendy blocked her path.

"No one ignores me, Cow Pie." Wendy cracked her

knuckles. Kisrie limped forward. Wendy's palms crushed into her chest a second time.

"Back off, Wendy."

"Cow Pie, you and I are having a little meeting today after school behind the stadium bleachers. If you don't show, don't say I didn't warn you, freakazoid." Wendy strutted on toward her entourage of glitter-laden goons.

Shivers pinpricked the skin on Kisrie's arms. Behind her back, Wendy extended her middle finger. Kisrie tripped her way to the double-glass doors of the library and grabbed the handle for support. The end of the sabre blade knocked against her hand and she froze. Her eyebrows joined forces above her nose. Swelling like a rising pastry, oven-hot anger replaced all fear.

"Hey Kiz, let's go grab a latte before band, okay?" Jacque said pulling out of an embrace with her new boyfriend.

"Latte?" Tammie swung her backpack into Jacque's bottom. "I don't like coffee."

Boy-toy backed away and Jacque said, "I wasn't inviting you."

"Ouch. If you're going all teeth and claws," Tammie said, "I don't want to be around you anyway, Jacque. Hey, Kiz."

"Kiz, latte or no latte? I'll pay."

What was up with these two? Was she not clear in her message to them? "I don't go out with strangers." Kisrie squeezed through.

"I still think you're mean, Jack." Tammie tapped her foot.

Jacque followed Kisrie. "Where you gotta go?"

"None of your business."

"She's got a creepy look, Jack."

"She always has a creepy look, Tam."

"She's got her sabre."

"We have band practice in twenty minutes, stupid."

"Then where are her flags?"

"In the guard room where they belong."

Skidding to a halt in front of the exit doors, Kisrie turned. "Would you guys quit talking about me like I'm not here?" She pushed through the doors.

Kisrie floated along in a plastic bubble. Where was the lot monitor? Usually some poor student teacher was assigned to supervise the parking lot at the end of the school day. Too many after-school fights, they said.

Another look around failed to locate a teacher. Leave it to Wendy to create some kind of diversion. Kisrie ran the silvery blade across her left palm. Its cool edge calmed her nerves. Watch out, Wendy. You won't find a defenseless wimp this time.

"And you don't even know who Miss Marple is!" A loud whisper from behind a Prius a few slots down drew Kisrie's attention.

"I know you're there, so stop trying to hide."

Two heads peeped over the shiny, burgundy hood. Jacque's brown eyes turned to black obsidian. She pressed her hands on the hood and rose to her full height. "Friends don't let friends do stupid things."

"And what stupid thing do you think I'm about to do, huh?"

Tammie jumped up and stood next to Jacque, hands on her hips. "You've got your sabre, no flags, and band practice is not in the stadium."

Jacque grabbed Tammie's arm and pointed to the stadium entrance. "There goes Wendy and her baffoons."

"I'm getting the principal." Tammie sprinted back to the school.

"No you're not!" Kisrie lurched forward, but the pain froze her in place.

"Don't do it, Kiz. You're gonna get hurt. You stay with me while Tam gets Dr. M."

"Get away from me, you little traitor!"

"The only traitor here is you, and you're traitoring yourself! Kiz, look at you!" Jacque moved from behind the car one step at a time. "What, you have a death wish? That—I can't bring myself to say the word—she tried to *kill* you. You want her to succeed this time?"

"Wow. Doesn't this look interesting." Wendy's voice shouted from a few parking slots away. Kisrie spun on her toes to see the goon squad emerging from behind a Nissan Murano. Her spit caught in her throat, trapping her voice.

"Nothing to say, Cow Pie?"

"Leave us alone, Wendy." With a few quick steps, Jacque skittered between Kisrie and the Queen of Mean.

Swallowing hard, Kisrie croaked in a hoarse voice, "This is between me and her. I'm done playing the victim."

39

The lot monitor was preoccupied with a fight over an MP3 player in Brittany's boyfriend's car. On the *other* side of the school. Prearranged, of course.

She had to make Cow Pie change her story to Dr. M. Wendy pushed Jacque aside. "You heard the bovine. It's between me and her."

She needed that scholarship, her ticket to freedom from being used and abused. But something fierce burned in Kisrie's eyes. Wendy's stomach flopped like a clumsy cheerleader. She had to make it clear that *she* was the one in charge of the situation. Wendy sucked in her gut, rolled her shoulders back, and took a deep breath. "Tell your little friends to back off."

Jacque whipped her hair back and hopped in front of Kisrie. She bared her teeth. What did she think she was, some kind of guard dog? Wendy let her breath out, loud and slow. "Why don't you go back across the border where you belong?"

"Wen! I can't believe you said that!" Sabrina put her hands over her mouth.

Jacque put her hands on her hips, like that made her look scary. "You're not gonna get away with this, Wetbottom!"

"Oh really?" Wendy's pulse pounded in her ears. She had not expected the other side to fight back.

Great. Jacque was determined to play hero. Kisrie had to take control of this nightmare. She grabbed the back of Jacque's shirt and pulled her out of the way. "Leave me alone."

Jacque grabbed Kisrie's left elbow. "I'm *not* gonna let you do this!"

Kisrie tore away from her.

Wendy's eyes narrowed to a squint. Kisrie rose to her full height.

Don't let her know you're afraid.

"So, what's this?" Wendy pointed at the sabre. "You gonna put on a stupid band show for me?"

"That's what you'll wish." Kisrie's heart thudded.

"That a threat, Cow Pie? Because if it is, I may not be as nice to you as I was planning."

"You're not nice to anyone," Jacque called over Kisrie's shoulder.

Wendy laughed. Brittany and Sabrina joined in. "Brush off your flea, Cow Pie. This chat is between you and me."

"I'm not going anywhere." Jacque butt-bumped Kisrie out of her way.

"That's just too bad. I was gonna give your, uh, *host* here a little break. But since you refuse to—"

Kisrie let out a loud yawlp and lunged for Wendy but got a face full of asphalt instead. Something crushed her. Her ribs creaked in protest.

"I. Will. Not. Let. You. Do. This!" Jacque was on Kisrie's back.

"Get off me!" Kisrie screamed, her voice echoing off the tar-smelling surface. Adrenaline surged. She drew her knees up under herself and shoved upward.

"Who needs Comedy Central when the world has you dorks?" Wendy doubled over.

"Teacher's comin'!" Sabrina yelled. "Musta heard the cow holler."

"What is going on here?" The football coach sprinted from the stadium.

Kisrie thrashed and bucked. She had to get Jacque off.

"You're gonna hurt yourself more."

Like being jumped on and tackled to the pavement wasn't going to hurt? "Get off me."

"No. Way."

An idea blazed in Wendy's brain as she watched Kisrie and Jacque wiggle like a pile of worms. Fixing her eyes on the coach, she yelled, "Kisrie Kelley hit me with that thing!"

The coach abandoned the circus show on the ground. Wendy breathed in a random, raspy pattern. Hopefully, that's how people breathed after getting stabbed in the stomach with a sword.

"Walloped her a good one," said Brittany, rubbing circles into Wendy's back. The coach stuffed his hand into a lumpy pocket and yanked out a walkie-talkie. Jacque rolled off Cow Pie, got on her knees, and grabbed Kisrie under the armpits, heaving her to her feet.

Don't give yourself a hernia, girl. This is my show.

Wendy rolled her eyes backwards and moaned.

The saber wasn't even in her hand! It had been knocked away when The Traitor jumped on her back. "Get your hands out of my pits." If she didn't hurt so much, Kisrie would have swatted the glittery, red-tipped fingers off her body. "I . . . I didn't hit her with anything."

The coach yelled into his radio for Dr. Martinez, who responded that he was already on his way.

"Where'd you get hit?" Coach asked.

Wendy moaned.

"Uh, Cow . . . I mean, Kisrie there tried to do a sumo thingy on Wendy. You know, cut her guts out," Sabrina said winking at Brittany.

"Yeah, hit her across the stomach. She might die."

Wendy raised her face to make eye contact with the coach. "My stomach hurts. Can you call my mom?"

"Do you need an ambulance?" Coach pulled an iPhone from his pocket.

"No. No ambulance. I'll be okay." Wendy gasped then cried out and cursed in a low voice. She forgot about the whole get-it-checked-out-by-a-doctor thing. "Call my mother, Iona Wetz. Britt has her number in her cell."

Brittany shook her head.

"What do you mean?"

"New phone."

Wendy grabbed the phone and poked its smooth touchscreen. She handed it back to Brittany.

Cow Pie was standing only because that skank, Jacque, held her up. Dr. Martinez arrived on the scene with Tammie trotting behind. He looked like an Olympic speed walker, hips gyrating with every step.

"She didn't do it!" Tammie said the moment Sabrina's cotton-candy lips opened.

"Do what?" The principal joined the coach in examining Wendy.

"Sir, this young lady claims she was stabbed with the sword."

Jacque waved her hands into a blur. "It's a sabre. Duh."

"Kisrie?" Dr. Martinez straightened his glasses.

"I didn't . . . hit . . . her." Kisrie's face was an ashy gray. Jacque's grip tightened to the point it hurt.

"Wendy set this up." Jacque said.

"She stabbed me. I've got witnesses."

"So does Kisrie," Tammie shot back.

"Iona's on her way." Brittany polished the phone with her shirt.

Coach finished poking his screen and held it up. "Should I call the police?"

Dr. Martinez waved his hand, commanding silence. He scratched his head. "I think we should call the paramedics to have Wendy checked out. She may have internal bleeding."

Wendy stood ramrod straight.

Can't go there.

"No. No paramedics."

"Paramedics, Coach. I want to make sure she's not hurt—"

"My mom won't let them touch me! I won't let them touch me."

"You're standing pretty straight for someone who was almost disemboweled." The principal spread his feet wider apart.

"I needed to stretch. My muscles were cramping. Oh!" She fell to her knees. Drama. Need more drama.

Tammie joined Jacque in propping up the pathetic Cow Pie. Fool doesn't even need to get beat up to look pitiful.

"I'm gonna puke," Kisrie mumbled and stumbled from between her friends. She didn't travel an inch before her lunch splashed on the ground.

"Ambulance is on its way," Coach said. Sirens wailed in the distance.

Kisrie felt like her ribs had gone through one of those wood-chipper thingies landscaper guys use. Jacque and Tammie jumped out of trajectory range when that awful turkey-breast-and-spinach wrap sought daylight. A white cloth materialized under her nose.

"Use this to clean up." Dr. Martinez gave his handkerchief a few quick shakes.

She grasped the cloth and wiped her mouth. Her body refused to straighten. Had one of her broken ribs punctured her gizzard? Do humans even have gizzards?

An ambulance tore around the back of the school, tires screeching and clawing at the asphalt.

Kisrie bent her neck upward to take in the scene before her. If she didn't hurt so much, she'd have a hard time keeping a straight face. This was gonna be good. Wendy was caught in a trap. Dr. M. sure knew how to expose the truth.

Paramedics poured out the back of the vehicle. The football coach waved his arms toward Wendy, who'd curled into a ball on the parking lot.

A small sports car jerked to a halt behind the ambulance, and Wendy's mom jumped out.

"You're lucky I was only a few blocks away—Hey! Hands off my daughter!" Wendy's mom wobbled into the stadium on heels higher than the Eiffel Tower. She tugged at a dark, suede micro-mini that threatened northern exposure.

"Oh. My. Gosh." Jacque dug her fingers deeper into Kisrie's arm.

Tammie pressed her lips to Kisrie's ear. "I hope she's got underwear."

"That red, leopard-print cami makes her look fat."

"Don't make me laugh," Kisrie said. "It hurts too much." Whoa, why was she laughing at something one of her non friends said?

"We need to check her out." One of the paramedics pointed at Wendy.

"No one touches her." Wendy's mom swayed her hips and stopped next to her daughter. "No insurance." Her red hair shone like polished copper under the sun's rays. To Wendy she said, "Come on. Get up."

"Ms. Wetz, she's accusing another student of assault. She must be checked for injuries should you choose to press charges. In fact, I'm going to call the police right now." Dr. Martinez pulled a sleek phone out of his back pocket and poked the screen.

"I would like to have an independent physician take a look at my daughter."

"Hey, ma'am." Coach stepped in front of Wendy's mom. "Your daughter claims to have been stabbed with a, um, sword. Injuries could be serious. At least let the medics assess her to see if a trip to the hospital is needed."

The paramedics surrounded a howling Wendy. Every time they tried to touch her, she would kick and scream and threaten to cut off choice parts. "Either we restrain her or sedate her for evaluation. My other thought is that her injury couldn't be *that* bad if she's able to move as she is."

"I was stabbed with a sword!" Wendy's face was red and swollen.

Dr. Martinez pushed through the paramedics and hovered over Ol' Wetbottom. "Where's the blood?"

"Hey, hey! What about patient privacy? Is there some kind of waiver I can sign to refuse treatment?"

"Hey, Kiz," Tammie whispered in Kisrie's ear. "I think we are about to witness Wendy finally getting caught in one of her own traps."

Dr. Martinez twisted around to catch Kisrie's eye. He winked. The Queen of Mean was going down! Exposed! Maybe, just maybe, the whole nasty rumor thing about Uncle Evan would go away. If only the pain would subside enough to let her enjoy the moment.

"You can refuse treatment at your own risk," an uber-handsome paramedic said.

"Gentlemen, you may want to take a look at her." Dr. Martinez pointed his thumb over his shoulder at Kisrie. "She took a hard fall and has a few broken ribs from a previous injury."

Jacque released her grip and swatted Kisrie's arm over and over. "Ooooh! He's so hot!"

Tall, dark, and handsome to perfection of the cliché. Hunky Paramedic's face lined with concern as he loped over. Kisrie's heart thumped wildly.

"I think I'm gonna have a heart attack," Jacque said.

"Jack, you're messed up. She's gonna get poked with needles and stuff. Probably end up in the stupid hospital again."

"Tammie, are you blind?" Jacque moved away.

With help from her mom, Wendy stood. Cold, hard eyes locked onto Kisrie. Hatred shot from them like high-velocity bullets. "You tried to kill me." Wendy faked a cough. "You're not gonna . . . get away . . . with this, Cow Pie." A few other nasty names were thrown in for effect.

Dark chocolate. No, dark chocolate with a latte. Yeah, that's more like it.

Kisrie stared into Hunky Paramedic's eyes, letting her imagination wander through the uncharted wilderness of romance. Swooning, Kisrie hardly felt the pain in her ribs as the emergency crew strapped her to a gurney.

Mr. Mocha, easier to say than Hunky Paramedic, leaned

close to her, whispering words of comfort. He smelled like the sun-baked pine needles on Mount Falcon. For him, she'd transform into the ultimate granola chick. Heck, she'd willingly scramble up a fourteener.

Kisrie closed her eyes and pictured Mr. Mocha and herself sitting along the glacial pond at Herman Gulch—her teeth rattling from the icy wind howling off the snow. He winks a dark-roast eye and sheds his North Face fleece. Wrapping it around her shoulders, he draws her toward him, his lips searching for hers—

"Kisrie. Kisrie!"

"Um, can't you see I'm busy?" Even to her own ears, she sounded drunk. Wrestling gravity, she lifted an eyelid and saw the principal. Ew. Embarrassment flushed hot over her skin.

"Your mom will meet us at Swedish Hospital," Dr. Martinez said. "I'm going to ride along if that's okay."

"Where . . ."

"You're in an ambulance. We need to make sure the, uh, pileup didn't create further injury to your ribs."

". . . is he?" she finished.

"Who?"

A shock of wavy, brown hair floated into view followed by those edible eyes. Drool dribbled from the corner of her mouth, and the IV tubes rendered her hand useless. She was turning into Jacque!

"Okay, Kisrie. I'm starting an IV. You're going to feel a little stick in just a sec."

"Stick me all you want." Her eyes widened. Did she say that out loud? A crooked smile tugged at his mouth. "I . . . uh, I mean, okay." Ripping her gaze from his face, she scolded herself. Lack of oxygen had to be causing brain damage. No male had ever made her act like an idiot.

Doc Martinez chuckled as the ambulance rolled out of the stadium.

Trinidad, Colorado may look like a quaint, old Western town nestled at the foot of the Rockies, but it has a surprising secret. To those in the know, Trinidad is the Sex Change Capital of the World." The camera pulled back for a wide-angle shot of the brick-laden city, revealing bridges arching over Interstate 25 and a flat-topped mesa.

The next frame was a close-up of a dark-haired, olive skinned woman. "Kinda looks like Jacque." Kisrie changed the channel. Weird stuff fascinated her, but she was craving something that didn't make her feel emotions. She flipped over to *Bizarre Foods*. Andrew Zimmern was in northeastern Pennsylvania eating snapping-turtle guts from Peck's Pond.

Kisrie's TV viewing choices were yet another thing that distanced her from her peers. She'd rather spend her time watching Discovery or Fox News than those dumb teen dramas.

She'd found that the living room couch was the only piece of furniture other than her bed where she could stretch out. She adjusted an ice pack. In the ER, the doctor said her innards were all in the right places, and she'd learned she didn't have a gizzard.

"Hey, Sweets!" Her father's voice cut through the narration about how turtle eggs were a delicacy. She fumbled for the remote, found it, then stabbed the Off button. Didn't want to get Dad into one of his adventurous moods. Knowing him, he would suggest a road trip to the Poconos to eat snapping turtles and scrapple.

By the time she set the remote down, her father had seated himself on the opposite end of the sofa and lifted her feet into his lap. "Just got off the phone with Dr. Martinez."

Kisrie pressed her lips together. Could it all be over? Wendy gets thrown away for good, like she deserves?

"We have a meeting with him, Wendy, and her mother at seven forty-five tomorrow morning."

Kisrie's tummy felt like a rock had just formed behind her belly button. "Wh—what for? Like, I mean, it should all be over by now, right? Especially after Dr. M. called her bluff?"

Dad patted her shin and stared at her leg. "Wendy's mother called to inform him that Wendy allegedly has deep bruising and a ruptured spleen."

"How can that be? She refused to go to the hospital."

"Claimed it was an independent evaluation."

"Yeah, right. And I have a gizzard."

"She's adamant about pressing charges."

"For what?"

"Assault with a deadly weapon." Dad leaned back and closed his eyes.

"Oh." What to say to that? A lie, all of it. Just like the lie about Uncle Evan.

"Dr. Martinez gave Detective Arbuckle a heads up about the whole thing. Tammie and Jacque practically chained themselves to his desk until he assured them you weren't going to wear a sea-foam-green jumpsuit."

Kisrie swung her feet to the floor and propped her chin in her hands. Why all of a sudden this effort to become super friends? Did her getting beat up guilt them out that much?

"Wendy's trying to make me change my story about what I heard in the bathroom, Dad. She wants me to say I'm just trying to protect my uncle and I'm trying to get her back for being mean to me." Kisrie took in a few short bursts of breath. "I didn't think anyone would take her seriously, especially after this afternoon."

Dad patted her back. "It's late. You've had a rough day. I want you to be prepared for tomorrow morning." He paused then added, "This is going to be very difficult for you." He stood. "I'll be praying most of the night."

"Like God gives a rip," Kisrie whispered to the remote in her hand.

Wendy and her mom sat across the table from Kisrie in the high school conference room. Wendy's eyes were cold and hard. The stench of Iona's cigarette breath made Kisrie's stomach lurch. Denver omelet wouldn't match the carpet. Mom and Dad sandwiched her, and the principal occupied an end chair. He tapped the ballpoint end of his pen on a blank tablet.

Detective Arbuckle and a uniformed officer walked into the room.

"Detective Arbuckle. Officer Schwartz." Dr. Martinez dipped his head to the new arrivals who sat down at the empty end of the table.

First up to speak was Wendy. Kisrie swallowed hard and chewed on the inside of her lower lip. What a liar! Wendy was making her sound like some sort of demon-devil. Iona kept interrupting Wendy, adding details Wendy had supposedly forgotten to mention.

Finished, Wendy leaned back in her chair. Her eyes narrowed, and the right corner of her mouth twitched upward. Iona shook her mane of hair and examined her glossy talons. Dr. M. raised his eyebrows above the frame of his glasses, signaling Kisrie to speak. Both of her parents rested their hands on her back.

"Uh, well, I was in the hall, and Wendy—"

"Kisrie Kelley tried to murder my daughter with a sword!"

"We could do without the dramatics, ma'am." Detective Arbuckle spread both hands open on the table.

The principal cut in. "Take a few deep breaths, Ms. Wetz. The police are here to help us work this out."

"There's nothing to work out. Our lawyer suggests attempted murder." Wendy didn't move at her mother's words. Kisrie had yet to see her blink.

"Attempted murder?" Detective Arbuckle asked, shooting a glance at the officer.

Mom rocked forward. She had the look of a mama grizzly bear having a stare-down with a poacher.

"She had a sword, didn't she, Wendy?" Iona elbowed her daughter's arm.

Detective Arbuckle looked at Kisrie. "Where'd you get a sword?"

"It's—" Dad said, but the detective cut him off.

"I want to hear it from her."

"I don't have a sword."

"Oh yes, she does." Wendy gave a perfect-teeth smile.

"I spin a *sabre* in color guard."

Officer Schwartz looked at the principal. "You let kids play with weapons?"

"It's not what you think. The sabre is made for twirling. Blunt edges and tip."

"Spin," Kisrie said. "We *spin* sabres, not twirl."

"Are you going to lock her up, or what? She tried to kill Wendy." Wendy's mom pulled at the shoulder strap on her bra. Red-and-black zebra print. Must have some sort of theme going.

Arbuckle ran his fingers through his hair. "Doc, Officer Schwartz and I need to interview the girls separately. Kisrie, come with me."

She scooted away from the table.

"Excuse me," Dad said. "Don't we as her parents have a right to be in the room while you question her?"

"Mr. Kelley, I don't want any influences or distractions."

Kisrie's entire body was sore. Each breath felt like she had a dagger lodged in her chest. The detective sat across from her. Staring. Kisrie wrapped a curl around her finger and twirled it round and round.

"Are you gonna tell me what happened after school yesterday?"

"You won't believe me."

"Try me."

"No one else does."

"That so?"

"Yeah," she said scratching her arm. "You didn't seem to believe me the other day." She raised her eyes. Detective Arbuckle sat up straighter.

"No one believed those two boys at Columbine could pull off the most horrendous act of terrorism in an American high school," he said.

Kisrie swallowed hard and looked the detective in the eye for a good seven seconds. "I'm not capable of murder!"

"Is that so?"

"Yes."

"People today wanna believe evil doesn't exist. Now, I'm not a religious man, but as a cop I've seen enough of this world to tell ya evil is real, and we all harbor it."

"I may hate her, but I wouldn't kill her. Like, I'm gonna mess up my whole life? She's not worth it."

"Under the right circumstances, we're all capable of murder."

Kisrie pressed her fists into the top of her thighs.

Arbuckle jumped out of his chair, his voice loud like a cannon shot, "Then why did you hit Wendy on the head with a sabre?"

Kisrie bolted upright. Philosophy time must be over. "I didn't."

"What was that? I didn't hear you?"

"I said I didn't. And it wasn't her head."

Arbuckle stood next to her. She could hear his breath sucking in and out as he let an uncomfortable silence cloak the room. "So you hit her somewhere else."

Kisrie's face flushed hot. "I didn't hit her anywhere." She bounced her toes.

More silence. Did he want her to make up a false confession? Get in touch with her inner evil side? Didn't her relationship with Jesus override that evil to some degree? "Mr. Detective, my friend Jacque tackled me before I could do anything, and I was on my face breathing in motor oil fumes when Wendy says I hit her. Look." Kisrie pointed to the scrapes on her face.

"Back up. Tackled? Why did your friend take you down?"

Crap. How *could* she explain the fact that she was in the parking lot with her sabre when she didn't have a car and band practice was in the other direction? And what *were* her deep-seated intentions? Heat flushed from her chest to her face. She looked down at her hands. Truth was, she intended to use the sabre as a weapon if need be, but Jacque never gave her the chance. Internal motivation not acted on wasn't some sort of death-penalty crime, was it?

"Miss Kelley, answer the question."

Could he see her wrestling with her answer? Could these hard-boiled cops read minds? That strange nudge returned. Instead of making her uneasy, it calmed her leaping nerves.

Truth!

"All right. Wendy wanted to meet me to discuss the situation with my uncle. Alone. But I don't trust her. I mean, look what she did to me." Kisrie paused to let the detective take in her yellowing bruises. "How am I to believe she won't hurt me again? Especially when I think she wants me to change my story, to almost take blame on myself for the whole thing with Uncle Evan . . . er . . . Mr. Plank. I *did* have band practice, so I had my sabre for when I was done. And also . . . well, I guess I did have it just in case."

Arbuckle slammed his fist on the table. "You still did not answer the question! Why did your friend feel the need to tackle you? Were you gonna go after Wendy?"

"She thought I was." Kisrie squeaked. Close enough to the truth. She couldn't possibly admit she had wished the sabre were sharp. Or that she had mentally disemboweled Wetbottom.

Kisrie looked up and made eye contact with the detective, who was now working his jaw into a bad case of TMJ. "I dropped my sabre when I fell, even scratched the new tape job on the handle. Detective Arbuckle, I did not stab Wendy with anything."

Arbuckle spent a few minutes jotting notes. Was she going to jail? Did he believe her? Was she gonna end up on some twisted reality show about the lives of troubled teens?

"Go back and send your buddy in here."

Kisrie avoided looking at the detective. She ground her molars and went to fetch 'her buddy.'

On the bus the following morning, no one spoke to Kisrie. Her little sister even kept a distance, huddling with her friends, pointing, and giggling. Pressing her head against the cool window, Kisrie stared at the beige homes blurring by.

"Would you quit it?" An eight-year-old Kisrie had demanded of the student behind her in the lunch line.

"Mooooo! Cows speak in moooo-language," some rat faced, toothpick-sized boy had said.

"I'm not a cow."

"Only cows are as big as you."

"I'm not a cow," Kisrie said.

"Well, if you're not a cow, then you're the cow pie! Ha ha ha ha ha. Cow Pie Kelley!"

"Are you planning to stare out the window all day?"

Kisrie bolted to attention. Her head swam as she realized the bus was parked in front of the high school and empty—except for her and the bus driver.

"Sorry." Kisrie swung her backpack over her shoulder and wiggled out of the seat.

Kisrie's brain didn't register the walk to her locker. Her hands dialed the combination with smooth, quick spins. She pulled open the door, dropped her pack to the floor, and leaned her forehead on the edge of the top shelf. Sticking her head inside her locker provided a refuge. She didn't mind the smell of her gym sneakers. Kisrie was an ostrich. Bury your head in the sand and the world goes away. You don't see them; they don't see you. Good deal.

Icy fingers impaled her shoulder. Something yanked her out of the locker. Her head and neck snapped backwards. Greenish glow from the fluorescent lighting assaulted her eyes.

"Listen to me, Cow Pie," Wendy said, her grip clamped on Kisrie's shoulder. "How many departments in the hospital do you want to visit?" Wendy released her hold. Kisrie turned and faced her. "We never got to have our little chat the other day, so let me give you the dumbed-down version. I suggest you give Hercule Poirot a call and tell him you lied to cover up for Uncie; otherwise, let's just say horizontal stripes won't flatter your figure."

"Poirot, huh? I'm surprised you read something other than *Cosmo.*"

Wendy jabbed a finger in Kisrie's face. "I mean it, Kelley. Today."

45

Given Wendy's track record for following up on threats, Kisrie toyed with the idea of recanting. Preserving her butt in school would guarantee slaughter at home. She'd be the family traitor. Forever. The anti-Megyn. She'd have to figure it out later. For now, more important matters loomed, like explaining to Mom why she wasn't at band practice this afternoon.

Gavin had called her out of class that morning and told her she owed the guard an apology for "misrepresenting the sport." She was sentenced to clean spit out of all the brass instruments before the next competition—all seventy-eight horns. He didn't want to see her at practice today, something about principle over performance. That'd go over well with the other guard members.

Boarding the bus, Kisrie cringed at the echoes of eighth notes ricocheting off the high school's walls. The drum line, as usual, was warming up early. Missing practice was a felony. Missing practice because your instructor didn't want you there? A death sentence.

"Why are you home early?" Mom asked as Kisrie lumbered through the kitchen door.

"Gavin suspended me from practice today." Might as well go with straight honesty. She dropped her pack on the floor and just stood there.

Mom squatted and picked up the pack.

"I'm gonna change my story so Wendy will leave me alone." Why she said that when she did, the way she did, escaped her. Facing assault charges and spending a lifetime lifting rusty dumbbells in a weed-choked courtyard with Rita, the chain smoker-serial killer, raised her anxiety level a teeny bit.

Mom's body froze in a Quasimodo-like position. She let go of the bag and stood tall. "What did you say?"

Kisrie rubbed her lips together until they hurt. Straight honesty. "I said I'm gonna go to Dr. Martinez tomorrow and tell him I misunderstood the conversation between Wendy and her dork-divas."

The color drained from Mom's face. Her jaw clicked open and shut.

"Mom, can't you understand? I'm just a kid. I can't live like this anymore. Wendy and her mom won't send me to prison if I admit I was making a vain attempt to protect a family member. You don't want to have to visit me in prison every day for the rest of my life, do you?"

"I don't believe I'm hearing this." Mom raked her fingers through her hair and paced. "Kisrie, he's your *uncle*, for Pete's sake. Besides, there's no physical evidence that Wendy was injured!"

"So? If one little lie will keep me from being mashed and tortured, then what's the big deal? *Uncle* Evan is a teacher. He's used to this kind of thing. I'm still a developing child." So Intro to Psychology had a purpose after all.

Mom turned, wrapped her arms around herself, and did some of her weird yoga breathing. Kisrie's throat constricted to the size of a soda straw. Mom spun to face her again. "Kisrie, your uncle has been accused of a heinous crime. Do you realize this is destroying his reputation?"

"But what about me? I'm only a sophomore. I have to go to that hellhole they call a school for two more years! Do I have to get beat up again and again before you see what's happening to *me*?"

Mom sucked in her cheeks and closed her eyes. She blew out long and hard. "If anybody should understand what it feels like to be falsely accused, it would be you. And you're the one who doesn't want to leave that school."

Kisrie felt a bomb explode in her head. She couldn't look her mother in the eye. She laced her fingers and tried to crack all of her knuckles at once.

"But it's still not fair!" She hurried past her mother, hobbled up the stairs as fast as her body would allow, and went to her room. A portrait of the Kelley family crashed on the hardwood floor.

Wendy took a sip of water, unable to concentrate on homework. Her cellphone sprang to life, skittering across the table with a loud buzz.

Wendy grabbed her phone and slid her finger across the screen, "Hello?" There was a lot of yelling in Spanish and English. It was the leader of the female gang that had shaken Kisrie. "You *told*?" Wendy leapt to her feet, banging her kneecap into the table leg.

"Look, it's my word against yours. And then there's this little issue of whether or not you're here legally." Wendy touched the End icon and threw her phone against the wall. Batteries and plastic sprayed the air. She wrapped her arms around her body, trying to squeeze away a rising tide of anxiety.

The doorknob jiggled and Iona staggered in with some guy in a suit. He stared at Wendy with the eyes of a starving wolf being offered a fresh kill.

Terror ripped through her like saw blades. She pressed her hands over her chest to hide the hammering of her heart. She scanned the room for some sort of weapon. Nothing that could do enough damage to stop the wolf as he prowled closer. "Oh, no you don't. Not this time. Not ever." Wendy leapt and shoved past Iona, knocking her off balance. All the more reason to make sure life went the way she wanted it to.

News trucks with satellite dishes on their roofs lined the curb outside the Smith home where Evan Plank was staying. Photographers and reporters loitered on the sidewalk, hoping to catch a glimpse of the condemned man. At least the predators weren't harassing Zena.

Three knocks shook the door. It cracked open. Rafe's face filled the gap. "Evan, Kathy made stroganoff. Wondered if you'd like me to bring some up?"

Words refused to form in Evan's mind.

"Evan?"

The door opened wider. Rafe squeezed inside.

Evan noticed a stale odor hanging in the air. He glanced below his arms at the yellow stains on his shirt. How much time had passed since his last shower? Dirty clothes hung limp from furniture. Who had he become? Normally, a speck of dust wouldn't have an extensive life span in his presence.

Rafe opened his mouth to speak but said nothing as he appeared to be shocked at the state of the room.

Evan's shoulders drooped, and his chin followed.

"Evan, are you all right?"

Evan's eyes roamed the room, resting on the window.

"The police made it clear—one foot on my property and they'll be slapped with trespassing charges." Rafe crossed the room and pulled the blinds. "Look, I heard on the news that the investigation is drawing to a close. The police will take the *lack* of evidence to a grand jury. You'll be cleared."

"It's already over."

"Almost."

"I'm not referring to this debacle." Evan looked up into his friend's eyes. "My life ended when Zena and I stood in the morgue staring at the remains of my daughter." His chin quivered. The muscles around his mouth pulled taut. "Megyn was robbed of life while trying to save another. Zena and I were robbed of our greatest treasure."

Rafe closed his eyes, a tear escaping and rolling down his cheek. "Man, what about Zena?"

"She has her job, friends, and God."

Rafe folded his arms across his chest. "Evan, *you* have friends, family, and God too." Rafe squeezed his arms tighter. "You're depressed. Get some help, will ya, before you make any rash decisions?"

Silence fell on the room like a wet, wool blanket.

"God left me when He took my daughter."

"God didn't take . . ."

Roots of grief plunged deeper into Evan's soul, twisting and winding their way to his extremities, rendering their extraction in this life impossible.

Kisrie fell to her knees beside her bed. Reaching between the box springs and mattress, her fingers closed around a plastic bag of contraband.

Peanut butter cups. Package half empty.

Jacque was gonna have to stock her up again. Kisrie plopped onto her bottom and grabbed a fistful of her only hope. Pieces of foil mounded in the triangle-shaped space between her knees. Desperately she wished the salty-sweet combination would numb the agonizing fire burning in her soul. But the candy ran out, and the flame still grew white hot.

Coming out with the truth was the noble, right thing to do. But the cost was way too high. Did her parents, her aunt, and her uncle expect her to sacrifice her whole teenage career over Wendy's stupidity? Really? Was accepting her own ruin the only way to earn any sort of respect from her mother?

Kisrie searched every crevice of her memory for the last time the svelte, health-conscious Gwyn Kelley, Ph.D. told her boring, fat, daughter she was proud of her.

Keri heard it all the time. Keri was the Kelley jewel.

"I was going to make Mom proud by winning that photo contest, but she ripped that away from me. I wish she could see

I'm good at guard and that I really, truly do have a future in photography . . . if she'd let me." Kisrie brushed the wrappers into a tighter pile and shoved them far under her bed, joining them with hundreds of others.

48

The stench of unwashed flesh—his flesh—assaulted his nostrils. Bile rose into his throat. Evan scuffled over to the window and rested his head against the blinds. Bronco colors of blue and orange squeezed through the slats as the dark night conquered day. Most of the media had left for the night.

Nice night for a drive in the mountains. He remembered placing his keys on the tiny card table on the other side of the room.

Evan swiped his hand across the table. A moldy sandwich fell, landing condiment side down, on the shag carpet. He felt the pointed edge of the keys that had been under the sandwich.

He wiped sticky food from the metal with his shirt and closed his hands around the keys until they bit his flesh. Megyn's face swam into his mind. She had a wide, bright smile and a contagious laugh. Those traits came from Zena. Megyn's love of literature and her habit of folding her socks and organizing them alphabetically by color came from him.

Archived memories paraded by—Zena cradling a prune-faced, pink infant. Megyn's first violin lesson. Megyn with her mouth full of hot dog, telling her parents she had Jesus in her heart. Megyn donning a purple-and-red robe, hand extended for high school valedictorian. Megyn jumping around the living room waving her acceptance letter into the pre-vet program at Texas A&M. Megyn, stiff, bluish, face frozen forever in a death mask of horror and determination. Blood stains on her chest and back where the knife had torn away her life, plunge by plunge.

Evan stared at his white knuckles. His fingers were numb. His beard was soaked.

He padded in silence to the door then sneaked down the stairs. Anguish, regret, and determination abducted his mind. He tried to pray as his car purred to life. Praying felt too foreign. Vibrations from the engine tickled his fingers as he shifted into gear.

Twenty minutes later, Evan was on Lariat Loop, the twisty corkscrew of a road leading up Lookout Mountain in Golden. Steamy-windowed cars dotted the shoulder of the road. Cool, night air slapped his face through open windows.

What had he done to deserve a life like this? Megyn's body had been imprisoned in the ground less than a year ago. Her killer was roaming free—free to kill again. And now never in his decades of teaching had a student taken such obscene revenge. Sure, there had been angry phone calls from parents, nasty emails. But this? Accusing him of—the word pushed against his skull—of rape. Rape! He never understood that kind of perversion. Now here he was, accused. No, he'd been condemned. Condemned before the investigation began. Condemned by students. Condemned by the community and his colleagues. At least Megyn had been spared this indelible mark.

Reflectors on the guardrail flashed by like ticks on a digital metronome as he wound his way upward to . . . where?

The hard truth was that Evan Plank had nowhere to go. He'd never be able to teach at Mountain Ridge again. Mere speculation of impropriety ruined an educator's career. Detective Arbuckle assured him that if the charges were dropped there would be no mark befouling his pristine record. He'd never even had so much as a parking ticket! Even so, people at

Walmart, King Soopers, and the Pepsi Center—all of Denver—would always wonder, did he really do it?

He couldn't stay.

The summit loomed black in his windshield. A large, gravelly area to the side of the road invited him. He accepted the invitation. He rolled to a stop, pulling the parking brake. White vapors twisted upward from his lips. A clean record didn't matter. The *Denver Post* had already branded him a felon. He'd even seen an AP report about his "alleged abuse" on Fox News.

All a small-town principal would have to do was Google his name, and these horrific charges would glare from the computer screen. He leaned back in his seat. Closing his eyes, he rubbed his temples. A migraine was coming on. He opened the glove compartment and searched for some Advil or Tylenol. Nothing.

Bright headlights stung his eyes. The car pulled up next to him, vibrating with a deep bass rhythm. The doors opened, and five teens with dark bottles in hand poured out and headed to a picnic shelter.

Evan shifted the car into first gear, easing onto the road, grill pointed downhill. Zena had handled Megyn's murder with faith and finesse. Her seemingly short-lived grief angered him. He punched the gas.

Thirty-five years ago at Houghton College, he had sat next to an amber-haired girl with chocolate eyes. It took him a month and a half to work up the nerve to ask her out.

He and Zena had said "I do" a few weeks after graduation before they both headed off to Wheaton College in Illinois for graduate school.

His eyes fixed on the double yellow line. He fought back tears. She'd be okay. Zena was always okay.

The guardrail reflectors flicked by faster and faster until they were a solid white line. More gas. Icy tines raked through his hair. Tires screamed as the momentum of the car tore them around a corner.

Faster, faster. Mind blank. Eyes unblinking. A yellow sign shouted a warning about a tight curve. For the first time in his life, Evan Plank broke a rule. Gravity and torque rocketed his car through the darkness, through the guardrail and into the inky sky over Golden, Colorado.

Kisrie bolted upright in bed, suddenly awakened from a deep sleep.

"Oh, dear God! Oh, Father God!" her mother's voice rose from the family room. Footsteps thudded down the hallway and then on the stairs.

"What is it, hon? What's wrong?" her father said.

Muffled sobs. What had upset her unflappable mother so much? In all her fourteen years, she'd never seen her mother cry.

"Kisrie," Keri whispered, her bare feet slapping on the floor as she approached Kisrie's bed. "What's wrong with Mom?"

"I don't know. Why don't you go to your room and I'll—"

"I'm scared. Can I stay here? Please?"

Searching her sister's face, Kisrie saw fear flash through those sapphire eyes, making Keri look like the small child she really was. "All right. Don't touch anything."

Kisrie made her way through the dark hall and down the stairs to the kitchen. From there, she saw the black silhouette of her parents in front of the TV screen.

A blond reporter with a microphone stood in front of a

gnarled guardrail. A second later, an aerial shot zoomed in on burning wreckage. Her parent's cries made it hard to hear what the reporter was saying.

"Mom? Dad?" Kisrie crept toward the family room.

Her parents pulled out of their embrace, slowly turning to face her. They didn't speak. Their eyes were red, cheeks shiny from snot and tears.

"Mom, what is it?" Panic rose in her throat. Ambulance and police lights flashed on the screen creating a weird disco effect.

"Dad, say something!" She ran toward them. Her father reached out his arms, catching her. His face snuggled into her bed-head curls. His body shook.

"Dad?"

Kisrie fixed her stare on the flat screen.

"Honey," Dad said, "there was an accident on Lookout Mountain." Stepping back, he put his hands on her shoulders and squatted to make eye contact. His eyes were glassy and red. Fear stabbed through Kisrie's chest. She wasn't sure she wanted to hear what was coming.

"Your uncle . . ."

Mom was on her knees hugging herself, rocking back and forth like some alien being was ripping out her intestines. "He's gone. Oh God, he's gone!"

Kisrie lurched away. A billion needles stabbed her brain. The temperature in the room seemed to plummet thirty degrees. Her teeth chattered. On the TV, a helicopter hovered over the smoking wreck.

"Rescue crews have been working for the past hour to cut through the wreckage to get to the victim."

"How do you know it's Uncle Evan?" Kisrie whispered.

The camera zoomed in on the firemen using the Jaws of Life. In the shot was a fragment of the front bumper with the license plate *EngLit.*

Her mother's forehead hit the floor, her hands pulling at her hair. "Oh my God, oh my God, oh my God . . . oh God!"

Waves of guilt crashed through Kisrie's chest. This was her fault. If something happened to Keri, would she be as devastated as Mom was losing her brother? The shivering rattled Kisrie's teeth until they hurt.

"Will you people—Mom? Dad? Kisrie?" Keri sprinted to the television set, her eyes tracking the crawling text on the bottom of the screen. Her hands flew over her mouth. Giant tears rolled down her face.

To eat breakfast or not to eat breakfast. Wendy rocked from one foot to the other in front of the refrigerator. She was finally down to a size two. Just right for the swimsuit competition.

Deciding she wasn't hungry, she slammed the door shut. Iona staggered out of the master bedroom in a new satin, leopard-print robe. This one was fringed at the bottom with tacky aqua feathers. Picking up a half-empty bottle of Coors, her mother slumped onto the couch and picked up the remote.

"You're up early," Wendy said as the TV screen started to glow.

"Couldn't sleep."

"I'm taking a shower," Wendy said as her mother flipped through the channels.

Wendy twisted the spigot, allowing the water time to heat. She hated the feel of cold porcelain under her feet. She stood, then stepped under the hot stream of water. The chill evaporated with the steam by the time she heard her mother yelling from the living room, "Wendy! Wendy! Get out here quick!"

Wendy let out a loud groan. What could possibly be on TV that was important?

She turned off the water. "I'm in the shower," she said and turned it back on. The bathroom door slammed against the wall. Wendy started, scrambling for balance. She let a few choice words fly. "What is it, Iona?"

"You gotta see this!" Iona flung the shower curtain to the side. Water spots added to the leopard print. "He's dead."

Wendy shut the water off and glared at her mother. Pathetic. Iona kicked her head back, taking loud swallows of her stale beer.

"Who. Is. Dead?" Dead people creeped her out.

The beer bottle fell to the floor with a thud. Iona's face lit up. "Mr. Plank."

Mom lay in the fetal position while Dad held her and prayed over her.

Kisrie felt an odd, tingling sensation pricking her body from the head down. Her heart skipped a few beats. She couldn't tear her eyes from the TV. A camera zoomed in on the burning wreckage just below a hiking trail on the north side of the mountain. A reporter's voice said it was fortunate this happened in the middle of the night; otherwise, someone might have been killed on the popular trail.

Unfolding before her was a scene more horrific than any of those *Halloween* blood-and-guts movies Jacque liked.

Guilt wrapped its tentacles around Kisrie's heart and squeezed. Grief added a painful weight. What if she'd immediately gone to Dr. Martinez and ratted on Wendy? Like, right from the bathroom?

Kisrie'd memorize *Moby Dick* word for word just to undo everything.

Uncle Evan had died a pervert, at least in the minds of most people. Or now, thanks to the news, all of Colorado.

Her body turned to the stairs and transported her to her room. Maybe she was dreaming. Her alarm clock would blare and she'd go to class where Uncle Evan would be at the white board with his favorite green marker. Kisrie never knew anyone who loved diagramming sentences more except for her mom. And Mom was a chemist.

Dr. Martinez paced the narrow hall in front of his office, chewing on the earpieces of his glasses. Mrs. Hampden had left a message on his cell saying she was on her way to the school. His stomach burned and bucked. There was nothing left to offer the great porcelain god. Not bothering to change out of his pajamas, he agreed to meet his secretary at 5:15 a.m.

He massaged the bridge of his nose, teeth hanging on to the glasses. Mrs. Hampden's sniffles echoed in the empty hall as she pulled open the door to the admin offices. Dark circles underscored her light blue eyes. Her hair resembled a rat's nest. She stood rooted to the floor, eyes searching his. Neither spoke for a few moments.

"We have two hours," he said.

"Do you want me to cancel classes?"

"I think that would be best." Dr. Martinez extended a hand to his secretary. "Are you all right?" Her eyes pinched closed. She shook her head side to side.

51

Kisrie and Keri sat at the dining room table. Keri took slow, deliberate bites without complaining about eating human food. Dung beetles seemed the farthest thing from her mind.

Kisrie pushed down the dark bran flakes with her spoon. They sank to the bottom of the bowl. For the first time in her life, she wasn't hungry. Her grief was beyond the comfort of food, even peanut butter cups.

"Good morning, ladies," Her dad called from the kitchen door. Aunt Zena followed behind him. Her eyes were red rimmed from crying and a sleepless night. Mom, who was elbow deep in soapy water, pulled away from the sink, ran to her sister-in-law, and flung her arms around Aunt Zena's neck.

"Zena and I just finished talking to the investigators at the scene of the accident. They'll let us know more when they hear from the labs."

Mom pulled away from Aunt Zena. "Coffee?"

While Mom busied herself with the coffee maker, Aunt Zena took a seat next to Kisrie, putting a soft hand over hers. "How are you?"

Kisrie counted the magnets on the refrigerator.

"Kisrie, your dad told me you're taking this hard. With the

allegations and the mess at school unresolved . . . What I'm trying to say is don't be hard on yourself. It was an accident." Her aunt pulled her into a sideways hug. "It makes no sense."

She got that right. None of this made sense.

52

"I need an inhaler." Wendy pulled open a cabinet near the stove where all the medications were kept.

"You don't have asthma," Iona said, checking her profile reflected in the refrigerator's shiny surface.

Wendy pressed her right hand flat against her chest. Her mother's hot, pink lips moved.

"We need to act quick." Iona grabbed her arm, pulling her off balance. "We have to use this to our advantage. Gotta make up for that mess you made about the sword. Good thing I have a client who's a doctor."

Wendy shook off Iona's grasp. Disgust coated her face as she said, "What kind of sicko are you? It was a car accident. The guy is dead."

She took a step backwards.

"Listen. We need to look at it this way—Plank's suicide could be seen as proof that he did it. An innocent man wouldn't kill himself."

"It was an accident," Wendy said.

"Well, now he's dead and no one will know for sure." Iona grinned and let loose a loud snort.

Wendy pushed her aside and stormed out of the kitchen.

Was a scholarship worth all this? Was all this drama coming back to bite her?

"I'm not done speaking to you!" Iona yelled.

"It's over."

"What happened to you? You grow a conscience all of a sudden?"

Wendy froze in the doorway to her room. She turned to face her mother. "You make me sick."

"Wendy, listen. What if the Kelleys come after you saying your accusations made him so distraught he couldn't drive safe? Think about it. We need to cover the bases."

Wendy rubbed her arms, willing the friction to erase the goose bumps. Could the police somehow tie the weight of her accusations to this accident? Would she be a murderer?

"Wendy, you gotta get rid of any doubts about your story. Now's not the time to back off. Tell the detective that Mrs. Plank knew what was going on, that she was his accomplice." Iona fished through a pocket in her robe for a pack of cigarettes. "Mrs. Plank let you into the house."

"You're drunk!"

"Creatively drunk." Iona laughed and coughed. "Maybe the wife got sick of being ignored by her man and cut the brake line for revenge?" Iona paused for a breath. "It's your life. I got mine. How bad you want to win that pageant?"

Wendy clenched and unclenched her fists. "You know, I don't think this is about me and my future anymore."

Iona's eyes widened. "Whaddaya mean?"

"I think it's your sick way of getting revenge for what that swimming coach did to you when your team went to Vegas for regionals way back when."

"That's not true!" Iona's hand shot out and made stinging contact with Wendy's cheek.

"Mr. Plank never laid a hand on me, and you know it! This is all about you. It always was and always will be. I'm done!" Screwing her eyes shut, Wendy slammed the door on her mother.

53

Solitude. The bathroom she shared with Keri was the only place it existed. Aunt Zena had been given Kisrie's room while the family dealt with all the details surrounding the death.

"Kiz?" Jacque's voice asked from behind the closed door. "Kiz, you in there?"

"Duh, she's in there," Tammie said.

Great. The non-friends.

The doorknob rattled. "No one answered your door, so we just came up," Tammie's voice yelled through the hollow wood.

"Go away."

The door opened.

"Ew. Stinks in here." Jacque waved her hand in front of her face. "Let's take it to your crib where we can open some windows and get some fresher air."

"I don't remember a crib in Kiz's room."

"You're such a lame-o, Tammie."

"Just leave me alone." Kisrie shifted her weight and faced the bathtub while she sat on the lid of the toilet. The plastic snaps attaching the lid to the seat broke apart. Her reflexes weren't quick enough to grab the edge of the counter, and she toppled backward into Jacque.

"Someone doesn't think you should be alone, either." Jacque jutted her chin at the ceiling then circled her arms around a now-wiggling Kisrie. To Tammie she said, "Don't just stand there; help me get her into her room."

Exhaustion refused Kisrie's body a good fight. She allowed the intruders to drag her down the hallway.

"Dang, girl! What a mess. I can't believe your mom offered this dump to your aunt. This is a tragedy."

"Bad choice of words, Jack." Tammie let go of Kisrie's feet. She bent over and picked a bra off the floor. It dangled from her fingers for a moment before she flung it at the open closet.

"It smells even nastier than usual in here," Jacque said, letting go of Kisrie's upper body.

"Owww." Kisrie tumbled to the floor.

"We know what happened. Mrs. Hampden had that computer thingy call everybody to cancel school. Jack and I figured you'd be holed up somewhere, beating yourself up."

Silence.

"Ya lose your voice, or what?" Jacque grabbed a stuffed animal from the bed and hugged it.

"I don't know what to say to you two. You don't want your lives messed up. Well, take a look around you. You can't get any more messed up than this, so go away and leave me alone."

"We've left you alone long enough. This is bigger than you, and you know it." Jacque paced.

"Well, we didn't *totally* leave her alone. Like, we tried to talk to her a few times, and then the parking lot thing. Anyway," Tammie said, shooting a deadly glare at Jacque before turning her attention back to Kisrie. "Kisrie, how many times do we have to say we were wrong for pulling away from you?" She clenched her teeth and mashed her eyes shut. "We're sorry, okay? Can you just forgive us so we can be those friends you so desperately need?"

"I don't need anyone."

Rocketing onto the bed, Jacque dug her fingers into Kisrie's shoulder and shook until Kisrie's curls rattled. "Stop it! Just stop it! This isn't just about you, you know. Lots of people are hurting over this. When are you gonna grow up and stop thinking of poor you? Geez." The shaking stopped. "Tammie, am I wrong here?"

Tammie shook her head. "What she said. Kiz, you can grow more prickles than a swimming pool full of porcupines, but it won't make us go away. Not anymore."

Kisrie flopped onto her back. Her brains felt like scrambled eggs. Jack and Tam weren't going away. Somehow that felt good. "I should've ratted her out."

Whump! A stuffed giraffe whipped over the top of her head. "Quit! I know where you're going with this. It was an accident!" Jacque yelled, arm arcing behind her head for another blow.

"Don't hit her Jack; she's hurting enough."

"You weren't driving the car. Lots of people . . . Those curves are nasty, 'specially at night."

"You know this 'cuz . . ." Tammie said walking toward the bed.

Silence filled the room for a few minutes. Squeaky, the cat, ran into the room and jumped on Kisrie's lap. She scratched the cat's ears.

Jacque sunk into the mattress beside Kisrie.

Tammie joined the other two on the bed. Squeaky purred while all three girls ran their fingers through her silky fur.

Tammie and Jacque remained stretched out alongside Kisrie for several hours. In silence. A new record for Jacque. But their grumbling stomachs finally got the best of them. Tammie and Jacque filtered out of her room, careful not to make any noise.

The visual of a car bursting through a guardrail exploding into a fireball on impact at the bottom of a ravine assaulted Kisrie's brain.

You caused this, a voice taunted.

Loud clattering in the kitchen brought her back to the

present. Sounded like a bunch of women from the church had come as promised to fix dinner.

The doorbell rang. Kisrie's body reacted as if someone slammed a railroad spike through her skull.

One of the church ladies answered. Her aunt and mom were out and about doing whatever people do to arrange a funeral.

The next day, students filed into the classroom as if walking into a haunted house. Everyone stopped in front of the teacher's desk, staring. Where piles of papers and books of classic literature once stood in perfect rank and file, naked Formica reflected the overhead lights. In the far corner of the room stood a young woman, hair pulled behind her head in a tight ponytail. She shifted her weight from one foot to the other.

"Looks like she just graduated from high school," Jacque said into Kisrie's ear.

"Yeah." Kisrie swallowed the lump forming in her throat. Both her mom and aunt had pressured her to go to school. Something stupid about keeping up her routine.

"Kiz, you're kinda creepy looking. You okay?"

Kisrie whipped her head around and glared at Jacque. "What do you think?"

Jacque's cheeks darkened. "Dumb question. Like, duh. Sorry."

Kisrie rested her head on her arms. The substitute teacher cleared her throat from the corner of the room. "Uh, you guys need to take your seats now. Can I, uh, get a volunteer to like hand out some books?"

"What're we readin'?" someone called from the next aisle.

The teacher bit off the nail tip on her index finger. "We're going to read *The Scarlet Letter*, a story of betrayal and uh . . . Hester Prynne's bad choices."

Desks and students melted before Kisrie's eyes.

"I'm the queen of bad choices." Ugh. Out loud again. Kisrie inhaled through her nose.

"What's the matter?" Jacque asked. "Smell something weird?"

"Um, everyone, please stop talking. We need to start class."

"I don't want to be here," Kisrie whispered to Jacque.

"Is there a problem? Um, you two are talking a lot." The teacher took halting steps toward them. Must be her first time in a classroom.

"She's having an allergic reaction to Fruit Loops," Jacque blurted. Other kids laughed.

"What?" The sub kneaded her hands.

"I bet her little sister snuck some in her breakfast," Jacque said, reaching across the aisle and hauling Kisrie to her feet. "Little sisters are known to do things like that."

"Jacque!"

"Act like you're about to die," Jacque whispered in Kisrie's ear.

Kisrie crossed her eyes and grabbed her throat and made gurgly noises.

"She needs to go to the health office and get one of those pen-thingy shots and she'll be good as new, won't you Kiz?" Jacque leaned in and whispered, "Nod your head."

Kisrie pumped her head up and down.

"So, I guess you could make sure she gets there okay. Um…" The teacher's eyes swept across the empty desk to the dry erase board. "Take that green marker for your pass."

Jacque shoved her from the room. Once in the hall, Kisrie put her hands over her face. Sobs shook her body. The marker fell to the floor and rolled away.

"Kiz, your mascara's gonna run."

"It's waterproof."

"Like that matters. Stuff still smears all over, making you look like—"

"Jacque, I can't do this. I need to leave."

Jacque grabbed Kisrie's wrists, wrenching her hands away from her face. "Yes, you can. You're a lot stronger than you think."

"Well, look what we have here." Wendy glided up to the duo, hands on her hips. Fake rhinestones spelled out the words *It's All About Me* across satiny, pink fabric puckering across her chest.

"Leave us alone," Jacque said.

Wendy stepped around Jacque to get closer to Kisrie. "Need some grief counseling?"

"Back off, Wetbottom, or I'll . . . I'll . . . uh . . ." Jacque perched on one foot, arms arched over her head.

"What, whack me with one of your pathetic flags? Dance for me?" Wendy pushed her jagged bangs out of her eyes. "Aren't you supposed to be in English? Later, you losers."

"That girl must eat pure evil for breakfast." Jacque fetched the fallen marker and tossed it, letting it flip around four times. It slipped through her fingers and bounced on the tile.

Kisrie watched the marker roll away. She tried not to feel. And failed.

"Kisrie, look. What Tammie and I said the other day is true. We're with you, no matter what." She bent down to retrieve the marker. "I just want you to know that . . . to know that I'm here for you. Tammie too."

Kisrie's eyes locked on to Jacque's. "The whole school hates me."

"I know."

Kisrie bent her neck down and toyed with a button on her shirt. "You can walk away, you know, and run for Homecoming queen someday."

"What's that got to do with being your friend? I'd win Homecoming today if I were a senior."

"Seriously, Wendy will do way worse than sexting to you and Tammie if you guys hang out with me. She'd make sure no one voted for you. I'm not worth sacrificing your social life."

Last thing she needed was more guilt about ruining lives.

"I doubt that." Jacque straightened her spine and combed her fingers through her long hair. "Wendy can say whatever she wants about me. I know it's not true."

"I don't get it, Jack." Kisrie leaned against a locker. "I mean, why are you my friend? You're popular; I'm not. People like you—they hate me. You give me so much, I—"

"Life with you is an adventure, Kiz. Those other people? Boooring. Why do you think I'm doing guard instead of being a cheerleader? Believe it or not, I don't want to live some cliché life. And you're the farthest thing from cliché."

"But—"

"However, Kiz, what *does* bug me about you is that you don't think you're worth it."

"Jack, I only—"

"Not listening . . . lalalalala!" Jacque pressed her hands over her ears. "Kiz, you look sick. Let's use this pass and fix you up. I've got a new flavor of lip gloss you gotta try. Pineapple Mocha Jazz."

Lip gloss? Fixing hair and makeup? What about fixing her life?

Wendy's comments proved she had a heart of pure evil. The Queen of Mean was not going to let this go. Not after the fake sabre attack, and now, not after Uncle Evan.

"Earth to Kiz." Jackie waved a hand tipped with metallic-gold nails in front of Kisrie's face. "Pineapple Mocha Jazz!"

"Sounds gross." She shrugged. What else was there left for Wendy to do at this point?

55

"Closed casket," Mom said to Aunt Zena as she poured a cup of coffee.

Rumbles shook Kisrie's tummy. She fished the fridge for something, anything, without fiber. Whenever something delectable appeared from one of the church ladies, like fried chicken or triple-layered chocolate cake, the leftovers disappeared. They weren't even in the trash under the sink. Kisrie checked.

"I agree." Aunt Zena added coconut creamer and stevia to the steaming, black liquid.

"Kisrie, you ate dinner less than an hour ago. The last thing you need is more food." Her mother's voice cut through her like a dull knife.

"Gwyn." A chair scraped on the floor. Kisrie slammed the refrigerator door shut, rattling bottles of organic condiments nestled in the door racks.

"You know, Zena, as well as I do, that she's not eating because she's hungry. This compulsive habit needs to stop."

Since when was putting fuel in one's body compulsive? Stomach growls; eat food. What's the problem?

"Now's not the time." Her aunt's voice was half the volume of her mom's.

Mom's jaw slid back and forth, and her lips pressed so tight the pink part was gone. "If she doesn't learn this now, she'll never learn." Her mom rolled her eyes at the ceiling.

"Teenager in the room. I hate it when you talk about me like I'm not here."

"You're right, Kiz. We're sorry," Aunt Zena said.

Kisrie's chin trembled. Aunt Zena was a widow. Alone. She lost her kid, then her husband. She had every right to be mad. But here she was, being all concerned about her stupid niece who had made such a mess of life, even leading to the loss of Uncle Evan.

Aunt Zena smiled.

"How can you do that, smile like that? Stop." Kisrie wrung her hands, then the bottom of her shirt.

Mom put her right hand over her face to hide her tears.

Aunt Zena faced Kisrie. "I cry enough tears to fill Lake Dillon every night when I slide into bed alone. It's just . . . just that each morning when I pray I ask God for strength, and He gives it to me."

"That's crap! God doesn't hear a thing you say! Look what he's done to you"—Kisrie swept her arm in front of her—"what He did to all of us." Her mom gasped. Kisrie pulled at the sides of her jeans. Sometimes she felt like she understood God, like in church. But ever since all this stuff happened, Kisrie felt like she had no idea who He was.

"Believe me, Kiz, there were times—" The phone rang. All motion stopped in the kitchen as if someone pushed the pause button on a remote.

"I'll get it." Mom sounded frog-like. Aunt Zena reached out and pulled Kisrie closer and closer until the space between them vanished. They listened. Mom didn't offer a greeting. Whoever called must have started talking the moment the phone was picked up.

High-pitched squeaks and shrill whistles sounded in the hallway. Keri slid sideways into the kitchen on socked feet.

"Feeding time."

A loud clatter startled everyone. Keri's feet lost traction, and she fell hard on her bottom. Kisrie and Aunt Zena tore apart and turned to stare at Mom's hands flailing for the fallen handset. All Mom's shyness about crying was abandoned as hard sobs threw her off balance. Aunt Zena rushed to help.

"Gwyn? What . . . are you . . . Do you …" Aunt Zena stooped for the phone.

"Don't!" Mom yelled, beating her to it and jabbing at the buttons to turn it off.

Aunt Zena's eyes widened. "Who?"

Mom unrolled her spine and leaned on the countertop. Red curls hung limp in her eyes. She didn't bother to tuck them behind her ears. "It was the traffic investigator."

"And?" Zena grabbed Mom's elbows.

"It wasn't an accident."

The two women fell into each other, crushing their bodies together.

Keri started to cry.

Kisrie's blood froze. It hadn't been bad judgment based on his emotional state. It was way worse.

He killed himself because of her.

56

Kisrie? May I come in?" Her dad said from the hall. She couldn't answer. She had nothing useful to say.

"Smells like rotting socks. I can't think of a locker room filled with sweaty football players that reeked more than this." He made a lame attempt to smile.

Dad pushed dirty underwear off the desk chair and sat down. Aunt Zena's suitcase sat upright in the corner.

"Either your aunt's nose doesn't work or she's got an unflappable stomach."

"Mom's already chewed me up." Kisrie gnawed on her lower lip. Her breathing was shallow. There was no putting this off. She had to know. "God's gonna hate me for this, isn't He?"

Dad's head snapped up. "Of course not. What gives you that idea?"

"It's my fault Uncle Evan is dead." She put her face in her hands. "I killed him."

A heavy silence smothered the room. Dad shattered it with a broken voice. "No, no, you didn't. Your uncle made a choice."

Kisrie could not hold back the agony dammed up in her

heart. "Yeah, but . . . but he wouldn't have done it if . . . if I wasn't a coward. I should've told! I should've told!" The last word came out as a strangled scream, and she threw herself at her dad. He held her until she could catch her breath.

"Why didn't God stop him?"

Dad lifted her head and looked at her with soft eyes. "We're not puppets on a string. He gives us choices."

Kisrie clasped her hands together between her thighs. "This is my fault. God didn't give *me* enough time to follow through with my choice to do the right thing. God hates me." Tears burned trails down her cheeks.

Dad rubbed his face with his hands. The blue in his eyes was punctuated by branches of red veins. "Can you make me stop loving you?"

Kisrie bit her lip and looked at her dad. "What does that have to do with anything?"

"If I choose to love you, even if you do the most horrible thing imaginable, can you make me stop if I don't want to?"

"But I did do a horrible thing. I killed my uncle. I am a murderer. Leave me alone!"

"Answer my question. Could you *make* me hate you?" Dad took her hands in his.

The only way to make Dad go away was to answer his dumb questions. "No. No, I can't."

"Why?"

Kisrie yanked her hands away. "Dad, I'm not stupid! Because it's your choice. Okay? Satisfied?" Did she just yell at her dad like that? Great. Just pile on the problems. What stinky mess would she have to scrub out now?

Dad raised his eyebrows in that "go on" way of his.

"God chooses to love me," Kisrie said. "No matter what I do. There. Now can you leave me alone?" It was obvious her dad didn't comprehend the magnitude of her crime.

"One more thing. You are not a murderer."

Kisrie vaulted away from her dad and paced back and forth, kicking any stuffed animals who dared be in her way. "I am! I am! What's the point? Why are you doing this to me? Can't you see how . . ." Her voice trailed off. What else to say?

Amazing how little one actually controlled in one's life, or for that matter, in the lives of other people. Maybe she *hadn't* killed her uncle. Maybe he'd done it to himself.

Sometime while she was lost in thought, Dad got up. Next thing she knew, his arms squeezed around her. "Now that I see you got my point, can you promise me you'll stop blaming yourself?"

Sure, but the fact still remained that her choices had consequences, one being that her family was now one member smaller.

57

Wendy swore at the stoned whack-job who ogled her from the front steps of the apartment building. The tenants in this place weirded her out, but Iona insisted it was safe and necessary for her 'work.'

Sighing, she opened the door to her apartment. Her mother lay stretched out on the sofa, basking in a shroud of tobacco smoke.

"How was school?" Iona asked, her eyes focused on the TV screen.

"Boring."

"English?"

"We had a dumb sub."

"Nice without old Plank, huh?"

A sour taste filled her mouth.

"I'm pretending I didn't hear that." Wendy made a beeline for her bedroom.

"Don't go too far. You gotta call that detective and tell him the rest of the story. Like that? The 'rest of the story' like that Harvey guy used to say." Iona threw her head back and laughed. Smoke curled from her nostrils, snaking its way toward the yellowed ceiling.

"Harvey? Never mind. How 'bout letting it drop? I need to focus on the pageant."

"It's your life," Iona said, tapping ashes onto the coffee table. "I'm just trying to cover your backside."

"I don't need you to cover my anything, Iona. It's done."

"If this doesn't pan out I lose too, you know."

Wendy made a slow turn to face Iona. "What do you lose?"

"Hey, if all goes well, you go off to college, get some fancy career, then come back and take care of your old mother."

"We've had this conversation before. This is all about you and the demons of the past."

"It's that, or you can work for me."

Wendy swallowed the torrent of insults bouncing off the back of her teeth. She wasn't about to let Iona get to her. "Never."

"Well, make sure you don't get dragged into some criminal investigation. You'll be outta that pageant for sure." Iona sat up. "Look. You gotta make up for your stupid antics over the sword. You owe Dr. Wan for making up that report. The detective was about ready to toss the whole thing out!"

"What was I supposed to do, let her get off? Let them think I was after her?" Seemed like the more the lies built up, the more lies were needed to cover the previous lies. And this is worth it because?

"Listen to your Ma. I have a solution. Say Mrs. Plank knew her hubby was fooling around with students and that she blackmailed him into silence. As a counselor, she's got lots to lose. Say she walked in on you and him at the house and tried to cover it up. You've got lots of options."

Wendy's face contorted into a mask of disgust. "Mr. Plank did nothing! I'm sorry I listened to you in the first place." She scurried down the hallway, slamming the door to her room behind her. It was time to chart her own course.

58

Don't let the door slam." Mom's fingers never stopped dancing over the keys of her laptop. An empty coffee pot sat on the kitchen table next to the computer. Clickety-click. Kisrie paused mid-stride, holding the screen door open. Then she let it go. The walls shook.

The clicking stopped. Mom glared at her with 'the look.' No, this look was different. Mom's eyes were harder than usual. The muscle cradling the right side of her jaw twitched. "Go to your room. I'll let you know what your consequence is."

Why couldn't she have a mom who greeted her with a bright, white smile and a plate of freshly-baked cookies when she came home from school? "Sorry."

The clicking resumed. Kisrie dropped her backpack on the floor and headed to the pantry.

"Pick it up."

Kisrie ignored her mother and pawed through organic nonperishables, settling for a bag of dehydrated apple chips. They were sort of roundish like cookies, at least.

A chair scraped on the floor. "The last thing you need to do is eat."

Defiance overwhelmed her senses. Kisrie tore open the

bag, stuffing a handful of dry, tasteless apple chips in her mouth. In a matter of seconds, a fire-breathing dragon materialized in front of her, tearing the bag out of her hands with its razor-sharp talons. "I said you don't need any more to eat."

Pressing her fingers over her eyebrows, Kisrie checked if they were still intact. "I hunnnry." One of Mom's pet peeves was talking with a mouth full of food.

This was the first time in days Mom had acknowledged her existence. Mom had been avoiding Kisrie since the news broke about the suicide. When Kisrie entered the family room where Mom was watching one of her Travel Channel shows, Mom had turned the TV off and gone somewhere else.

A blast of classical music accompanying a live flute floated downstairs. Stop. Reverse. Replay. Keri was practicing for a recital next month. Mom was always chiding Keri to practice more, then praising her for adding dynamic or connecting the phrases in her part.

"I said. Go. To. Your. Room. You have homework to do." Mom squeezed the bag, crushing the apple chips.

"I got it done in study hall." Kisrie refused to break eye contact. Not this time. No more. Sadness ached through her, coaxing her eyes to drop. Kisrie refused. Looking down would confirm she was weak in Mom's eyes. Kisrie was tired of being labeled as weak and lazy.

Mom opened her mouth then snapped it shut. Kisrie pivoted hard and marched toward the stairs to her room.

Hangnails hurt. Especially on the big toe. Kisrie tried to pick the sliver of skin off, but it only tore deeper into the sensitive nail bed. Toenail clippers were the answer.

She limped to the bathroom, pulled out the junk drawer, and rattled the odds and ends around. Nothing. Maybe they were in Dad's toiletry kit under the sink. Kisrie dropped to all fours, shoving her head around shampoo bottles and that bubble bathroom cleaner stuff. A loud sound shot through her brain.

Kisrie jolted, the back of her head smacking into the sink plumbing.

"Hello?" Who was in the bathroom with her?

Silence.

Pray!

"Great. I'm hearing voices." But it wasn't exactly audible. Or was it?

She shook her head and resumed her search.

The imperative bounced around in her head again.

It was the same voice or nudgy thing that had pestered her about telling the truth.

She backed out of the cabinet. "God?" Kisrie looked up at the ceiling, rubbing the back of her head.

Pray.

"Why should I?"

Find the toenail clippers.

Why in the world was God talking to her, asking her to pray? For Pete's snakes, she was the last person He should trust to pray. She hated youth group and only read her Bible when forced. Sugar. Her blood sugar was probably low and she needed some Reese's.

Images filled her brain. Ideas flooded her senses. She pulled herself out of the cabinet and rocked back on her haunches. Kisrie put her hand on her forehead. "You've got to be kidding me. I can't. Can I?"

59

Sabs, it's me. I was hoping you had your phone on, because I need to talk." Wendy stared out her bedroom window watching the traffic zoom by on Colfax. Creepy Weed Guy leaned on the brick wall of the apartment building, inhaling from a tiny tube between his pinched fingers. That'll never change now that marijuana was legal in Colorado.

"Well, knowing you, you probably forgot to charge your phone again. I guess I'll catch you tomorrow. Later." Wendy poked the red rectangle on her new phone's screen.

Something disturbed her from the inside out.

On her desk, the computer screen glowed with the web page for the Colorado Teen Queen competition. Her coach had said her walk was strong and her interview skills were excellent. But Wendy worried if she could hold up mentally. Mr. Plank's death haunted her. She never envisioned any repercussions other than him losing his job. As much as she couldn't stand him, she never wished him dead.

Knots tightened in her stomach. Could she be held culpable for causing his death as Iona suggested? Did she have to push this farther and make up one more story?

Muffled laughter peppered through the sheetrock wall

separating her room from her mother's. Wendy gritted her teeth. She would *not* end up like Iona. Winning the pageant meant money toward a scholarship to a state university of her choice. Wendy wished she could go out of state, far away from Denver.

More drunken laughter flittered through the shared wall. Far away from this.

Wendy pounded on the wall with her fists. "Child in the house! Have some respect!" Like that would do any good. Wendy swore, giving the wall a final beating before heading out of her room. Shame coursed through her veins. Her friends thought Iona was a lawyer. This was why Wendy never had friends come to her house.

Kisrie paced back and forth in her room. The location of the toenail clippers remained a mystery.

"Why should I talk to you? I'm more than a little hacked off. And now I'm talking to the honkin' ceiling!" She paused in the middle of her bedroom, squinting at the popcorn texture. How long was it since she last prayed, seriously talked to God like He was real?

"Why'd you let him die? You made dead people like Lazarus come back to life. *You* came back to life." Kisrie was crying now. "Yet you sit up there on a golden throne letting my life rot in high school hell." Oh, dear. She said hell. "Yeah, I said hell. It's the best description I can come up with. You know I'm talking about the place, not using it as a curse word."

She jabbed her pointer finger upward. "You let people like Wendy be all popular and have it easy. No one makes fun of her. She's at the top of the class in grades. Don't let me forget to add she's a beauty queen, too. How fair is that? She probably doesn't even know what a Bible is!"

Since she was talking and He was listening, might as well let it all out. Cast her burdens.

"About that mutant sister of mine that everyone thinks is so—"

Pressure built in her chest. An undeniable sense of knowing hijacked her brain. She knew beyond a shadow of doubt she *had* to pray for Wendy, just like she *had* to take another breath. But it rubbed raw every wound on her body and in her soul.

"Why? I can't." Her hands covered her head like she was shielding herself from falling rocks.

Kisrie plopped onto the bed, her nose wedged between her palms. "What if I don't? I'm the one getting beat up. It's my family that's grieving Uncle Evan. Don't you think somebody should be praying for me?"

Her heart accelerated and her breathing shallowed. Looked like no peace until she caved to that—what in the world do you call it?—voice of God? Schizophrenia?

"You want me to pray for her? Okay. Here goes. Dear Lord, I *pray* Wendy burns a chunk of hair off her head and loses that stupid vanity competition so she can have empathy for everyone she's been mean to. There. I prayed. Are you happy?"

In addition to a pounding pulse and rapid breaths, sweat poked through her pores.

"I'll take that as a no."

61

Kisrie cradled the wooden pole. Bright jewel-colored silk and lamé tickled her sandaled feet. She pushed her arm down, the pole popping out of her elbow and into the air. Her hands rose above her head as she turned away from the lofted flag. Three beats later, it landed with a quiet smack in her left hand behind her back.

"Whoa! Pretty cool," Jacque said, getting out of her mom's car.

Kisrie shrugged. "It's no big deal."

"I've been working on that since Gavin taught us, and it hits me on the head every single-dingle time."

"Because you swing your release hand to the right and don't put enough pop in your toss. You have to keep it in front like this."

Kisrie executed the toss with precision.

"You know, you gotta stop saying you stink at stuff," Jacque said.

"I do though."

"Nuh, uh. Kiz. Do you realize the section leaders can't do that, uh, what you just did?"

"Whatever."

"Don't 'whatever' me, you dork-butt. You're the best one in this guard. That's why they pick on you so bad."

"It's 'cuz I'm fat."

Jacque threw her hands up in the air and rolled her eyes. "You can't take a compliment, can you? Every time anyone tries to tell you something good about you, you argue. You're such a poopyhead."

"What's with the names this morning? So far you've already called me dork-butt, and now it's poopyhead."

"It's because I love you so much. Hey, did you hear Wendy's got a pageant thingy this weekend? She still thinks she can be the next Miss Teen Colorado. I heard Sabrina and Brittany yapping about it while I was looking for you in the hall."

Like this was news? If it weren't for the stupid pageant, Uncle Evan would be alive and assigning them some boring book from ancient Rome. "I hope she loses," Kisrie said. A stab of conscience shot through her mind. Kisrie did a set of drop-spins.

"Yeah, then maybe she'd realize how much like the rest of us she is." Jacque kicked a small rock across the parking lot.

"Trying to break a window, Jack?" Tammie called from the band room door. "That'd get you suspended for sure."

"Get over here, girl. We gotta come up with a plan to sabotage Wendy's pageant. Like throw rotten tomatoes at her like she did to Kisrie back in—"

Tammie cut in, "You couldn't pay me to go sit through some show where girls with big heads compete for Ego of the Year awards."

"You realize how peaceful life would be 'round here if Ol' Wetbottom got put in her place?" Jacque said. Metal studs on her low-rise belt glinted in the morning sun.

"Maybe we can start a nasty rumor or Photoshop a picture about her and post it on Facebook or something like she did to us," Tammie said, grabbing the flag from Kisrie. She started to do some pull-hits then stopped.

Wrapping both hands around the pole, Kisrie reclaimed her flag. "I don't know." She fluttered a hand in front of her eyes to ward of tears. "Nobody'd listen to us, and I'm sure she'll figure out where it came from and add slander to the assault charges."

Jacque shook her head, glossy, black hair spraying her face. A few strands stuck to her lip gloss. "Do you really think the adults believe her anymore?"

"They'd be stupid if they did." Tammie danced a few steps.

Grabbing the flag on the tape with her right hand, Kisrie did a reverse flourish, grabbed with her left hand, and buzzed a single. It *did* seem like the principal was finally working to expose Ol' Wetbottom.

"Look, Kiz, maybe we wait until this thing blows over. Dr. M. seems to be on our side now. I think he's on to Wendy. When everyone starts forgetting, we strike. My boyfriend can hack into the school web page and maybe even mess with her Facebook or something. We can claim she's selling secrets to some Middle Eastern terrorist or something."

Kisrie pulled the pole to flat.

"We need justice." Tammie snatched the flag after Kisrie tossed a horizontal. "Wendy deserves to lose. I hope one of her stupid high heels breaks and she falls on the floor, splitting her bikini bottom while barfing on a judge."

"Maybe she'll fall off the stage after barfing on the judge and fall into a forever-coma thingy."

As fun and intriguing as her friends' wishes sounded, that weird thing poked Kisrie's soul. Her head wanted Wendy to be eaten by a shark, but something deeper inside knew such desires were wrong. Very wrong. "Jacque!"

Jacque pointed a thumb toward Kisrie. "I didn't say she'd croak or anything!"

"Well, I hope the heel snaps off and gets stuck in her nose as well," Tammie added.

"I gotta get my stuff for class." Kisrie turned away from her friends. She ripped her flag out of Tammie's hand then let out a gasp. The urge to pray for Wendy struck her like a falling tree. Her hands flew to her chest.

"Kisrie, are you having a heart attack? Is your left nostril numb?" Jacque rushed to her side.

"It's her left arm that'd go numb, not her left nostril! Move over." Tammie hip-thrusted Jacque out of the way.

"If I was having a heart attack, I'd be dead before you two quit arguing." Kisrie squeezed her eyelids shut, hoping to quiet the persistent urge.

She felt all the energy drain from her body. Her arms hung slack. Her fingers relaxed.

"Huh?" Tammie and Jacque said together, their eyes searching Kisrie's.

"Nothing. Just leave me alone," Kisrie said in a quiet tone.

Jacque grabbed Kisrie's hand. "We're not letting you go anywhere. By yourself, that is."

"Just leave me alone! I don't want to talk about this anymore."

"Come on, Kiz," Tammie said. "Don't be mad."

Jacque pulled Kisrie off balance so she stumbled closer. "Talk."

The first block bell rang.

"Bell rang," Kisrie said, ripping away from her friends.

"Uh-uh. We'll get a late pass."

Kisrie looked from Tammie to Jacque.

"You're gonna think I'm a psycho."

"S'okay. We already know that about you. It's why we love you so much. Right, Tam?"

Kisrie ran a hand down her face. "Yeah, but what I'm about to tell you may make you reconsider."

62

Accusing glares pierced her skin like those big IV needles at the hospital. As she figured they would, Tammie and Jacque freaked about the whole idea of praying for Wendy. Jacque insisted God had more common sense than to ask Kisrie, the victim of all Wendy's crimes, to pray for her.

Kisrie needed to find a place of solitude. What parts of the school did Jacque avoid? Fortunately, Tammie usually followed Jacque.

The school library was the last place Jacque would go. Mrs. Van Wooten, the librarian, took extreme measures to keep the library nosh-free.

Kisrie hung her backpack on a chair in the Science and Technology section and headed toward the magazine rack. Midway, she stopped to browse the Suspense section. Stephen King. A crooked smile cracked her lips. Her mother would have a stroke.

Bending her knees, she pulled *Carrie* off the shelf. The bell above the entry door dinged. She looked up. Wendy and her goons.

"Listen, let's grab a table in the back. No one will bother us there."

"Hey look, Taylor Swift is starting her own brand of snacks!" Sabrina squealed as the trio passed the magazine stand.

"Really?" Brittany said.

"You can read about it later. Come on."

Kisrie stood, pressing her back against the bookshelf. The girls passed by on the other side. They pulled out three chairs and sat, crossing their legs as if their movements were choreographed for a Disney movie. Curiosity simmered in Kisrie's chest. She crept closer.

"This better be good," Sabrina said.

"I need your help. Need extra insurance."

"Help? Don'tcha think this whole thing's gone far enough?" Brittany pressed the back of her hand on her forehead.

"Since when did you become the voice of reason?" Wendy snapped. "Look, I'm not sure what to do here. Iona wants me to add to the story and make sure there is no doubt about this whole mess. I think Dr. Martinez isn't buying the sabre thing."

Sabrina pulled a book off the shelf and flipped through the pages. "Ya think?"

Wendy ripped the book from Sabrina's hands and flung it away. "Shut up and listen, would you? Iona's afraid the Kelleys will come after me in some way for—It wasn't supposed to be like this, okay/ I almost wanna just drop the charges and forget about it."

Brittany toyed with the hem of her sock. "I'm confused. What does that mean?"

"What does *what* mean?"

"Drop the charges?" Brittany snapped her gum.

"I can't believe you're this stupid. It means I'd tell Detective Dude to just forget about it."

"No way," Sabrina said.

Wendy slammed her hands on the tabletop. Kisrie jumped. They didn't notice. "I'm asking you for help here. Help me figure this out!"

"Uh, your mom's a lawyer, so can't she sue Cow Pie or something?" Brittany squeaked.

The three girls stared at each other. Wendy lowered her voice to a near whisper. Kisrie pressed closer to the bookshelf, straining to hear every word. Dust motes from forgotten books made lazy circles in the sunlight. "No, she wouldn't waste money on that. Court costs, you know. I need to come up with something like Mrs. Plank is trying to blackmail me to keep my mouth shut so her hubby's post mortem reputation can be—"

"Yo. Slow down with the big words, Wen. You may be smart, but Britt and I . . ."

Wendy rubbed her head and sighed. "Here's the kindergarten version for you two idiots. My story is falling apart. I think Martinez suspects something. I made a mistake with the sword thing."

"That's a problem." Brittany abandoned her sock and reached for a book.

"Well then, help me come up with something to convince them that my story is true."

Sabrina picked at her thumbnail. "But it's not."

Wendy clenched her fists and pumped them at her sides, looking around. Kisrie imagined herself shrinking.

"I don't know what to tell ya, Wen. Britt and I aren't the most creative people on the planet."

"What if I say Mrs. Plank is trying to blackmail me, that she is threatening to put in my records that go to the pageant people that I'm psycho unless I change my story."

"Or you could say she found out about you and Plank and tortured you in a dark room with biting ants."

"Seriously, Sabrina? Biting ants?"

"What if you say she pulled a gun on you and threatened to shoot your brains out?"

Kisrie hugged *Carrie* against her chest, fearful the loud thumps from her heart were audible. A weird, tickly feeling buzzed in her right nostril. She closed her eyes, fighting the inevitable sneeze. Her foot turned the wrong way. She lost her balance, body slamming into the metal shelving unit with a loud "Ahhchoo!"

"What the—" Wendy appeared from around the fallen bookshelf.

"OMG, Cow Pie!" Sabrina said, both hands on top of her head.

Kisrie lay on the floor, dusty novels on top of her like a lumpy blanket. A scene from several weeks earlier flashed through her mind.

"She heard everything," Brittany said, circling her two friends.

Wendy stooped. Her dark eyes bore holes in Kisrie's face.

"You can't do this," said Kisrie.

"Do what?" Wendy said.

Kisrie propped herself onto an elbow. Her heart jackhammered. "Make up more lies about my family, that's what."

"Who said anything about lies?" Wendy let out a low chuckle.

"My uncle was innocent, and you made up those lies." Kisrie stood, brushing dust off her clothing. The librarian headed toward them, looking like she could bite all four of their heads off in a single chomp.

"That's your story," Wendy said, her eyes flicking toward the prune-faced teacher. She mouthed "jail bait."

"What's going on? Passes. Now." Mrs. Van Wooten propped one fist on her hip, her other hand held flat out waiting for a pass.

"It's lunch. We can be here," Sabrina said with a smirk on her face.

Van Wooten lowered her hand and brushed at her burlap-like skirt. She narrowed her eyes at the tangle of books and shelving. "And I suppose you are going to tell me the ghost of an old gold miner made this mess."

Three pairs of eyes landed on Kisrie. The librarian took a step toward her. The bell rang.

"Gotta run. Can't be late for class, can we?" Wendy said, grabbing her goony friends by the arms and booking it out of the library. Kisrie tried to make a break for it, but Mrs. Van Wooten blocked her. Kisrie knew there'd be no late pass. If she even made it to class at all after cleaning up the mess.

Another mess Wendy created. And got away with.

63

It's at the Hilton in the Tech Center," Dad said from behind the *Denver Post.* Kisrie poked at the fibrous vegetable goo on her plate. This organic thing should be classified as child abuse.

"What's that, Dad?" Keri twisted around in her chair so her knees rested on the seat.

Dad folded his newspaper and bopped Keri over the head. "A hotel."

Keri giggled, grabbing the newspaper. "No, what's going *on* at the hotel?"

"The Colorado Teen Queen pageant."

Kisrie put her fork down and glared at her dad. What did he care about that?

Mom walked over to the coffee maker and poured herself a cup of black. She leaned against the countertop with her hip.

"Why're you interested in *that*?" Keri sprang off the side of the chair, landing in a crouch.

"Because we're all going." Dad stood up and tapped his left palm with the folded paper, his perfectly-straight teeth exposed in a wide grin.

Time froze.

Mom set her cup on the counter, a little hot liquid spilling over the side. Keri plopped onto her bottom. Kisrie stared. She shook her head and blinked. What alien had hijacked her dad's brain?

"A family outing. We'll hop on the light rail at Englewood and get off at the DTC." He panned the room. Kisrie closed her eyes. He was serious. If it was a joke, he'd be on a new one by now.

"I have a band competition this weekend," Kisrie said.

"No, this is the one weekend off," Dad said, "so you can come too."

"You couldn't pay me to go!" Kisrie shot up out of her chair, slamming her toe against the chair's leg.

"Bern, we need to talk," Kisrie thought her mother said. It was hard to hear what anyone was saying while she yelped and hopped around the kitchen clutching her foot.

The smile fell off Dad's face like an old magnet falls off a refrigerator door. "Listen, I've already talked to Zena about this, and she agrees it would be good for us as a family and as a way to start reaching out to Wendy."

"Bern. Seriously. We need to talk."

"That's so lame. But I'll go with you, Dad, as long as we can swing by the zoo on the way back. I'm feeling homesick," Keri said with a chirp.

"Kisrie?"

Looking from Dad to Keri, Kisrie's mouth flapped open and closed like the salmon at the aquarium. Was her dad for real? How did he think this hairbrained idea would make Mom feel? Wendy's antics had pushed Uncle Evan to his death. And Aunt Zena—had she gone senile in her grief?

"Reach out? Reach out?" Kisrie said. "She's the one who wronged us! Why should we reach out to her? Shouldn't it be the other way around? Shouldn't she be paying restitution or something?"

"Bern, I don't think this is a good time." Mom folded her arms, tucking her hands into her armpits. The grief lines on her face deepened.

"Oooh, can we get ice cream too? How about we go to

the Cheesecake Factory? It doesn't hurt me too much to eat people food sometimes." Keri got up.

"Shut up, you little skunk! Number one, the zoo is on the northern side of town, and the Cheesecake Factory is downtown. Nowhere near the DTC! And people think you're a genius?" Kisrie said limping toward her sister. Keri's eyes widened.

"Kisrie, go to your room." Mom's voice was a low growl.

"She's gonna hit me!"

"Stop it! Just stop it." Mom had moved to the middle of the kitchen, both hands on her head, fingers pulling at her hair. Tears pooled at the corner of her eyes. Her jaw sawed back and forth. "Bern, we need to talk about this. Upstairs. Now."

"Dad's in trouble," Keri whispered.

Kisrie's arm shot out and whapped Keri across the back of the head.

Keri shrieked.

"Shut up! How can you act so silly at a time like this?"

Mom and Dad stood frozen, staring.

"She hit me!" Keri scurried toward Mom and Dad.

"Uncle Evan is dead. *Dead!* And you don't seem to give a rip." Kisrie whipped around to face her father. "And neither do you." She rolled her lower lip into her mouth and bit down until she tasted blood.

"Come again, Kiz?" Dad asked. Mom linked arms with him.

Should she speak her mind? Ask what had gotten into all of them? She'd probably be sentenced to cutting the grass with her teeth or something if she didn't hold her tongue.

Mom moved away from Dad. "To your rooms. Everyone. Kisrie, go to the spare, since your aunt is in yours." Mom and Dad headed to the stairs.

Keri bounced out of the room. Kisrie stood statuesque in the middle of the parquet floor.

It hit her. Like a bag of bricks to the diaphragm. That urge. To pray for Wendy.

Whoa, hold on. Now where did *that* come from?

Pray for Wendy.

Like, seriously? Now? Wasn't God supposed to have perfect timing or something? Last thing Wendy deserved was prayer. Probably would turn her into a pile of ashes if she tried doing it herself.

Didn't God hate evil? Wendy was the epitome of evil.

The urge became a pain. A moan bubbled up from Kisrie's throat and poured over her bottom lip. Her fingers crawled into her hair and twisted deep into the curls. Since when did God start speaking to teenagers, and why her? Why now?

Rhyme and meter poured in one eyeball and spilled out the other. Kisrie shoved the *Anthology of American Poetry* off the rolltop desk in the guest bedroom. The book hit the floor with a resonant thunk.

"Kisrie?"

Her body jerked, and the chair lurched backwards. Her dad lunged into the room, catching her head before it made contact with solid oak.

"Dad!" She screamed once her breath returned. "Why'd you sneak up on me like that?"

"The door was open."

"Ever hear of knocking?" Kisrie rolled from her dad's grip onto her knees.

Dad stepped backwards. "The hostility!"

"I'm not hostile!"

"Can we go for a walk? I have peanut butter cups." Dad patted a bulge in the thigh pocket of his cargo pants.

No, no, no, no, nooooo.

"Sure," she said, eyeing the bulge. Her desire for the candy overruled common sense. Plus, it might get that whole 'pray for Wendy' thing out of her head.

Amber circles of light illuminated Kisrie and her dad every few houses. A shrub on her right rustled like a paper bag. An orange tabby with a whiskery scowl skittered past, followed by a stooped old woman and a little old man cradling an oxygen bottle.

"Sorry 'bout that. Wish Marmalade'd keep to the walkways," the old lady said while the man wheezed by.

"Keep to the walkways," the man said.

"Do you need help catching her?" Dad took a step toward the woman.

The old lady rubbed her hands together. "Oh, no! She's an outdoor cat."

"Outdoor cat, dadgum cat."

"Hector and me, we're keepin' an eye on her. Don't want her to cause any trouble, you know."

"No trouble, no trouble, no—"

"We'll let you catch up with, er, Marmalade." Dad waved. "Nice evening."

"They are so weird," Kisrie whispered, reaching into Dad's pocket for a peanut butter cup.

"To each their own. Now. About Saturday." Dad sure didn't waste any time getting to the meat of the matter.

"I'm not going." Kisrie rubbed a fist against her eye then stared at the dark form of the elderly couple as they slipped through the gate of a neighbor's backyard.

"Keep moving, Kiz. It's chilly."

Father and daughter crossed the street in silence. A muffled shriek followed by crashes and thuds colored the breeze. The little old lady and man scurried out through the gate they had entered a few minutes prior. An orange streak of fur shot between them. "Don't know why women these days breastfeed in the wide open. Didn't bother to close the drapes."

Hector took a drag from his oxygen bottle. "Dang nab breasts."

Kisrie looked at her dad who cocked his head away to hide an ever-expanding smile. Not waiting for conversation, the pair changed direction. After a few steps, Dad turned his attention back to Kisrie. His blue eyes seemed to glow in the dark. Creepy.

"Stop looking at me like that."

"How am I looking at you?"

"All creepy like." She shoved her hands into her pockets.

"Dad, I'm not going to that stupid pageant. I mean, have you started drinking or something? Are you coming down with Alzheimer's?"

"No." Dad gave a few short laughs. "I'm not losing my mind, and it wasn't my idea. It was your Aunt Zena's."

Incomprehensible. Why would Aunt Zena want to go to a pageant to cheer on the girl who slandered her husband? Maybe it was about revenge.

"That doesn't make sense! If it weren't for Wendy's rotten lies, Uncle Evan would be alive!" Kisrie spotted a long stick lying on the sidewalk. She picked it up and whacked it against fence posts, tree trunks, and fire hydrants.

"Wendy isn't responsible for your uncle's death. And neither are you. Remember our conversation about free will?"

"Unfortunately."

"Well, then?"

Gripping the stick in both hands, she snapped it in half. "Come on! Don't you think making him a criminal pushed him too far? Can't you even suppose he might be alive today if that—I can't say what I want to call her—kept her mouth shut, Dad?"

"Kisrie, I can't say for sure one way or the other. Truth is, your uncle suffered from depression. His illness goes way back before Megyn was even born. None of us this side of Heaven will know his motivations at that moment."

So not what she wanted to hear. She wanted her family to band together and to stick it to Wendy. Lock *her* lying butt up behind bars. Even then, justice wouldn't be served. Because Wendy would still be breathing.

"Kisrie, I can't make you go. I won't tie you up like a canoe and strap you onto the roof of the car and haul you to the Hilton. But I will challenge you to consider doing what you believe is right in God's eyes."

Kisrie stopped walking and stood to face her dad. "Right now, I don't care what Jesus would do. I care that my uncle is dead. I care about Wendy getting what she deserves." Deep breath. "And speaking of God, I had another, um, incident."

"Incident?"

"Like, what does He want with me? If He's such a loving God, why doesn't He punish Wendy? What's up with that? She needs to suffer for what she did, not win some stupid pageant and go on trips with the rich and famous or whatever people who win those things do. Plead for world peace, maybe? Like, that would be quite the irony. Wendy, the peace destroyer, Queen of Mean—"

"Are you done?" Dad had crept closer during her little rant. He wrapped his arm over her shoulders and pulled her into a warm embrace.

"Honey, you're going to make yourself nuts by trying to figure God out. God sees things we don't. His ways are beyond our little brains. Just trust."

Like a water balloon on pavement, Kisrie's emotions burst. She couldn't hold back any longer. "But what she did was *wrong!* How come God blesses people who are so evil and who destroy people who try to do what He says? Megyn died helping some lady. Aunt Zena and Uncle Evan loved Jesus more than the average person." Her sobs picked up, breaking up her speech. "How come they've suffered so much for doing good?" Kisrie buried her face into Dad's coat. "How come?"

Squeaky dug her claws into Kisrie's shoulder. Deeper. Deeper. "Ow, that hurts." Kisrie grabbed the cat around the middle, pulling her underneath the covers. Sleep wasn't within the Denver zip codes.

The walk with Dad had left Kisrie feeling all mixed up. She hated the fact that life wasn't nice and easy for Christians. Why would anyone *want* to be a Christian if they knew life was only gonna hurt more?

Dad had tried to explain to her that it was about a personal, intimate relationship with God, not about having some sort of genie-in-the-sky thing going on who gave you what you wanted when you wanted it. And then Dad hand gone back to this whole free will thingy.

Yeah, it could all be true what he said, but that didn't mean she had to like it. Was it okay to not like the truth?

Her breath caught in her throat. Her heart hammered faster and faster. Images of Wendy's face swam through Kisrie's imagination. She tried to imagine Jacque or Tammie's face, a peanut butter cup. But breathing got harder, and Wendy's image grew clearer. There was no way to stop it.

What if she gave in? What if she said a for-real prayer for Wendy?

Obviously, she wasn't gonna get any sleep unless she did. But she had to mean it, right?

Squeaky purred, her furry body massaging Kisrie's achy ribs.

"Okay. Dear Lord . . . um . . . You do realize you're asking me to do something I don't want to do? So, um, You gotta help me out here. You gotta help me get past, well, how much I hate Wendy."

Nothing could have prepared Kisrie for what happened next.

Please tell me this is all some sort of twisted joke," Jacque whispered through the corner of her mouth.

Kisrie's eyes scanned the field. Gavin was yelling at one of the captains for cutting the wrong plane with her flag—again. Tammie stared straight ahead. Her lips pursed, and her cheeks puffed out with unmoving breath. Kisrie turned her head a fraction of an inch, giving it a quick shake.

Jacque blew the air out of her lungs. Gavin's head popped up. "Miss Gonzales? Do you have asthma?"

Jacque stood at attention.

"I didn't think so. Breathe quietly, please."

Gavin ran the flag feature in the opener several times. Poor Jacque looked as though her flag moved through wet concrete. The gawk block clicked faster and faster, imitating the acceleration of the music. Kisrie lunged forward, pushed a big circle alongside her body through a front slam before stirring the silk by her feet. She drew her left hand sharply behind her head, pushing the right high and forward. She launched a perfect forty-five. She turned under the airborne pole and caught it with her left hand, sweeping it in an arc.

"Cut! Run that again. Most of you are late on the slam,

making you even later for the release. Oh, and don't forget to pass through flat in front of your eyes. Set!"

Poly China silk flapped in the afternoon breeze as the guard reset to count one.

Gavin stood feet apart in turnout, hands on hips. His chin arched from left to right. He examined body shaping and equipment angles. His hands slapped against his bald head. "Do we need another geometry lesson? For the sake of Marvin! Can somebody show me what a forty-five-degree angle looks like?"

"Kisrie's not paying attention," someone called out from behind.

"She looks like a pregnant cow when she does the leap in the next set."

Snickers rippled through the guard. Kisrie's cheeks burned. Did she look that bad?

"Let me make something clear. This is not Pick on Kisrie day. Worry about yourselves. Take five." Gavin massaged the back of his neck.

Kisrie relaxed the hold on her flag, letting its butt slide to the ground. Jacque loped toward her.

"Girl, you *gotta* tell me your dad's taking drugs or something. Only someone with a serious brain injury would think of doing something like that." She blinked hard. "It's child abuse!"

"Do I totally look like a pregnant cow in set twenty-three on the leap?"

"We can kidnap you," Tammie said. "I'm reading this novel where these bad guys sneak in a girl's room in the middle of the night, put a pillowcase over her head, and drag her out."

"Do pregnant cows leap?"

"We should knock her out first. Knowing Kiz, she'll fight us." Jacque pantomimed bonking Kisrie over the head. "That way she won't scream."

"Should I even bother trying out for winter guard?"

"No! What if, instead, we—all three of us, after we kidnap Kiz of course—go kidnap Wendy and tie her to a tree in Bear Creek Lake Park?"

"I should've taken up something that doesn't require grace. Like, maybe I'd have been better at marbles." Kisrie squatted down and balanced on her toes. Her fingers tore up chunks of grass.

"Dude, are you even listening to us?" Jacque nudged Kisrie in the back with her foot.

"I'm not a dude."

"We're standing here trying to figure out how to help you, and you sit there and whine over some comment made by a big dummy," Tammie said. "Have some respect, will ya?"

Kisrie tilted her head up and looked at her friends. "Do you think I'd be any good at knitting?"

Jacque's foot shot out and clobbered Kisrie between the shoulders. Hands flailing, Kisrie landed flat on her face. "Ow! You kicked me!"

Silence dropped over the entire guard. Every head turned toward the action. Jacque helped Kisrie back up and put her mouth to Kisrie's ear. "You're right. I smacked you one. You're meaner to yourself than Wetbottom is to you. I'm sick of it."

"Hey Jacque, if you're into girls now, can I have your cast-offs?"

"You can do better than that, Gonzales!"

"What's wrong with you people? Get a life!" Tammie yelled.

"Enough!" Gavin jogged into the middle of the gathering group. "What's the matter with you ladies? Bicker, bicker, and bicker. You are not going to win any championships this way. We're doing silent rehearsals for the rest of the afternoon. Open your mouth, and it's thumb-roll prances around the field. Got it?"

"You're not getting off that easy, Kiz," Jacque whispered.

"Gonzales? Pick up your flag and start prancing. Now!"

"Slimy banana slugs!" Jacque rolled her eyes as Gavin frowned, clapping off a double-time tempo.

One talent Kisrie knew she had was getting her friends in trouble. If Jacque freaked this much over Dad making her go to the pageant, how much worse would it have been if Kisrie had told her what happened in her room last night?

65

Kisrie plopped two iced caramel mochas on the table at the Village Roaster in Lakewood City Commons. Jacque groaned, eyeing her drink. "I don't know if I can pick this thing up, let alone hold it. Like, find out if they have one of those sippy-cup thingies."

"I'm sorry about the laps." Kisrie stood. "I can get you a straw."

"Gavin needs a megadose of Ex-Lax. I mean, how're we supposed to spin after doing those high-knee-run things while doing thumb rolls from the lower third on the pole? That's child abuse! I'm gonna be in pain for the next year."

"Sorry."

"Kiz, the comfy chairs are free. Hurry before someone else gets them." Jacque slid off her stool and limped to the pair of plush chairs in the corner.

Kisrie picked up a newspaper off the coffee table and flipped through, skimming headlines.

"You never told me the whole story about your dad's whacked-out idea of going to Wendy's dog show. That's, like, so wrong."

Kisrie recounted the conversation she had with her dad

the night before. And her prayer. All of a sudden, her hand flew to her mouth.

"Oh, no!"

"What's wrong?" Jacque craned her neck around, looking for some perceived threat.

"Oh, no."

"You're scaring me, Kiz."

"I forgot to talk to him."

"Who? Stop being a dork-butt! Who?"

"Dr. Martinez."

Jacque knocked her forehead on the table. "You're giving me a migraine."

"Oh. Oh. Oh!"

"Kisrie!"

"I gotta stop her."

"Who, her?"

"Wendy!" Kisrie twirled her hair around a finger. "I was in the library and heard Wendy and her pet snakes brainstorming ways to make her lies more believable! They're gonna say Aunt Zena blackmailed them or something like that."

Jacque laid a hand on Kisrie's arm. "You don't have to say any more. I think I get it. Wendy knows no one believes her about the disem . . . you know, where she says you cut her guts out with a sabre! Girlfriend, she's trying to cover her mosquito-sized hiney!"

Kisrie bolted to her feet and circled the table. She had to get to the school. Principals stayed all kinds of weird hours. They didn't have lives outside of running schools.

"Stop getting distracted. We need to be the first two people in that school office tomorrow morning, and you need to know what you're gonna say." Jacque took a huge gulp of her drink. "I'll be Dr. M. and you pretend you're you, and let's get this figured out."

"But I need to go now. What if Wendy beats me to him? Come with me."

"Uh . . . you expect me to walk forty-five miles, in this condition?"

"It's only, like, six."

"Tomorrow, Kiz."

Kisrie plopped onto the cushioned seat. "Tomorrow will be too late. I know it."

66

Mrs. Hampden rubbed her lower back and picked up the stack of purchase orders on her desk. Why did teachers wait until the deadline for next semester's POs? A single strand of hair fell from her bun while she leaned forward. She was in for a long day.

Her fingers danced over the keys of the adding machine, double-checking the sums. The hairs on the back of her neck rose. Her fingers froze.

She rolled her eyes upward. Two students stood in front of her desk. One was Evan Plank's niece. She pushed the loose strand of hair behind her ear. "Can I help you?"

"Is Doc M. here yet?" The long-haired Mexican girl standing beside her asked.

"Doctor *Martinez* will be available any moment. May I ask what this is about?"

"It's about my uncle," Kisrie said.

Mrs. Hampden's hand flew to her hair. A dull pain zinged through her chest. This whole thing was beyond horrible.

Before she could answer, three more students pushed through the glass office door. Wendy Wetz and several of her friends.

"Look, it's 'ol Cow Pie!" A white blonde-haired girl pointed a hot-pink, manicured nail toward Kisrie.

"May I help you?" Mrs. Hampden asked. She folded her hands on her desk.

Wendy eyed Kisrie. "Yeah, we need to talk to Doc Martinez. It's an emergency."

"*Doctor* Martinez is not yet available." She closed her eyes and swallowed. Whatever happened to the theory that teens liked to sleep in late? "Have a seat, and once he settles in, I'll let him know you ladies are here waiting."

All five girls glared at each other. Mrs. Hampden reached toward the stack of purchase orders. Her shaking hand upset the pile, scattering it through the air.

Dr. Martinez saw an explosion of paper in his secretary's office. Several students dove into the paper blizzard. Mrs. Hampden's bun hung limp at the nape of her neck.

He took a deep breath and placed his hand flat on the door's glass. A few steps later and he was in the midst of a pile of POs, Kisrie Kelley, Wendy Wetz, and three others. This was not a good sign. He tugged at his collar.

"What's going on in here?"

Everyone froze.

Dr. Martinez spread his feet apart. "I asked a question. Does someone have the courtesy to answer?"

Mrs. Hampden looked up at him. "Dr. Martinez, these girls would like to speak to you."

"It's important!" Wendy jumped up from the floor, re-scattering the papers she'd collected.

Dr. Martinez panned the room, taking a moment to look each girl in the eye. "All of you. In my office." He did an about-face and reached his office first.

Five teens scampered in like puppies being offered a treat. He slammed the door shut behind the last one. He pointed to the wall across from his desk. They lined up execution-style. "Now, will someone please tell me what this is about? No more games."

"It's not a game." Wendy stepped forward.

Kisrie studied her sneaker. He barked her name. She jumped. "She's gonna try to convince you her lies are true."

Wendy's nostrils flared. "You're the liar, Cow Pie."

"I will have none of this. Do you all hear me? Nod your heads. Now Wendy, what did you want to tell me?"

Wendy's face went scarlet. She turned her back to Kisrie. Her two friends pressed into her shoulders.

The girl on Wendy's left said, "Mr. Plank's wife, like, she—"

"Cork it, Sabrina!"

Wendy whipped her head around toward Kisrie and Jacque.

Dr. Martinez positioned himself between Wendy's gang and Kisrie.

"It's a lie. Just like the first lie about my uncle!" Balled fists were cocked and ready in front of Kisrie's chest.

"I need all of you to calm down and tell me what this is about."

Kisrie lifted her chin a little at Wendy, almost like a dare.

The second hand on the wall clock ticked away the seconds. The other girls slunk away from Kisrie and Wendy, who locked eyes in silent battle. Dr. Martinez glanced at the clock. Wendy's shoulders dropped, and she turned away from Kisrie. "We still have that assault issue to talk about. This other stuff doesn't matter as much now."

For the first time ever, Dr. Martinez saw Wendy lose steam. Hope swelled in his chest. She was *not* going to get away with it this time. Her wrongdoings were going to catch up with her. Evan Plank's reputation would be reconciled.

Leave me alone, you freaks." Wendy narrowed her eyes at her friends, who peppered her with dumb questions.

"How come you caved to *Cow Pie*?"

"You think the principal knows you weren't hurt by that sword thingy?"

"Can you still compete in the pageant?"

Sabrina grabbed Brittany by the purse strap and dragged her away. "I think Wendy needs to be left alone for a while."

"Good call. Now go away, both of you." Wendy waited until they were out of sight before heading to the bus stop.

Leaning against a pole holding the red-and-blue RTD bus sign, emotions too powerful to describe roiled through Wendy. One moment, she felt capable of murder. The next, she was overcome by the urge to cry. She had assumed Kisrie'd be her usual chicken-livered self and keep her rotten beak shut.

The bus rolled to a stop, its brakes hissing. Foul exhaust filled Wendy's nose, making her cough. She glanced at her watch. Thirty-four minutes to hide her sense of utter failure from Iona.

"You should've seen her, Tam! I mean, like, Wendy was all in Kiz's face, and Kiz was all 'don't mess with me,' and Wendy was all nasty, and Kisrie was all heroic-like. It was intense, girlfriend." Jacque rocked backwards until the trunk of an aspen tree in Kisrie's backyard caught her back.

"And I missed it. Rats."

"You said 'rats,' Tam," Jacque said, digging in her purse for her cell.

"Sooo?"

"It's lame, and you know it."

Kisrie sat cross-legged on the grass, pulling out individual blades by the root. "It wasn't that big a deal."

"But Kiz, you stood up to Wendy. You didn't just roll over and die or pretend you died."

"I'm telling you, Tam," Jacque said, "you so should've seen it. Now Ol' Wetbottom's probably gonna spend the next sixty years in the slammer for vernacular manslaughter!"

"Jack, you really need to develop a relationship with a dictionary." Tammie stretched her arms over her head. "But it would be cool if the police came and hauled her away in the middle of the pageant. Kiz, maybe you can film it and post it to YouTube."

"I don't know."

Jacque bent forward until her forehead touched Kisrie's. "What? This is the perfect chance to get that you-know-what back for all she's ever done to you!" She pulled back and examined Kisrie. "Wendy's been mean to you, like, forever. Remember when her mom and friends booed you in the sixth-grade Christmas musical?"

"You can borrow my phone to video it," Tammie said.

"I can't."

Lifting Kisrie's chin, Jacque said, "What is it you can't do?"

Kisrie brushed a clump of grass off her leg. "I'm not gonna sabotage her beauty parade. It's not worth it."

"Maybe she's coming down with Congo fever or . . . or Ebola," Tammie said, reaching out to check Kisrie's temperature.

"Quit touching me! I'm not sick." Kisrie slapped Tammie's hand away.

"Then what's your problem?"

Would they think she was nuts if she told them? Should she tell them? Would they believe it? "I . . . I had this . . . experience."

"Serious conversation alert!" Jacque waved her hands above her head like she was flagging down airplanes.

"Stop being weird, Jack." Tammie drew up her skirt and crawled on her knees to where Kisrie sat. "What kind of experience, Kiz?"

Hands resting in her lap, Kisrie's shoulders sagged like the bags under her grandmother's eyes. "You guys won't believe me."

"Um . . ." Jacque tick-tocked a raspberry-pink-tipped finger in the air. "Yes, we will."

Kisrie studied the two faces before her. "Promise you'll hear me out."

Jaw dropping, Jacque gasped. "You're not gay . . . are you?"

"Jack!" Tammie rocked forward and shoved Jackie to the ground. "I can't believe you said that! The way she's been fantasizing about that hunky ambulance dude?"

"Can I continue?"

Jacque sat up. Tammie nodded, settling onto her bum.

"All right. I've been getting these weird . . . impressions. Like someone's saying stuff in my head and it isn't me, and *no*, I'm not schizoid."

"What do they say?" Tammie flicked a bug off her sleeve.

"Pray for her."

"Who?" Jacque asked and cut a glance at Tammie.

"Wendy."

"For reals?" Tammie said.

Kisrie nodded. "I think I told you about it before, but I was determined to ignore it and hoped it would go away. It didn't. The other night I was in bed all mad, and then I couldn't breathe. I saw Wendy's face in my mind."

Jacque put both hands over her eyes and shrieked, "Nightmare!"

"Shush." Tammie pulled Jacque's hands down. "Let Kiz finish."

"I knew it wasn't going away. I . . . I prayed and told God how mad I was at Wendy and that I felt He was asking me to do something impossible." Should she tell them the rest? What would they think about her?

"Go on," Tammie urged.

"Well, as I was telling God I had no clue *why* I should pray for Wendy, or *what* I should pray for Wendy, these things came to my mind, and before I knew what was happening, I was praying for her." Tammie and Jacque's eyes grew large. "Not that she'd fall or die or anything like that. But for . . . for her soul. I had this sense that she's in some kind of trouble."

Jacque snorted and tore out a handful of grass. "Well, duh, she's in trouble! She created all the trouble."

The kitchen door slammed. All three girls sat ramrod straight. A blood-freezing scream tore through the air. "Grass killers!" Keri dove into the trio, shielding the violated grass with her body.

Could her sister have interrupted her at a worse time? What did Keri hear? And if she heard something, it would only be a matter of minutes until Mom and Dad knew.

Mom poured a box of sprouted-grain noodles into a pot of boiling water. "Hand me a wooden spoon, will you?"

Kisrie slid off the stool and shuffled to the utensil drawer, yanking it open. It rolled off its track. Spoons, spatulas, and a few other odd kitchen things clattered around her feet. Her mom never flinched.

"Are you ever going to talk to me?" Kisrie asked.

She knelt, grabbed a wooden spoon, and smacked it into the hand Mom extended without taking her eyes off the pot. Mom stabbed the bubbly surface and stirred the noodles. "Did you even hear me, Mom?"

"I heard you."

The muscles in Kisrie's chest tightened. She rubbed her sore ribs.

"Vivaaaaa! Viaagggrrrrraaaaa!" Keri spun into the kitchen, arms and legs pumping in time with her song.

"Keri, that's not appropriate." Mom let go of the spoon. It swirled in the vortex created by her stirring.

"Vivvvvvaaaa Viagra! Viva—"

"Quit, you little pustule!" Kisrie kicked at the utensils, spreading them across the floor.

"Kisrie, clean that up right now and go to your room. I will deal with you later."

Kisrie dropped to her hands and knees and crawled around on the floor, grabbing at her mess. All she wanted was for Mom to talk to her, treat her like a human being.

"It's an Elvis song," Keri said. "Mother, were you alive when Elvis was popular?"

Mom resumed stirring, slower. "It was 'Viva *Las Vegas*.'"

Keri scratched her head and screwed her mouth to the side. "Yeah, but on TV they sing those other words. What's Viagra?"

"Not something little girls need to know about."

"I'm not little."

"It's inappropriate. End of discussion."

Mom's posture deflated over the pot. If she bent a few degrees lower, she'd have a hump like those little old ladies picking through crocheted coin purses at the craft fair.

Keri rose up on her tippy toes, lifted her arms up high, then inhaled. "The sun'll come out, tomorrow. Bet your bottom dollar that tomorrow there'll be sun." The word sun was dragged out over what seemed like an eternity. So not fair that the little brat could probably catch the attention of a Broadway scout with her vocal talent.

Mom turned from the stove. A faint smile flickered and was gone. It was enough encouragement for Keri to pick up where she left off.

Kisrie clutched a bunch of spoons and spatulas to her chest and wondered when Mom last smiled at something she said or did. Now, without her camera, there was no way to prove to Mom she had talent. Mom must be sorry Kisrie was ever born. Probably wished Keri came first and would have stopped there. If she had, Uncle Evan would still be alive.

Wendy twisted in front of the three-way mirror and examined the rear profile of a deep-navy evening gown. "I don't like that ruffle. It makes my butt look big."

"Ah, but it's what they are wearing in Paris."

"I'm not going to Paris. I'm competing in a pageant. In Denver." Wendy tugged the offensive ruffle.

"But that shape . . . such an elegant line."

"Your store has on-site tailoring?"

"*Oui*, I mean, yes."

"So you can take this hideous ruffle off my butt?"

"*Oui.*"

"What's up with the French? You don't have an accent." Wendy pursed her lips and blew out a long stream of air. Waiting until the last minute to get an evening gown was never a good idea. Good thing Sabrina's mom kept a stash of cash in an upper kitchen cabinet. Stashes like that were rarely counted. And who knows? Maybe it could be reimbursed before being noticed.

Pink spots dotted the saleswoman's face. She was attempting to sound all *haute couture*. "Go ahead and get out of it. Bring it to the counter, and I'll make sure the bow is off in the next two hours." The saleslady backed out of the changing area and yelled something unintelligible to an older Asian lady behind a sewing machine.

Wendy faced the mirrors again. The neckline plunged deep enough to capture the attention of any breathing male. Tiny gold threads woven through the silk created a subtle glow under the store's bright lights. The dress almost looked spray-painted on until it flared away in swirls of fabric from her knees to the floor. Sophisticated. Confident. Sexy.

Wendy on the outside.

Sure wasn't Wendy on the inside.

The band director called for a break. Kisrie shot her flag pole to the front sideline, missing a baritone sax by less than one nose hair.

"That was close, girlfriend!" Jacque blew a long, low whistle.

"You almost owed that dude a few thousand bucks," Tammie said.

Kisrie turned to face her friends. "You know, I sometimes feel like I've got warts. Two of them."

"Warts? Owww-eee." Jacque grabbed her water bottle from the sideline. "So, you still gonna go to that prissy parade this weekend?"

"Well?" Tammie nudged Kisrie's shoulder.

Swallowing a mouthful of water, Kisrie shrugged her shoulders. A wet spot appeared on her chest.

"You're leaking." Tammie brushed at the beads of water.

Kisrie stepped back. "Don't touch me."

"Are you still wanting to pray for Wendy? If not, maybe we should go and put itching powder in Wetbottom's bra." Jacque's dark-brown eyes narrowed. Her perfect smile seemed to glow.

"I'm in." Tammie and Jacque exchanged sweaty high fives.

"I bet Kiz's dad would get us tickets. I have his cell number on my phone." Jacque reached down into the neckline of her tight, gray T-shirt and pulled out a hot-pink phone. Tammie side-stepped closer to block any band staff's view.

"You have my dad's cell number?" Kisrie took another sip of water.

"Duh," Jacque said, poking at the touch keypad.

"I want an iPhone," Tammie said. "No buttons. And you can fit it in your pocket."

"If you don't have the guts to do the right thing, Tam and I are gonna have to do it for you. Found it! I'm calling him now."

"No!" Kisrie whacked the phone out of Jacque's hand.

"Kisrie, I love you and all, but you have contracted some serious mental illness. Wendy is the *enemy*. What part of that don't you get? Don't you hate her? She messed with you. She messed with all of us, right, Tam? I'm sure God understands."

Kisrie crossed her legs at her ankles then sank to the ground. "I did."

Tammie pursed her lips. "Did what?"

"Hate her."

"Whoa, *did* is past tense."

"Really? Where'd you learn that, English class?" Tammie said, slapping Jacque's arm.

Gavin and the band director checked their watches and called for the low brass.

"I was going to explain it all to you before we were so rudely interrupted by that rodent sister of mine."

"Well, I have a hard time believing you. I think you're crazy."

Kisrie tossed and caught her water bottle. "I'm not. And I tried to tell you the other day."

Jacque let out a loud laugh. Conversations around them fell silent. Jacque twisted her mouth and crossed her eyes at the closest group of kids. "Mind your own business."

Three sharp whistle blasts ended the break.

Jacque grabbed Kisrie's arm. "Your aunt is a psychologist. She can help you."

"Everyone set up at the accelerando," The band director said into his megaphone.

"Five! Four! Three! Two! Who wants to run with the cymbals? One!" Gavin clapped his hands. The guard snapped to attention, and the band played the first note of the B-flat concert scale.

"I don't need that kind of help." Kisrie muttered as she sprinted to her spot. She should have kept her mouth shut.

70

Why did *this* weekend have to be the one weekend when there was no band competition? What did she ever do to her dad to deserve being dragged to a stupid beauty pageant? Mom didn't have to go. Why did she?

"Thunder Thighs isn't out of her room yet!" Keri shouted down the stairs. Dad was in the kitchen brewing coffee. The earthy scent slid under the bedroom door.

"Keri, what have I told you about saying things like that?" Dad answered back.

"Well, her thighs are huge!"

"Keri? Get down here and eat."

Watching a bird molt would be more interesting than a dumb anorexia convention.

"Kisrie!" Dad called over the clinks of silverware on plates.

An urge to pray for Wendy knocked the breath from Kisrie's lungs. Weird, how it hit when she was thinking not-so-nice thoughts about the Queen of Mean. The only way to find peace seemed to be to obey the urge.

Kisrie prayed.

Wendy waited for the next train at the light rail station to take her back to the pageant. Dawn peeked over the Eastern Plains, casting the Rockies in a purple glow.

Iona hadn't answered her phone when Wendy called from the hotel where the pageant was being held, asking her mother to bring a pair of shoes she'd accidentally left behind. Real mothers were waking up in hotel rooms *with* their daughters ordering coffee from room service. Real mothers checked and double-checked their daughter's garment bags to make sure all the necessities where there. Real mothers did everything Iona did not.

As always, Wendy had to come to her own rescue. So, here she stood. In the cold, heading back to the hotel. Her stomach lurched. Dread washed over her like battery acid. Hopefully, her sneaking out to retrieve the shoes wouldn't be discovered.

The train blew its horn, warning people to stay clear of the tracks. Wendy shifted her shoe bag from one arm to the other and back. Her brief run back to the apartment had flared a gnawing uneasiness in her chest, adding to the distress in her tummy.

It had looked like Iona never made it home last night.

Metal screeched on metal as the light-rail cars shuddered to a stop.

She stepped over the yellow line and climbed up the steps onto the train. Every seat was occupied. The train lurched forward. Wendy stumbled onto another passenger. The lady turned and gave her the Look of Death. Embarrassed, she retracted into herself, cursing under her breath.

"Kiz, we need to leave *now.*" Dad tossed the keys into the air and caught them in his hand. "I know how much you hate running."

Tipping the bowl to her lips, Kisrie swallowed down her mushy fiber sticks. That stuff was not meant for human consumption! "Okay. Ready." She slammed the bowl on the table. She had seven hours of band practice to figure out how to avoid going to the freak show that evening. A trip to the ER?

Amazing how they can make you wait for hours while you lay in a pool of blood at death's door. Nah, she'd had her fill of hospitals.

"Seriously, Kiz. I will ask Gavin to have you run extra laps if you don't get a move on."

She took the bowl to the sink to rinse it off before putting it in the dishwasher. "Do I really have to go tonight?"

"We've been over this. Yes, you do."

"Even if the world explodes?"

"Yes, Kisrie, even if the world explodes."

"Star crunches! Twenty-five!" Gavin twiddled with his iPod attached to the amp.

"One!"

"So Kiz, your dad still making you go tonight?" Jacque crunched up and reached through her legs, which pointed to the sky.

"Two!"

"Unnngh." Kisrie lifted her legs high into the air and split them apart. "Unfortunately."

"Kidnapping offer still stands."

"Three!"

"I bet my dad hid a tiny GPS tracking device in my cereal. No matter where you took me, he'd find me and make me go."

"Sorry, that just stinks."

"Tell me about it."

Bare feet flopped into Kisrie's peripheral vision. "Kelley and Gonzales! Three laps! Now!"

Wendy's roommates were gone when she burst back through the door of the hotel room to grab her interview suit.

From the time she'd left this morning, the temperature seemed to have gone up a hundred degrees. Sweat trickled down Wendy's face. Hopefully, her makeup would cover the flush in her skin so she'd look calm and collected in front of the interview panel.

Scooping up her garment bag, she jogged out of the room to the backstage area where everyone was prepping. Why did it have to be at the farthest point of the hotel complex from her room? Maybe someone brought extra tissues for mopping up perspiration.

Backstage, the dressing room was loaded with mother daughter duos. Wendy's coach assured her she could hold her own just fine. Iona had never attended a pageant, let alone helped her daughter get ready for one. But it still stung.

The only empty space was next to a blonde girl with hair that would make a freshly-groomed and fluffed Keeshond jealous. Taking a deep breath, Wendy dumped her garment bag over the back of the chair and dug inside for the little baggie holding her interview makeup.

First things first. False eyelashes. Wendy laid out her supplies and got to work. She needed to focus.

Loud laughter echoed off the smooth walls in the changing rooms set up behind the stage. Mothers and daughters tried to calm jittery nerves by telling stupid jokes. Opaque clouds of hair spray made it hard to see a clear image in the mirror.

The frizz-headed girl plopped down in the chair next to Wendy, her pastey-white face filling the glass. Wendy dropped the toothpick with lash glue on the tip. "Do you mind?" Wendy said, leaning hard to the left to capture her reflection.

Miss Fuzz Ball shot her a nasty look and seemed to expand.

"Move it, already. You're in my space!" Wendy picked up her toothpick and wielded it like a dagger.

"Touch my daughter with that and I'll sue your sorry—"

"Mother!" Fuzz Ball squealed like a rusty gate. No chance her talent was singing. "Get real. Like *she's* going to be a threat. Look at her."

Fuzz Ball's mom wore a suit that would make a circus clown appear minimalist. Sparkling gemstones glinted on her fingers under the lights. The woman's face looked like she had a whole lemon in her mouth. Eyes traveling up and down Wendy's stature, she grunted and wrapped her talons around Fuzz Ball's arm, dragging her to an open station across the room.

Hot tears stung Wendy's eyes. She waved her hand in front of her face to preserve her lash job.

Think about the scholarship. Colorado State or University of Colorado?

Wendy finished pressing on her lashes and picked up her hair spray. In the mirror, she saw dozens of moms wrapping hanks of hair around steaming curling irons and poking bobby pins into updos. Updos. The first thing they had to do was dance, so pinning up hair made a lot of sense. Maybe some of those pins would shake loose off their pretty, little heads.

The flashing light on her straightening iron stilled to a steady glow. Wendy combed a section of bangs and placed it between the ceramic plates. She'd never had the luxury of someone else styling her hair. No one seemed to notice in the smaller pageants; it wasn't too unusual. But at this level?

She pulled the iron down, angling the plates away from her head. Wendy left her hair alone for a moment and slid her cell phone out of her makeup bag. No message from Iona. Where was she? A text from Sabrina wished her well. Brittany sent the "break a leg" line.

Disappointed, Wendy threw the phone onto her garment bag. She resumed styling her hair. Pulling another section of bangs across the middle part, she rounded the ends under, giving the hair a little dimension. Sleek and professional; that's the look she needed. And it would survive the group choreography number.

"Ten minutes!" A contest staff member yelled over the din of voices.

Can we still go to the Cheesecake Factory after?" Keri bounced on her toes and tugged Dad's coat.

"What did I tell you before?"

"This is so wrong." Kisrie kept her face down. She didn't belong here. A trip to the gynecologist would be more relaxing than standing in the midst of a bunch of Miss-America types. Every now and then she scanned the room, looking for someone close to her size. So far, they'd been in the hotel eight minutes and she was by far the biggest person around. All the doting parents, grandparents, and siblings of the contestants were slim, sleek, and stylish. Must be genetic. Wait, that didn't make sense. Considering her parents, what had happened to her? Mutation? Switched at birth?

Dad took her hand and Keri's as the wave of spectators swept them through the auditorium doors. Dad let go of Keri for a moment and pulled out four tickets. "Looks like we're in for quite a show. I hear these girls have a good chance at Miss America someday."

The ticket taker nodded. Claustrophobia had never been a problem before, but Kisrie felt her skin prickle. Beads of sweat dotted her forehead, and her breathing grew rapid and shallow. She twisted to look behind her as Dad dragged her and Keri to their seats. No way out. There was no way she'd be able to claw through the wall of beautiful people unnoticed.

The lights flickered on and off three times.

Keri announced to the seven rows or more around her that three blinks was the universal cue that a show was about to begin. It was something she learned at that performing arts school where a select number of kids with extreme musical talent populated the attendance charts.

Kind of like this pageant. One must be beautiful to qualify. Beautiful on the outside, that is. Didn't matter if one or more contestants had less internal appeal than a maggot-infested corpse. Why didn't they give away scholarships for something that mattered, like a brain?

Kisrie slumped as low as she could in her chair.

Some cheesy hip-hop-funk loop played, and an emcee burst through the scarlet curtains.

Tightness squeezed Kisrie's chest. She pressed her head between her hands. Not this. Not now. She tried to take a deep breath to ease the tension.

"You okay?" Dad asked as the guy with the mic yakked on and on about the competition.

"I'm okay." She rubbed her chest in a circular motion. "Maybe a little heartburn from that dinner you made."

"Relax and enjoy, all right?" Dad patted her thigh.

"Sure." She flashed a fake smile.

Dad and Keri jumped to their feet, hooting and clapping.

The pressure increased. She was at a loss. When it happened before, she was at least in a place where she could clear her mind and sort of let thoughts and words fill her mind. Kind of like in the Bible where it says the Holy Spirit fills in the blanks if you hit a brain fart during prayer.

But to do it here? Now? With all this noise?

Girls in black shorts and white T-shirts pranced onstage to a techno mash. Several had some gravity-defying piles of hair. This could get interesting. Kisrie pushed up to see better. She made a bet with herself about whose hair would be the first to fall.

Applause roared in Wendy's ears as the entire group of contestants ran off the stage after their opening number. Why they assumed everybody could dance Wendy would never know. Some red-headed chick kept going the wrong way, knocking into the girls all around her.

Five minutes was all they had to get out of their short shorts and T-shirts and into their power suits for a public interview question. Hurdling over a girl hurling the contents of her stomach onto the floor, Wendy hustled toward her station. Fuzz Ball was nearby shimmying into a ridiculously shiny, hot-pink skirt.

Wendy reached her chair. "Where'd my garment bag go?" She called aloud, noticing the back of her chair was empty. Few people looked up.

"Three minutes!"

Heat flashed through Wendy's chest. "Did anyone see my garment bag with my interview suit? The bag was dark green, the suit gray?"

A few heads shook. Fuzz Ball grinned, exposing horsey-looking teeth.

Someone tapped Wendy's shoulder. She spun around to see a petite, Asian girl holding out a bag. "Um, I'm not sure if this would fit, but I have an extra dress you can borrow if you want."

The girl pulled out the suit. It was gorgeous, but there was a five-inch height difference between them. Wendy forced a smile. "Thanks for the offer, but I think it'll be too short." Time froze as the nice girl slunk away in slow motion.

Wow, a genuinely nice girl.

"One minute!"

Squeals echoed off the walls as girls hopped along, shoving shoes onto their feet. A contest staffer arranged contestants in order of appearance.

"Wendy Wetz? I need Wendy Wetz right here, right now."

Wendy looked down at the white Keds on her feet. She

smoothed her damp T-shirt and tugged the shorts lower on her hips to cover her buns a little better. What choice did she have? It was do or die trying.

72

Kisrie couldn't help but compare the ensemble dance to color guard. Frankly, the guard could outdance that group. Some of the girls were really good. Others weren't. Didn't they know they had to do the dance thing at a pageant? That girl with the red hair, she seriously could've killed somebody. And the way that blonde girl's hair flopped off her head? Not quite as boring as she thought it would be.

A tap on her shoulder broke her reverie. Aunt Zena had arrived and needed to get to her seat. Kisrie stood up and tried to contract as much as possible. Once Aunt Zena passed, Kisrie plopped back in her chair.

A blast of pain filled Kisrie's chest. It was as if someone or something was poking her from the inside. Pray about what? Pray that Wendy would win the pageant? Did God really care about things like that? And wouldn't that be like rewarding her for her evilness?

The emcee announced the public interview section of the pageant. The contestants would be dressed in business attire and answer whatever question a judge posed.

People cheered.

Kisrie fought to hone in on her thoughts. If she wanted

this feeling to go away, she had to pray. But if she couldn't hear herself think, how could God hear her pray?

The first few interviews were boring, stuff about world peace and issues of foreign investment. One girl, when asked about the biggest problems facing education today, said the solution would be to allow kids to bring pets to school because pets give a feeling of calm. Oh, how Kisrie needed a feeling of calm. So much so, she'd rob a pet store right about now.

"Kiz, I think she's next." Aunt Zena pored over her program and nudged Kisrie to sit up.

Wendy entered the stage.

Words and thoughts flooded Kisrie's mind. She wasn't the one needing peace and calm. Wendy could probably use massive doses about now.

The entire audience fell silent.

A big grin split Wendy's sparkly lips. She winked and waved.

"Oh my." Aunt Zena put her hands to her mouth.

At the judges' table, there were a few coughs and some shuffling of papers as Wendy approached the mic, still in her opening-act shorts, T-shirt, and sneakers.

"Hi, I'm Wendy Wetz, and I'm from Lakewood, Colorado."

Polite golf-like clapping.

A male judge cleared his throat. "Good evening, Miss Wetz." He paused and looked at the other judges who were leaning forward, elbows on the table. "What are the best values a parent could pass down to his or her child and why?"

Values? *Lord, give her words to answer that one, because I think they are speaking a language Wendy doesn't understand.*

Intense light made Wendy's eyes water as she stepped forward to take the mic. She ignored the snickers coming from Miss Fuzz Ball and a few of her friends.

I'm wearing a business suit, the classiest one of the bunch. I'm not in shorts and a T-shirt. I'll impress them all with my knowledge of the global economy.

". . . values a parent could pass down to his or her child and why?"

Values? Did she just say values? What happened to possible solutions for the tsunami of poverty ravaging the world? The down economy? Global warming?

Concern over her appearance faded. Iona didn't know a value if one managed to wedge itself up her nose and scream out the Ten Commandments.

Think. Think.

Wendy froze a few feet from the mic stand.

The judge exchanged a sideways glance with a colleague. Her words sounded like hammer blows as she repeated the question. One. Word. At. A. Time.

Wendy's cheeks ached. Hopefully, that knock-off brand of whitening strips worked as well as those expensive Crest ones.

Think!

The judge finished repeating the question.

Dust motes swirled in the spotlights. Was the audience even breathing?

"What kind of values do I wish Iona taught me?"

"Excuse me, Miss Wetz, would you please approach the mic?"

Did she really speak that out loud? Ten eyeballs stared at her from the judges' table. As if on cue, they all leaned forward. What the heck. Dressed in this get-up, Wendy had nothing to lose. Might as well tug at the heartstrings.

With a confidence that caught her by surprise, Wendy took the last few steps to the microphone, and words tumbled from her mouth.

Aunt Zena handed Dad a tissue. He balled it up and blew his nose. She gave Dad's hand a sisterly squeeze.

Kisrie rose up from her seat a little and looked around. People dabbed their eyes. Even the stony judges seemed moved by Wendy's I-wish-these-were-the-values-my-mother-passed-along-to-me-but-she-was-too-busy-pursuing-her-career speech.

At first, there was a moment when Wendy looked like she'd witnessed the judges morph into snakes, but then she changed. Right as Kisrie started praying. As ideas filled Kisrie's mind and she asked God to intervene on Wendy's behalf, it looked like Ol' Wetbottom grew a few inches. Then an undeniably heart-wrenching speech came out of Wendy's mouth.

There was no sign of the earlier turmoil left in Kisrie's chest. On one hand, she felt calm. On the other, she was miffed. What was God up to here? And why was He dragging her into it? If Wendy actually won this pageant, what about all the horrid things she had done at school, to Kisrie's family?

And what was up with Aunt Zena? The woman was cheering. Cheering for the very creature who had practically killed her husband.

This was so confusing.

73

As soon as she turned her back to the audience, Wendy balled her fists and took deep breaths. The tremors that had started in her ankles were working their way up her legs and into her knees, threatening her practiced pageant walk.

Asian Girl waited for her on the other side of the curtain. "Wow. You handled that so well."

Blow by or stop and chit chat? It was five minutes before the next onstage moment. Wendy looked into the girl's narrow eyes and saw a softness. "Thanks."

The girl nodded and turned to leave.

"Wait." Wendy touched the girl's arm. "What's your name?"

"Anna."

"Thanks, Anna. Thanks a lot."

Anna smiled. "We better hurry. Wanna help each other?"

"Sure . . . that'd be great." What was happening to her? Wendy slid her arm through Anna's, and they dashed to their stations.

"Bern, there's something going on with her. I think we only heard a sanitized version of the story."

"I agree." Dad turned to face Aunt Zena. "Why didn't anyone at school ever pick up on this stuff?"

"Children become adept at keeping family secrets. Even the best school psychologist can be clueless if the deception is played out well by the family."

"My gut is telling me that young lady is teetering on a precipice, like her whole life hangs in the balance of something."

Hot tears sprang to Kisrie's eyes. What was happening to her? Is this how God saw Wendy? In that moment, Kisrie caught a glimpse and knew He loved her. God had a plan for Wendy, and she, Kisrie was to be part of it.

"We are down to the last two contestants, ladies and gentlemen. Who will be first runner up? Who will walk away with the title of Colorado Teen Queen?"

Second and third runners up huddled in a mass, smiling fake smiles through real tears. Wendy was either a big loser or a big winner. Kisrie twisted a strand of hair around her finger.

"First runner up is . . ."

A girl with hair like a poodle waved and winked as if she had already been called the winner. Wendy stood stoically like a marble statue.

"Phoebe Delonger!"

"Phoebe? Sounds a lot like Fifi to me," Keri snorted. Aunt Zena scooted to the edge of her seat, ready to launch into space.

Phoebe, a.k.a. Poodle, stretched her smile. Her eyes hardened as she did that model-wiggle-step thing across the stage to collect her banner.

Yep, just like a dog at a dog show. Wendy stood frozen, void of expression.

"Now it's my pleasure to crown this year's Colorado Teen Queen."

A gaggle of gowned girls huddled and held hands. The energy of anticipation vibrated the stage. It was evident most of them were pleading to whatever power they believed in, "pick me, pick me." Wendy stood alone, her chin lifted a tiny bit.

"Miss Wendy Wetz!"

Kisrie gasped. Aunt Zena, Dad, and Keri shot to their feet.

Wendy stood, rooted like a tree. Had she heard her name?

In the cluster of contestants, hands dropped for polite clapping, except for one girl. The girl hopped up and down on her toes and rushed over to Wendy, throwing her arms around her neck and dragging a stunned Wendy toward the emcee.

Kisrie could tell the girl was trying to convince Wendy of her win.

Kisrie sat and stared. She felt as stunned with disbelief as Wendy appeared to be. Part of her rejoiced at the unexpected win; another part of her seethed at the injustice of it all.

"You won!" Anna danced a circle around Wendy. "Go get your crown!"

"Pinch me, Anna." Wendy extended an arm and tried to focus on what the emcee was saying. Her name. Again. Anna obliged. "Ouch."

"Go, go, go, go, go." Both hands on Wendy's back, Anna pushed her toward the waiting emcee and last year's Teen Queen, who held a huge bouquet of flowers.

She did it. She won. Money in the bank toward freedom from Iona's lifestyle. Time to start planning for her future. Wendy lifted her lips into a huge smile. Through the glare of lights, Wendy could see most of the audience was standing. Sympathy for the underdog?

Who cares. A crown was goin' on her head.

Last year's queen settled the crown onto Wendy's head. A wave of sadness wilted the happiness of the moment. She had no one to share this with. When the event was over, the photographers and reporters would pack up. Then what? Back to her grimy apartment and groping drunks?

Maybe Iona had grown a conscience and shown up for her only daughter's Big Moment.

Scanning the crowd one last time, Wendy searched for her mother. All she saw was most of the Kelley clan hopping around like the freaks they were. Except for Mr. Kelley. He wasn't a freak. He could jump around for her until her hair turned gray and fell out. Why in the world did the universe see fit to give a worm like Kisrie a dad like that? If there was a God, Wendy would have been a Kelley, and Kisrie would have been Iona's burden. Life was not only cruel but unfair.

The music cued, contestants lined up for photos, and reporters swarmed the stage. TV crews stood at the ready for interviews. Wendy noted with horror that some of the interviews included her competitors *and* their moms. What would she say if asked about her mother? Tell them she died of cancer? She was out of town on a business trip? The latter was closest to the truth. Or could she find a way to get Mr. Kelley to stand next to her and let the world assume she had a dad?

Better think quickly. The paparazzi were headed her way.

Most normal people were leaving. Kisrie's family squished against the current toward the stage and photographers where Wendy basked in her glory. *National Geographic*, for sure. As a photographer, she would have no part of this chasing down celebrity stuff. Kisrie'd rather shoot a real dog show than this.

"I think she sees us," Zena shouted back to Dad.

Wendy's eyes lit up, and she waved. Whoa, was she actually waving them up to the stage? What was this all about?

"I don't think we should go up there guys," Kisrie called. "I think it's for family members only. We are *not* her family."

This time, Wendy distinctly pointed at them and used both hands to motion them on. Kisrie read Wendy's lips, telling the event staff that it was okay. Nuh-uh. So *not* okay. What was she planning to do? Publicly embarrass them all on the nightly news?

"I really don't have a good feeling about this."

"Kisrie, she wants us to share her success. She's alone. You'd want familiar faces with you in a big moment like this." Dad grabbed her hand and pulled.

Praying for Wetbottom was one thing. Throwing herself at Wendy was another.

Seriously, what harm would it do if people assumed the hunky middle-aged man smiling proudly behind her was her dad? She would just steer questions away from family and focus on her goals and ambitions and the future. After all, the future was what this was all about.

75

Standing outside the apartment complex on Colfax, Wendy let out a deep sigh. For the first time ever, the future looked bright. No more living in trashy apartment buildings with slime-ball tenants. Nope, a fancy loft in LoDo or along Downing would be more like it. She just had to make sure she chose a respectable profession that would survive any economy and rake in the big bucks.

Wendy tucked her garment bag under her arm and bounced up the stairs. The creeper drunk was not in his usual spot. In the hall, she noticed it was eerily quiet. Usually someone in the building was screaming or throwing things, but not tonight. And where was Iona? What could have been so important that she couldn't bother to show up?

Wendy threw her stuff on the floor outside her apartment door. Turning her fist sideways, she hammered on the door. Nothing.

"Iona? Open up!"

Nada.

The key was buried deep in the garment bag. Wendy didn't want to hang out in the dimly-lit hallway any longer than she had to, but it looked like she didn't have a choice.

Once inside, Wendy noticed the apartment was cleaner than usual. She must've come home after Wendy had returned for her shoes. This was weird. More than weird. Iona's stuff was not strewn over the furniture and the floor. It looked like one of those Merry Maid services had scoured the place.

"Iona?"

Silence.

Wendy tiptoed down the hallway and peeked into her mother's bedroom. Her heart skipped a beat at the sight.

The bed was stripped. The closet doors were open with a few wire hangers dangling from the crooked metal pole. Wendy sprinted across the room and yanked open dresser drawers, flinging them onto the floor. Empty.

Panic wrapped its fingers around her throat, making her feel like she was breathing through a kinked straw. She ran to her room. On the bed propped up against her pillow was a stained, white envelope. The *W* of her name drooped down vertically toward the bottom. Hands shaking, Wendy lifted the envelope and pried open the flap. Inside was a folded piece of spiral notebook paper.

> W,
>
> You won. I told you this would happen if you listened to me. Now I can get on with my own life. You can make it on your own. I did. Maybe our paths will cross again someday.
>
> Iona

"What the—" Wendy's words exploded with profanity as she re-read the note three times. Iona had left her. All alone. In an apartment where rent and utilities needed to be paid. And at age fifteen, with her prize in a college fund, that would be impossible.

76

"You're kidding me." Jacque proceeded to make gagging sounds through the phone.

"No, I'm not. She won." Kisrie lay on her bed, running her toes through Squeaky's soft fur.

"There's something so not fair about that. Wendy cheated! She had to have!"

"Actually, it's a miracle she won. Looked like one of her dress thingies went missing, and she had to do an interview wearing shorts and a T-shirt."

"And she still won? But she's evil."

"They didn't ask about her evil deeds."

"They shoulda. Doesn't sound like you're too hacked off about this."

"Not sure how I feel. Part of me is glad she won; the other part feels like something grossly unfair happened."

"Well, something unfair *did* happen! Kiz, how can any microcule of you be glad for her? She deserves the death penalty for her crimes." Jacque panted into the phone. "She killed someone."

Jacque had a point. No matter what Aunt Zena said about depression, Wendy and her stupid lies had played a big role in

Uncle Evan's death. And so had Kisrie's silence. That fact made it hard for Kisrie to throw blame on Ol' Wetbottom. And then there was God.

"I think you mean molecule."

"Yeah, sure. Whatever. Microcule, molecule. Same thing."

"Jack," Kisrie paused. Would her friend understand the conflicted emotions roiling through her soul? She needed to talk about it to someone. "I think that prayer thing is doing something to my attitude."

"Girl, I still think that was a bad burrito or some rotten almond milk. God doesn't speak to kids like us. He only speaks to pastors or missionary-type people. Or dudes like Matthew West. Or—" The phone went silent as if Jacque had suddenly fallen into a coma.

"Jacque? Hello? Earth to Jacque?"

A deep exhale. "Everfound."

Kisrie rolled her eyes at the mention of Jacque's newly-discovered obsession. A teen boy band from Bear Valley Church in Lakewood. They were amazing. They were hot. But Jacque only cared about the hot part.

"Well, I'm not so sure about that."

"Oh, I'm getting a text from Chris. Gotta go!"

"Wait! Who's Chr—?" Kisrie heard the click and frowned at the phone. Something important was going on, something she needed to figure out, and no one seemed to care.

Rent past due. Figures Iona would go off and leave the previous month's rent unpaid. Wendy slammed the notice on the table. If she didn't find a way to pay it, there'd be an eviction notice. Worst case, she had a month and a half to figure it all out. Problem was, everyone at school believed Iona was a lawyer and that Wendy lived in a big, beautiful home in a gated community on the far side of town. Wendy always told her friends Iona didn't allow anyone over when she wasn't home. In elementary school, kids had asked questions, but now all her friends were used to the no-visit policy.

Over the past two weeks since winning the pageant, the scholarship money had been put away in a special fund in the bank. Wendy couldn't access it until she was eighteen, and it could only be spent on tuition at the college of her choice.

Reporters hounded her, wanting to know more about her life, but Wendy held firm on her need for privacy. Instead, she told them she was researching causes to take up. Everyone needs a cause, right? Especially winners of beauty pageants. If she had known everything that'd be expected of her, she probably would have rethought her strategy. How could she have been so naive?

At least one good thing was that the Plank mess was calming down. Zena Plank didn't want to pursue anything. Not that she had much of a case, anyway. Apparently, false reporting by a minor wasn't exactly a high crime.

Brittany was being forced to attend some stupid classes on the dangers of sexting. All the content had been pulled down. Again, no one wanted to press charges, at least not right now. Tammie's family didn't have much money, and the Kelleys said they forgave her. What the heck did *that* mean?

It looked like nothing bad was gonna happen. She had gotten away with it all. Again.

So, why this uneasy feeling?

"I don't know, Kiz. I still think it's creepy how your dad is in that picture with Wendy on the front page of the *Denver Post.* Totally creepy." Tammie dumped her equipment from its bag onto the field.

"Kinda makes him look like a proud father."

"I think he was yawning." Kisrie glared at Jacque and unrolled her silk.

Tammie stretched her shoulder. "Hey, at least he wasn't identified."

"I still don't like it."

"Whoa, Kiz, you really are conflicted about Wendy."

Kisrie pressed her lips together and then spoke. "I was trying to talk to you about that the other day when you got a text from *Chris.*" Kisrie drew out the 'i' sound for several seconds, enjoying Jacque's worm dance. "Besides, how am I supposed to feel? None of this makes sense. Part of me hates her guts for everything she's ever done to me and my family. Yet, when I start imagining mean ways to get back at her, God interrupts my thoughts and tells me to pray for her."

"So you pray for her?"

"Yes, Tammie, I do. Because if I don't, God won't stop bugging me."

"My pastor says God doesn't talk to people today. Everything He had to say, He wrote in the Bible." Tammie pulled her arm behind her head to stretch her triceps ."I *know* the Bible does not say, 'Kisrie, pray for Wendy, thine enemy of thy loins.'"

"Yo, girlfriend, I don't think she's got loins." Jackie snickered.

Frustration boiled under Kisrie's skin. "Look, none of this is making sense to me either, and alls I'm trying to do is figure it out by talking to my best friends. So what do I get? A debate over whether or not I have loins!"

Jackie sidled up to Kisrie. "Okay, new topic. I hear they're gonna be announcing the winner of the photo contest at the end of the week." Bobbing on her toes, Jacque wrapped her flag's silk around her shoulders.

Kisrie threw her flag down. "Are you out to make me feel extra horrible today or something?"

"No, I uh—"

"Sore subject, Jack. Let's focus on something else like State, which also happens to be coming up this weekend."

"Color guard, please set up for the flag-and-rifle feature at the end of the closer." Gavin clapped his hands in rapid succession. "Hurry! Time's wasting."

Could life get any more complicated? All the planning for Uncle Evan's funeral, State Championships being moved up two weeks earlier due to a venue conflict, and now she was trying to decide if God really was "speaking" to her or if she was just plain crazy.

Wendy stood in line behind a smelly, homeless woman with a grocery cart stuffed full of empty juice boxes in various stages of decay. At least at this food bank at the Catholic church down the street, nobody asked questions. Fear of social services discovering her alone in that seedy apartment made Wendy extra vigilant in keeping up appearances. The world expected the new teen queen to be better than okay, which wasn't easy without any money to take care of herself. If anyone from Mountain Ridge knew she was here right now with homeless people, she'd die.

Wendy rummaged in her purse and pulled out a newspaper clipping. She smoothed it out across the palm of her hand and stared. What would it be like to have a real family, a dad? To fall asleep knowing she wouldn't be awakened by a rapacious stranger?

And what kind of cruel joke did God, if there even was a God, play by giving Cow Pie all of that while Wendy was literally moments from becoming Juice Box Lady's neighbor?

For now, pretending things were okay had to suffice.

"Kisrie! Kisrie!" Students tilted and stumbled as Tammie and Jacque tore down the hallway like two piglets in a race at the fair.

Kisrie buried her head in her locker, hoping to avoid detection. Jacque and Tammie skidded to a halt, slamming into her back. Epic fail on the invisibility thing.

"You gotta come see! You gotta come see!" Tammie flapped her hands up and down in a most Jacque-like way.

"Can't you just tell me? I still have to finish my English homework."

Jacque wrapped her fingers around Kisrie's arm. "Oh, no, no, no. You gotta *see.*"

"Do I have a choice?"

Tammie latched on to the other arm. "Nope."

As soon as she was steered in the direction of the photography lab, Kisrie knew where her friends were taking her. She locked her knees and dug her heels into the tile floor. "Is this some kind of sick joke?"

"Aw, come on Kiz, you gotta see! Trust us." Jacque bent down and swept Kisrie off balance. Tammie tugged her forward.

"Clear the way!" Jacque yelled. Dozens of students huddled around a glass-enclosed display board.

"Don't do this to me!" Kisrie thrashed as hard as she could, only to be met with sharp fingernails in the flesh of her arms.

"Okay, now quit wiggling and take a look." Jacque and Tammie dropped her arms simultaneously.

Kids turned to look at her. Smiles crept onto their faces. What was going on here? A shudder worked its way down Kisrie's spine. This was the photo contest announcement. Yippee. Like, why should she care?

Someone grabbed her wrist, pulling her closer. A colorful 8X10 glossy blazed from under the case. Leaves. The perspective was taken from underneath a leaf pile using a macro lens backlit by the sun. Who stole—

"Congratulations, Kiz! You won!" Tammie and Jacque squealed and screamed, arms waving above their heads. Other kids stepped back and started clapping.

"But . . . but I didn't enter. My mom—"

Stepping in front of the display, Jacque slapped a flat hand on her chest. "I entered you in the contest. Well, Tam and I did. We split your entry fees."

"Yeah, and the photography teacher helped us keep it a secret from you." Tammie beamed, grinning from ear to ear as if *she* had won the grand prize.

"We love you, Kiz. I hope you get that now. Oh, and the fact that you aren't stupid and untalented." Jacque wrapped her arms around Kisrie's shoulders.

"I . . . I just don't know what to say. I—"

"Shut up and enjoy your moment."

"Yeah, what Jacque said."

But none of them had to deal with Mom, who would see this as nothing more than an act of defiance.

79

The click of high heels zapped Wendy back into the present. She folded the newspaper clipping and shoved it into her front pocket. No way would she let Sabrina or Brittany catch her looking at it.

"Hey, Wen." Sabrina halted and kicked off her shoes. "Did you hear about Cow Pie winning the photo contest?"

"What photo contest?"

"Something the district was doing. Apparently, one of her weird, little friends entered a photo for her."

"How cute." Wendy looked down at her nails, which were a little more interesting than this conversation.

"Ooh, look, here comes Cow Pie and friends."

Kisrie stumbled down the hall like a drunk. A goofy, lopsided grin spread wide across her face. That freak better not be expecting a word of congratulations or anything.

"I'm wondering if they're still selling smoothies in the commons area." Anything to avoid a run-in with the moo crew.

Brittany shrugged. "Not sure. What's that noise?"

A roaring sound echoed off the locker-lined walls, growing louder by the second.

"It's not a tornado is it?"

"Sabrina, really?" Why did Wendy have a penchant for picking friends who lacked in the intelligence department? She wished that nice Asian girl from the pageant went here. What was her name? She needed to find it. *That* was the kind of friend Wendy needed.

A horde of boys clad only in boxer shorts came tearing down the hall behind Kisrie and freaks. The one in the front was waving a bottle full of clear liquid at the floor. Kids behind him dove onto the ground and slid across the tiles like they were some sort of slip-and-slide at a water park.

"What the—?" Brittany grabbed Wendy's arm.

"Let go of me!"

Cow Pie and herd flattened themselves against the lockers to let the shiny, slimy crowd through. Wendy felt as if her feet were rooted to the spot. She saw the unmistakable pink-and-white label.

Baby oil.

Nobody behind the leader stayed upright for long.

"Wendy, move!"

Oil sprayed across her knee. The crowd splattered and slid by. Sabrina pulled her out of the way. Wendy stared at the shimmering trail oozing down her leg.

"Think it's senior prank day." Brittany checked a text message on her phone.

Dr. Martinez's voice came over the PA system. "All students report to the nearest classroom immediately, and stay put until further notice."

"That's real swell." Wendy looked up and down the hall. "Nearest classroom is photography, and guess who's headed there."

Kisrie pressed against the cold metal, letting the psycho senior mob slither by. Most of them were on their bellies slipping and sliding along. Some tried to surf and fell hard on their butts.

"I'm not sure if I want to laugh or scream," Tammie said. "Someone could really get hurt."

"If I knew it wouldn't ruin my clothes, I'd go for a slide." Jacque grabbed Kisrie's face and pointed it at the back of the group. "Did you see the guy with the bottle? He was hot!"

"Don't look now, guys. Here comes Ol' Wetbottom and her goons."

"Thanks, Tam."

Wendy and her stupid friends all wore ridiculously high heels. A brand new pencil would seem stubby next to those poles. Sabrina tentatively put out a toe to test traction. It kept going forward. She screamed and latched onto Wendy.

"Dog pile!" Jacque whispered.

Free arm flailing, Wendy knocked Brittany across the face before Sabrina hit the floor hard, sending Wendy down sideways.

The Queen of Mean pulled her arm free in enough time to try to break her fall with a fully extended elbow. The joint crumpled upon impact. Wendy's screams cut over all the other hall noises.

"Oh my word, she's hurt." Jacque flapped her hands like hummingbird wings.

Brittany pulled her hand away from her face, discovering her nose was bleeding.

Wendy's screams became gasps. She tried to roll onto her back and cradle her arm, but she couldn't get traction to do so with all the oil. Her face paled. Her lips went white.

"She's really hurt." Kisrie slid a foot in front then followed with the other. The floor was slicker than an ice rink.

"Where ya going, Kiz? You're gonna get hurt too!" Jacque said.

"I gotta help her. Her friends are in no shape to."

"Tammie, give me a little push. Not too hard."

"Are you sure?"

"She's not too far."

The principal's voice thundered through the halls commanding all students to get into classrooms before anyone gets hurt. Too late. Wendy's arm wasn't bent the way normal arms bend.

"Wendy." Locking eyes with Wendy, Kisrie braced for the

gentle push from Tammie. She held her arms out to the sides and slid precariously forward.

"What are you doing, Cow Pie? We don't need your help!" Sabrina fought to sit upright.

Kisrie slid forward another foot or two. Almost there. Compassion for her enemy in pain overwhelmed her. "Can I have your sweater thingy, Sabrina?"

Sabrina took one look at Wendy with wide eyes then tore her cardigan from her shoulders and tossed it over Wendy who lay still, shivering.

"Wendy, I'm going to try to help you, okay?"

Wendy closed her eyes, and her lips trembled.

Kisrie looked to her friends. "Can one of you get to the photography classroom? We need an adult to help us."

"I think Jack and I can do it if we hug the lockers."

"Hurry." Inches from Wendy, Kisrie kneeled down and braced herself on the slippery floor with her hands. "I'm gonna put this sweater thing over you."

"D—d—don't t—touch me, C—Cow Pie."

"I want to help."

"That's bull—"

"Shut up, Sabrina, and help Brittany," Kisrie said. Whoa, where was that boldness coming from?

"Teacher's coming!" Jacque yelled from the photography room.

Kisrie avoided touching Wendy's arm and gently spread Sabrina's cardigan out. "Keep breathing."

"W—who are y—you to tell me what to d—do?"

From the moment she'd hit the floor, a nuclear shockwave of pain had torn Wendy's breath from her lungs. Laying on the slimy, cold tile, she knew it was pretty serious. Her arm had to be broken, and there was no way to avoid a trip to the hospital.

She wanted to go. Pain overrode her fear of discovery that Iona was long gone. Tiny breaths sent waves of fresh pain through her arm, and to make matters worse, the ugly mug of Cow Pie floated into her field of vision.

It was like she was in some kind of Plexiglas tube. Time outside the tube moved at normal speed. Time inside moved a hundred million times slower.

Cow Pie said some stuff.

Wendy replied.

Something was said about a teacher coming. Then a call to 911.

Violent shivers wracked her body, but there was nothing Wendy could do to make them stop. It wasn't like it was cold in the school.

Someone wanted to roll her over and try to splint her arm. Wendy screamed.

Someone suggested waiting for the paramedics to arrive so they could drug her up real good. Someone else said her mom needed to be called.

But she didn't care. Pain was her all-consuming reality.

Kisrie, I need to talk to you." Aunt Zena leaned against the doorjamb at Kisrie's room.

Nodding, Kisrie motioned her aunt in. She was too tired to use words.

"It's about Wendy."

Kisrie froze. Aunt Zena crossed the room and sat on the bed, patting the mattress in a gesture for Kisrie to join her. "I don't know if you've heard, but Wendy's mother has gone missing. The media's making a big deal of it since Wendy won the crown at the pageant."

Plopping onto the bed, Kisrie nodded.

"After some intense prayer, I've decided to take her in. Emergency foster care."

"What?" Kisrie bolted to her feet and wobbled to gain her balance. She really didn't hear that, did she? Aunt Zena just lost her husband and is now taking in the girl responsible?

Aunt Zena stood up and put an arm around Kisrie. "I can only imagine what's going through your mind right now. We haven't even had the memorial service for your Uncle Evan."

"I just don't understand. What does that mean? What about *you?*"

"Honey, life isn't about me. It's not about any of us. Just God. Whatever brings Him glory. Whatever the cost."

"Why can't they, like, find a grandparent or something, another family member? It just doesn't seem right."

"Kiz, there's a whole lot about Wendy we don't know." With gentle pressure to her shoulders, Aunt Zena turned Kisrie and sat her back down. "This wasn't easy for me to surrender to. Believe me. I shed enough tears to fill Sloan's Lake, but when I finally told God I'd do it, a peace I can't explain poured over my pain. Besides, who better to help someone deal with loss than one who's been there?"

"But this is Wendy."

"I know. I know. That's why I wanted to talk to you. Your mother is having a hard time with it, too."

What to say? What would she do if *her* parents disappeared? How could she pay the bills, keep the house, and still go to school?

But Wendy had done this to herself. She deserved it. Right?

"I'm sorry, Kiz, but your family has lost it. Are you sure there's no poison in your water supply or something like that?" Jacque swiped gloss over her lips.

Tammie sat curled in a ball with her hands over her face, silent.

"I don't know if I should be in awe of Aunt Zena or mad at her." Kisrie dug her fingers into her curls. "I mean, I don't like Wendy. But she's in a bad place. Can you imagine if your parents walked out on you when you were hurt real bad, like she was?"

"I'm not sayin' throw her to the street, but can't they put her in an orphanage thingy or something?"

"There aren't any orphanages in America." Kisrie dropped her hands and blew a stray lock of hair off her face.

Ugh. Why were her innards at war with each other?

"So, when does the invasion . . . I mean . . . you know what I mean."

"Aunt Zena is cleaning out Megyn's room as we speak. Wendy's with her already."

"Kiz, I still don't get it."

"Aunt Zena thinks God is telling her to do this."

"I wish people in my church did things like that." Tammie wiped at her nose with the back of her hand. "If all people did stuff like that, this world would be so different."

Whoa. Where did that come from? Tammie was always so adamant about God not speaking to people today. Kinda shocking she didn't jump on that again.

Kisrie knelt beside her friend. "Don't people in your church help each other when bad things happen?"

Tears dripped from Tammie's red-rimmed eyes. "Kiz, they won't let my family come back after what Wendy did. They said because my parents chose to put me in a public school rather than their private one, we deserved it and it was payment for our sin."

Jackie plopped on her butt on the other side of Tammie. "How come you didn't say anything about this to us before?"

"I didn't want you to think I was a freak."

"Girlfriend, I hate to break it to ya, but we're all freaks. That's why we're such good friends."

Tammie covered her face in her hands. "I'm having a hard time with what your aunt is doing. My family is paying for a sin we didn't do."

Wendy swore, knocking over the water pitcher on the coffee table with her foot. What kind of sick joke was the universe playing on her? The moment her future brightened, it was all blown into black oblivion. Literally. And, crossing the line into absurdity, *Zena Plank* planned to be her foster mom?

Fear rippled through her body, causing spasms of pain in her elbow. What was Zena's motive? Did the grieving widow plan to suffocate Wendy in her sleep with a pillow? Maybe there was something to the whole karma thing after all. *So* not a comforting thought.

As soon as she was able, Wendy called her friends, searching for options other than becoming a victim of the Plank woman.

Brittany's older brother was coming home from his deployment. Sabrina's excuses ranged from her parents working weird hours to her brother driving down from Fort Collins to do laundry on weekends. Her friends were bailing on her now that her life stunk. Her boyfriend dumped her via text. No reason, just "It's over."

Wendy cursed Mrs. Plank and the stupid plot she birthed. She cursed the whole senior class and their stupid idea of a prank.

Or was there really a God up there who was doing His vengeance thing? No. She wasn't gonna take this on. It was all Iona's fault. Iona was the one who had said the original plan wasn't solid enough. Iona had pressed Wendy into making the accusations personal. Iona, Iona, Iona.

If there was a God, He would have given her a normal mom. A mom with a job she didn't have to hide. A mom who kissed her boo-boos. A mom who didn't coerce her daughter into criminal behavior. No, it was clear God did not exist.

Cradling her arm, Wendy squeezed her eyes closed and did something she hadn't done since she was five.

She cried.

Darkness cloaked the Plank kitchen as Wendy padded to the refrigerator. The bright LED light inside made her eyes water.

"Hungry?"

Wendy stifled a scream. What was up with all this emotion? Now was not the time to come unglued.

"I didn't mean to scare you." Zena's voice was as soft as red-velvet cake.

"Don't tell me you're one of those nocturnal rodents like your niece."

Zena laughed. Her laugh reminded Wendy of the wind chimes hanging from a neighbor's balcony at the apartment on Colfax. "No, no. I'm all human. You don't have to worry."

Wendy shifted her weight from foot to foot. A hammer pounded in her shoulder. "What do you want from me?"

"Truthfully? Nothing."

"I'm on to you." Wendy slammed the fridge door shut. Glass bottles rattled. "You're playing the good little Christian woman until you find a cell for me somewhere. Then, *wham!* Bye-bye Wendy. Hope you rot in Hell! Perfect revenge for what I did to your husband."

Zena crossed the floor and grabbed a glass from one of the overhead cabinets. She side-stepped over to the sink. "Wendy, may I ask you something?" The voice had a sharp edge to it, but not the kind of sharp that wounds. Zena opened the faucet and filled her glass with water.

Wendy pressed her arms to her chest, hoping to slow down her heartbeat. "Ask away."

"You think I'm out for revenge?"

"What else is there?"

"Do you know what forgiveness is?"

"Just do me a favor, okay? I want another placement. I'd rather go to a women's shelter than stay here." Wendy smirked as she watched shock and hurt flicker across Zena's face. Good. The farther away from this mess, the better off she'd be. "I'm going back to bed."

I thought people were supposed to wear black to funerals?" Keri sunk her teeth into a celery stalk, sawing it back and forth to break the fibers while playing with the magnets on the refrigerator.

"Keri, that's nasty," Kisrie said, peeking at Wendy from the corner of her eye.

Aunt Zena had to be at the church extra early and had dropped Wendy off on her way.

Keri slid the stalk from her pursed lips and pointed at Wendy with the stringy end. "She looks like she's auditioning for the part of neon road sign."

"Aunt Zena must not have minded if she's still wearing it."

"And I thought all public buildings banned rodents." Wendy put her good hand on a jutted hip.

"I'm not a rodent. I'm a primate."

Clamping her mouth shut, Kisrie swallowed the caustic comment burning in her mouth.

"You girls ready?" Dad descended the stairs, smiling and tugging his tie to the right.

Wendy let her hip-propped hand drop against her thigh.

"I don't get you people. You're getting ready for a funeral like you're getting ready to go to a musical or something."

Mom clicked into the kitchen on heels. "You were all supposed to be in the car by now." She snapped the top back on a tube of lipstick and slid it into her purse. Her outfit reminded Kisrie of one of those old black-and-white TV shows—what was it called?—*The Monsters . . . Munsters*?

Dad opened his arms wide and took a step forward. "I was in the process of herding these young ladies out of here, but I haven't succeeded. Herding hamsters is easier."

"You tried to herd hamsters, Dad?" Keri hopped on one leg while Dad nudged all three girls closer together.

Kisrie broke free from the cluster and skulked toward the door. She had mixed feelings about this whole Aunt Zena Wendy thing.

Wendy was so rude to Aunt Zena. She didn't deserve any kindness from Aunt Zena, who kept talking about forgiveness. But then again, the same could be said about her. Nobody would be headed to a memorial service if she had had the guts to go to Dr. Martinez in the first place. Wendy wasn't the only one who needed forgiveness—just the most obvious.

Conversations waned to hushed tones as the Kelley family picked their way down the auditorium aisle to the reserved pew. Jacque and Tammie sat with their families in the middle section. Each girl gave a timid wave as Kisrie lumbered by.

How insulting that Wendy was going to be seated with the Kelley and Plank families while Kisrie's *real* friends had to sit elsewhere. Sick and wrong. Everything about this whole situation was just sick and wrong.

Wendy wanted to disappear. Plank's funeral was the last place she belonged. There were so many people, the Kelley family had to park six blocks from the church, and that was after circling through several neighborhoods. Mr. Plank had friends. Lots of them.

Wendy's stomach roiled and lurched. Good thing she refused breakfast.

Mr. Kelley's eyes blazed bright blue in the rearview mirror. "You okay back there?"

"I hope Aunt Zena ordered those dung beetles for me for the reception," Keri said. "If not, I told her mice would suffice."

Wendy put her uninjured hand over her mouth and mumbled, "I think I'm gonna be sick." It took some contortionist twisting to reach across with her good arm and get the door open. As the car stopped beside the curb, Wendy leaned out and dry heaved. Dung beetles. That was too much.

Mrs. Kelley twisted in her seat. "Do we need to take you home?"

Wendy shook her head. She lifted her upper body back into the car and closed her eyes. "Someone must've poisoned my breakfast."

"You didn't eat breakfast," Keri said.

Mr. Kelley was already out of the vehicle, smoothing his suit coat. "If we don't start walking, we'll miss the whole thing. Come on."

Over a thousand people, Wendy figured, crammed into the church auditorium. Men with name tags jogged up and down the aisles with folding chairs hung like shopping bags on their arms.

A yearbook head shot in a simple, black frame sat on a rectangular table surrounded by bright flower arrangements. Zena sat in the front pew, chatting with some lady while dabbing at her swollen eyes with a crumpled tissue.

Wendy lagged behind the weird little family, hoping to snag an empty corner in the back. She wanted to be there as much as she wanted to be in a dentist's office getting a root canal minus that numbing stuff.

One of those name-tagged clones appeared alongside Mr. Kelley. "Bernard. Gwyn. Children." The man's head bobbed with each greeting.

This isn't jolly old England.

Pointing toward Zena, he told them about the reserved space in the front pew.

Spinning on the ball of her foot, Wendy turned to head for a back corner, but before she could escape, Mr. Kelley caught her arm and gently escorted her down the aisle like a reluctant bride.

"So glad you came." Zena's voice puffed into Wendy's ear during a soggy embrace.

Wendy grunted.

Zena released her and hugged Mrs. Kelley. Wendy's legs trembled as she lowered her bottom onto the padded bench. So many people. Most of them red-eyed and snotty. For Mr. Plank.

Sneaking a glance at Cow Pie, Wendy saw the fat blob sitting at the other end of the pew, head down and eyes closed.

A band filed out on stage, and music with a light beat erased the babbling din of conversation. People hopped to their feet. Some raised their hands; others clapped. What the—? Plank was dead. Gone. And people were singing like it was Sunday?

Zena swayed in time with the music, palms facing up at hip height. Wendy tugged her elbow. "I'm going to the bathroom." Zena gave a slight nod.

Mr. Plank obviously hadn't been on her list of favorite people, but Wendy found it odd to feel more disturbed about his death than those who claimed they loved him.

A flash of color grabbed Kisrie's attention. She turned her head in time to see Wendy skitter toward the back of the sanctuary. Good. She didn't belong here anyway.

Music from the worship song caressed her skin like a cheese grater. God is good. Praise Him. Was faith supposed to be this confusing and contrary?

Kisrie clamped her head between her hands. Guilt over her own negligence prickled through her chest cavity. No one else seemed to blame her. Why did she continue to blame herself? Why not let Wendy carry it alone?

Pastor Dan climbed the steps onto the stage and cleared his throat. Something about a home-going party.

Waves of thunderous applause pummeled her.

"I gotta get out of here!" Kisrie rolled up and over the edge of the pew into the aisle. She had to go somewhere quiet where she could think. Somewhere she wouldn't run into Wendy.

Pulling open the bathroom door, Kisrie poked her head in to make sure she'd be alone.

"We really should stop meeting like this." Wendy's voice echoed over the hard, bathroom surfaces. Kisrie's heart skipped a beat. Duh. What was she thinking? This whole mess *began* in a bathroom.

"And why is that, Wendy?" Kisrie laced her fingers behind her back.

"Well, if you think about it," Wendy circled her head. Her neck popped. "Nothing good ever comes out of our little chats."

"Only because you opened your big ol' mouth and spread rumors about my uncle." A surge of anger powered Kisrie closer to her nemesis. "Now look where he is." Kisrie poked her pointer finger a few millimeters from Wendy's nose.

Wendy's hand shot up and snapped shut over Kisrie's finger. "You could have stopped it."

In a microsecond, Wendy released the finger.

Kisrie stepped back. There would've been nothing for her to stop if Wendy hadn't made her stupid claims.

Leaning over the sink and checking her teeth, Wendy said, "Yeah, we're both guilty. Never imagined we'd have something in common."

"Yeah, but you started it. And Uncle Evan made a choice of his own. A choice neither one of us could see coming."

God, help me here.

Wendy looked up and pinned Kisrie to her spot with an obsidian glare. "Y'know, it's people like you who make me so freakin' sick. People like you who make life intolerable for the rest of us."

Where was this coming from? "What are you talking about, Wendy?"

Looking around, Wendy swept her free arm in front of

her. "You live in a dream world! Perfect little family. Perfect little future. Perfect little church where everyone goes to pay homage to an imaginary god. And yet you walk around like you're a victim. Oh, poor Kisrie." Wendy got in Kisrie's face and snarled. "Cow Pie, you have *no* idea what it's like to be a victim."

Kisrie tried to pull away, but Wendy grabbed hold of her wrist.

"Uncomfortable?" A laugh. "You should be."

"You don't know what it's like to be me," Kisrie said.

Wow. That was lame.

A four-letter word tore the air. "You don't get it." Wendy yanked Kisrie's arm. "Not you, not your weird, little family or your poser aunt."

"What don't I get, Wendy?"

Kisrie's body slammed into the frame of a stall. "Stuff someone like you'll never understand." Wendy shook Kisrie free and stormed out of the bathroom.

Trembling, Kisrie slid down the door frame to the tile floor. There was a lot about Wendy that didn't add up. That girl needed help, serious help.

Where were you?" Mom was perched inside the doorway to the reception hall like a snake poised to strike an unsuspecting mole.

Kisrie jumped then twisted to face her mom. "In the bathroom."

"You missed the whole thing!" Wet, angry eyes pierced the distance between her and Mom.

"I . . . I . . ."

Jacque approached with a plate full of food. How could Kisrie use this as an out?

Mom clamped her jaw and spoke through her teeth. "You're right; there is no excuse. Life's all about you, isn't it?"

"Hey, Kiz." Jacque nodded at Mom. "Mrs. Kelley."

Mom backed up.

"Just came to tell ya there's some good stuff over there." Jacque grabbed a cream-cheese pinwheel from her plate and popped it in her mouth.

Mom folded her arms tight against her chest. Kisrie backed away. Jacque stood facing Mom and chewing. If Jacque didn't move, Mom could strike out at her.

"Why couldn't she be more like her sister?" Mom mumbled.

A knifing pain seared Kisrie's heart. It was The Dreaded Comparison. Like, did Mom expect Jacque of all people to have an answer?

"Honestly, Mrs. Kelley—"

"No. Oh, no. Jacque, don't." Kisrie took a step forward.

"You have no clue what kind of talent lies in Kisrie's bones."

Mrs. Kelley dropped her arms and curled her hands into fists.

"I think you need to see what I'm talking about." Jacque set down her plate on an empty folding chair and fished through her purse.

"Jacque, what are you doing!" Kisrie positioned herself between her soon-gonna-die friend and Mom.

Knocking Kisrie aside, Jacque handed Mom a folded certificate.

"What's this?" Mrs. Kelley's brows pressed down. Her eyes rolled back and forth, taking in the print on the paper. "But I pulled her out of photography!" Fierce eyes nailed Kisrie.

"You know, all Kisrie wants is for you to be proud of her and see her for what she's good at. Not what she's not." Picking up her food and shrugging her purse into place, Jacque headed for the food table. Then she stopped and glanced over her shoulder. "Just so ya know, I entered Kiz in the photo contest. Kiz-o didn't do anything sneaky. Just so ya know."

Mrs. Kelley stared at the paper, then at Jacque, then Kisrie. Her jaw hung so low, if it were a rusty hinge it would have squeaked.

Now would be a good time to go invisible. Forever.

85

"Kiz, I wish you could just move in with me. My mom wouldn't care if all you ate for dinner were peanut butter cups."

Jacque ran her hand up and down Kisrie's bowed spine.

"I just want to forget any of this ever happened and move on." Kisrie stood up and shuffled the length of her bedroom. "Actually, I want to go into the Witness Protection Program and start over."

"What about us?" Tammie asked.

"I'd take you with me."

"Kiz, I don't think you wanna run away from what happened. You wanna run away from *you*. And even I can tell you that's impossible." Jacque went to Kisrie, cupping Kisrie's face in her hands. "Kiz, you need to learn how to be okay with who you are. Tam and I must think you're pretty awesome, sticking with you through all this crud."

Tammie nodded. "What she said."

"Girl, you're your own worst enemy. Even Wendy Wetbottom can't do the damage to you that you do to yourself."

"Again." Tammie wrapped her arms around Kisrie. "What she said."

"But my own mom tells me over and over how I'm not… like Keri."

"Parents aren't perfect. I think your mom just doesn't understand you. She's a scientist-type person. Think of O'Neill, our bio teacher. Is she anything close to normal? Like, who keeps dead things floating in jars on their desk? That woman has issues."

"I think Jack is onto something. I know people in my old church came across as mean because they were afraid of things they didn't understand—"

"Like the twenty-first century," Jacque cut in.

"Look, Kiz," Tammie squeezed harder. "You know how you told us you prayed for Wendy? That's not normal—I mean that in a good way. I've been doing a lot of thinking about what I've been told all my life. Because you did something so radical like that and stuck to it, you made me realize God is personal. Am I making any sense?"

Kisrie pulled away. "But where did it get me? I did what I felt God was asking of me and ended up with Wendy as a new cousin!"

"What if it's not about you?" Jacque swiped her toe back and forth on the floor.

"She's right, Kiz. You're the lucky one. Wendy's life is a mess. You . . . we have way more than she does. Probably more than she ever did. It looks like God cares about Wendy. It also looks like He's using you and your family to show her. And He's also probably trying to show you who you are to Him."

Jacque slid her hair behind her ears. "Whoa. Tammie, the theology professor. Who knew?"

Tammie shrugged. "Y'know guys, maybe this is about all of us, not just Kiz or Wendy."

"If you wish to opine, just go to Bill O'Reilly dot com. That's Bill O'Reilly dot com."

Kisrie jabbed the remote at the screen, turning the TV off. The living room fell into darkness.

Her pleas to be sent to a remote island had been met with

have-you-lost-your-mind looks at the dinner table. Dad gently told her the Witness Protection Program is only for people who need to be hidden from bad guys. So, starting over wasn't an option. And her friends were acting bizarre, like Aunt Zena had invaded their brains.

What Tammie said was true. Kisrie knew it. And the truth hurt. All of them were way better off than Wendy. Wendy's whole life up to now had been a lie. Made up to cover a horrible truth. The encounter in the church bathroom haunted her. Did she want to know what Wendy meant when she accused Kisrie of not knowing what it was like to be a real victim?

"Kisrie?" Mom's voice cut through the darkness.

Shivers rippled through every muscle in Kisrie's body. What kind of trouble was she in now?

"Can we talk a minute?"

Footsteps thumped down the stairs. Like there was a choice.

The light flicked on. Mom was holding up a copy of Kisrie's photo, the one that Jacque submitted. Tears bit Kisrie's eyes. This had to be a death sentence for her photography dream. Mom probably thought Jacque had been trying to cover for Kisrie's disobedience. Kisrie closed her eyes and rose from the couch.

"I want to talk about this." Mom wagged the photo. Her face was flat.

"Mom, I didn't know. Honest. Jacque, she—"

"You took this?" Mom held the photo in one hand and ran her other hand over the surface.

Nodding, Kisrie swallowed. Hard. "But I took it before—"

Mom didn't look up. She stared unblinking at the image of leaves. "It's good."

"Wha—what did you say?" Kisrie dug at both of her ears.

"I said it's good."

"Good?"

"Yes."

Silence.

"Kisrie, I had no idea. Actually, I, um, I never took the time to get an idea."

Of course, she didn't have an idea. Mom was too busy trying to mash her oldest daughter into a mold that was the wrong shape, size, and color. What had changed?

"If you'd like, you can enroll in any and all photography classes the school has to offer."

Okay. Who was this woman, and what did she do with my mother?

"I'd like that." Kisrie croaked the words out around a growing lump in her throat.

The corner of Mom's mouth lifted—into a smile? "Well, I need to figure out where I can hang a framed"—her voice cracked—"a framed print in the house where everyone will see it." Tucking the photo under her arm, she left Kisrie alone with a seed of new confidence planted in her heart.

"I don't see what's so special about that." Keri folded her arms and stomped her foot. Mom kneeled on the back of the couch in the family room, holding a large, framed and matted print of Kisrie's winning photo against the wall.

"It won the district contest, you little piece of slimy, maggot mucus."

"Kisrie, that's not necessary." Mom called over her shoulder.

Could the little monster do no wrong? Wendy leaned against her good arm over in the corner with a stupid grin on her face.

Aunt Zena felt it was best that cousin Wendy not be left home alone to dwell on her abandonment and loss issues.

Wendy pushed off the wall, scuffed to the center of the room, and cocked her head to the side. "I like how it goes with the furniture."

"Can someone tell me if this picture is straight?" Mom tipped the frame to the side.

"You like it, Wendy?" Keri looked at Wendy and snickered.

Kisrie froze. Wendy better not say something dumb.

"It's not quite straight. Raise it up on the left a bit." Wendy hugged her body.

"Hey." Keri poked Wendy in the side. "I'm asking if you like Kisrie's picture."

Turning her head to catch eyes with Kisrie, Wendy answered, "It's not bad."

Whoa. Stop the bus. What was going on here?

Mom made the adjustment and hopped down from the couch. "Kisrie, Wendy just paid you a compliment."

Kisrie's mouth flapped open and closed. It was like her vocal chords had turned into cement. Her expression of thanks sounded more like a burped sneeze than anything.

"Well, I like it too." Keri stepped back and mimicked Wendy's posture.

Wait. Was she really hearing things right? Was this some kind of sick, cruel dream? First, Mom being proud of the very thing she tried to rip away from Kisrie's life, then Wendy's admission of liking the print, and now the vermin approved?

Kisrie decided not to waste time analyzing the situation. She was going to relish the moment. Bask in the glory, however small. A compliment from her arch enemy? It wasn't much, but it was a start.

About the Author

Darcie J. Gudger has fifteen years experience as a competitive color guard director and was on staff for a WGI Semi-Finalist team, Malachi Independent. Darcie lives near Casper, WY with her husband, son, dog, and a cat called Blob. If not at her desk, she's likely to be found stalking moose, bison, or antelope and considers coffee a form of currency. Darcie has a B.A. In psychology from Houghton College in NY and a M.A. in special education from the University of Colorado, Denver.

Visit her website: www.darciejgudger.com

Discussion Questions for Spin
(Warning: Contains Spoilers!)

1. A common mistake we humans make is not thinking through the chain of events a single decision can set into motion. What were the consequences of Kisrie's initial decision to keep quiet? In your opinion, is she directly responsible for them all? Why or why not? How does the idea of personal responsibility fit in here? Who was responsible for what? If you were Kisrie, what choice would you have made? Why?

2. It's pretty clear Wendy is a bully. She is mean. She is cunning and calculating. And out to further her own cause no matter the cost to anyone else. As you learned more about her, did your feelings about her change? What range of emotions did you experience about Wendy? Are bullies simply mean people, or are they complex? Does what you know about Wendy justify her behavior? Why or why not?

3. Wendy's torment of Kisrie goes way back to kindergarten. In spite of all the anti-bullying stuff being done by schools, bullying isn't going away. Why do you think that is the case? Why aren't these programs working? What is the best way to confront bullying?

4. Social media is a world of its own. Kik, Snapchat, Facebook, Poof, Tumblr . . . you're probably familiar with those and more. In what ways is social media constructive (good?) In what ways can it be used as a weapon (bad?) How are *you* using social media? Did you know that what you post online is forever? Sure, they tell you the image is gone in ten seconds—from your device! There are servers holding all those "deleted" images. Discuss your feelings about the "foreverness" of online images, statements, and behavior. How will this knowledge affect how you use social media?

5. So how did Wendy use social media as a weapon? If you were on the receiving end of the attack, how would you handle it?

6. Mr. Plank commits suicide. This is a tough subject to think about. But it is a "solution" many people seek. Do you think the situation at school drove him to that point? Why or why not? Did he give off clear signs of what he intended to do? How or how not? Do you know what signs to look for in your friends and family? Do you know what the local suicide hotlines are in your area should you, a friend, or family member feel suicidal?

7. Kisrie and her dad hang out a lot. What kind of relationship do they have? How did her relationship with her father influence her actions in the story? Think about Wendy. Why does she *really* hate Kisrie?

8. How does Kisrie's faith play a role in the story?

9. Is holding to a faith-based world view easy to do in a school setting? Why or why not? How do you see people of different faiths being treated around the world today? If you hold to a faith, how do you live it out in your everyday life?

10. After all the mess Wendy caused, why in the world did Zena Plank of all people, take her in after she was injured? How does that make you feel about Zena? What kind of person is she? Could you do something so extreme to help a person who hates your guts? Why or why not?

11. Jacque and Tammie get sick of Kisrie's victim mentality and call her out on it. How does Kisrie handle this? Do you see her start to grow out of that mentality? How or how not? Discuss how identifying as a helpless victim impacts bullying. How would you advise Kisrie moving forward?

12. Does Wendy see herself as a victim? Why or why not? Do you think she is doomed to follow her mother's example? Is she a lost cause, or can she rise above circumstance and make something of herself? How? What kind of advice would you give Wendy moving forward?

Made in the USA
Lexington, KY
10 November 2018